CLAN NOVEL:

TREMERE

ERIC GRIFFIN

author	eric griffin
cover artist	john van fleet
series editors	john h. steele and
	stewart wieck
copyeditor	anna branscome
graphic designer	aaron voss
cover designer	aaron voss
art director	richard thomas

More information and previews available at
white–wolf.com/clannovels

White Wolf Publishing
735 Park North Boulevard, Suite 128
Clarkston, GA 30021
www.white–wolf.com

First Edition: June 2000

10 9 8 7 6 5 4 3 2 1

Printed in Canada.

For Susan—

(Because real magic is matrilineal)

TREMERE

part one:
the dragon's graveyard

Sunday, 18 July 1999, 2:00 AM
Manhattan cityscape
New York City, New York

Aisling Sturbridge sluiced through the rain-slick streets. The city towered above her on all sides in colossal glyphs of pitted steel and sizzling neon. The jumble of arcane signs and sigils that assaulted her senses seemed haphazard. The city streets were piled high with half-forgotten ambitions rendered in concrete and raw altitude.

This was the Dragon's Graveyard—the place where the lumbering juggernauts of unbridled industry came to die. Sturbridge could feel the weight of old bones looming over her.

She ducked through a low archway and found herself in the midst of a vaulted colonnade of jutting ribs. Each of the gently curving monoliths was yellowed and pitted through long exposure to the elements. She absently ran a hand down the nearest ivory pillar. Its surface was encased in a nearly invisible envelope of cool water, tricking over the pocked surface in dozens of miniature fountains, cascades, waterfalls. As if of their own volition, her fingers searched for and traced out the letters of the logo— the sacred name that the faithful had carved into the obelisk all those years ago.

The Plaza.

She smiled at a distant memory, recalling a lobby on the scale of a cathedral, filled with the luminaries of the American aristocracy gliding among peerless marbles. After only a brief contact, her hand fell absently to her side and she moved on.

In the rigors of the hunt, there was little room for nostalgia.

Through careful scrutiny, Sturbridge began to discern that hers was not the only sign of life among the ruins. She was amazed that the castoffs of two hundred years of avarice and ambition were not content to lie still and be dead. All around her, the city clamored heavenwards, clawing its way upward, trampling upon its own shoulders in its rush. The glass-walled towers seemed to shift like liquid under her gaze, flowing upward toward some unguessed sea amid the night sky. Experimentally, she put one hand out and broke the mirrored surface of the nearest building.

The tingling was not the expected rush of cool water, but something different—the scurrying of thousands of tiny legs across her skin.

The touch of Sabbat sorcery.

The vision shifted abruptly as the enemy attack erupted all about her. The alien mindscape pulsed like a migraine of flashing red lights. Fire engines emerged from the glaring light and screamed toward the Harlem River where a great funeral pyre tore free from the low-lying tenements. It cracked skywards like a whip. There were figures among the flames. Long, lithe, gibbering figures. They danced the primacy of the flames—the legacy of Heraclitus.

In the beginning, there was the flame. And the flame was with God and the flame was God. The same was in the beginning with God.

Through it all things were made; without it nothing was made that has been made. In it was life and that life was the light of men. The light shineth in darkness, and the darkness comprehended it not.

Sturbridge could feel those flames reaching out to embrace her, to engulf her. She staggered, throwing one arm before her eyes to block out the light and heat. They bore into her skull. She stumbled against the nearest building, but its shifting surface would not bear her up.

Instead of the unbroken towers of still water she had envisioned earlier, the buildings now seethed in carapaces of teeming insect life. Sturbridge recoiled, stumbled. She could feel the wave of scurrying life break over her. She felt herself going down beneath the weight of it—clinging, crawling, stinging. She sank to one knee.

Immediately, there were hands beneath her arms, steadying her. The ancient chant that formed the backbone of the ritual reasserted itself. The distant voices rose to a worried crescendo. Although the singers were all miles away, secluded within the walls of the Chantry of the Five Boroughs, the voices imposed themselves upon the vision.

She could see the individual voices, distinct and radiant, like strands of colored light. They wrapped around her, supporting, caressing. Where they touched, the clinging insects burned away.

Sturbridge caught at the nearest snatch of song and latched on to it. Held firm.

She recognized something familiar in the bright but tentative strand of amber light—it was Eva. Sturbridge smiled. She felt the novice stagger under the unexpected tug from no discernable source. Sturbridge could almost see Eva flailing wildly, trying to catch her balance and momentarily losing the rhythm of the chant.

The amber light flickered and vanished, but immediately there were a dozen others to take its place. Sturbridge could no longer see her surroundings for the glare of them.

She was exalted, bathed in their light. The adepts, Johanus and Helena, were twin pillars of smoke and fire, rallying and guiding the chosen. They shepherded the novices who flickered uncertainly like fragile phosphorescent tubes. Sturbridge could not quite stifle a smile of amusement and pride in her young protégés.

But where was Foley? She took a quick headcount of her forces. He certainly could not have forgotten about the ritual. The secundus regularly regaled the novices at great length about his infallible mnemonic powers.

Her mind leapt to thoughts of treachery and then quickly discarded them. No, Foley was ambitious, but not so foolish as to attempt to dispose of his superior in such a clumsy, imprecise and public manner.

That probably meant trouble back at the chantry. It might be something as innocent as an unexpected guest, or an inadvertent trespasser. Or it could mean an intruder, a would-be thief, a Sabbat scouting party or even an all-out assault.

She took another rapid count to be sure that no other forces were being withdrawn from the ritual to deal with the crisis at home. No, everyone seemed accounted for with the curious exception of Jacqueline. And here, at last, was Foley. His affected royal-purple glow was flushed and pulsating as from great exertion.

Sturbridge grabbed Foley and held him back from taking his rightful place at the head of the adepts. It was a gentle reminder that his absence had been noted and would be addressed as soon as the ritual was concluded. Foley was unflinching in her grasp. His light grew more stable. Good, he was not wounded at least. Nor did he try to draw her back to the chantry. Situation under control.

Sturbridge gathered the varied and multicolor strands of light to her. She stroked each one reassuringly, drawing from its strength, returning its strength twofold. She was the conduit. Her entire body thrummed like a taut string. Twisting. Tuning.

There. She was again perfectly in pitch with the pulsing lifelines and she rode the rising chant toward the very crux of the city.

The tops of neighboring skyscrapers rushed angrily toward her, intent on pinning her, wriggling, against the night sky.

But even as they closed upon her, she was already conjuring up her defenses. Her armor was forged of the materials abundantly at hand, the cast-offs of the city streets. She girded herself in the overturned trash cans, the abandoned cars, the gutted apartment buildings, the rusted iron gratings, the bodies (some stirring, some not) in the alleyways—the detritus of the city, jettisoned in its heedless skywards rush.

A vast pyramid of rubble and refuse was taking form around her. The vengeful thrust of the skyscrapers crashed against the sides of the pyramid but could not avail against it. They fell away harmlessly to feed the tangle of ruins below.

Sturbridge broke from the press of voracious buildings like a predatory bird rising above a forest canopy. Suddenly, she could see for miles in every direction. Any minute now... There.

She sighted the main gathering of Sabbat forces along the burning river and swooped down upon them. She could now pick out individual figures capering through the flames. Her prey was there among them. The Koldun. The spawn of the Dragon.

The Tzimisce sorcerer had the aspect of a broken mirror, his body a jumble of cruel, jagged angles. Looking at him, Sturbridge expected that his movements would be tortured and ponderous, but the fiend was inhumanly lithe. He seemed to flow without effort in and out of the dark pauses between the tendrils of flickering firelight. His slightest movement was accompanied by the music of fine crystal.

The fiend sensed her approach. Looking up, he thrust one accusing finger toward her. Sturbridge felt the impact of the blow despite the intervening distance. She tumbled in the air, careening wildly toward the waiting arms of the inferno below.

The Koldun curled the upraised hand into a fist with the shriek of diamond cutting through glass. Sturbridge plummeted like a stone.

She struggled to right herself as the flames roared up at her—to regain some control over the direction of her unchecked descent. To hurl at least her body at the Koldun like a projectile. It was no good. She tumbled end over end, unsure even which way was up any longer.

She knew the first caress of the flame would remove all such uncertainty. She thought of Icarus, of the boy who, refusing to heed his father's warning, flew too close to the sun. In her mind, she could trace each detail of the intricately handcrafted wings. She could see the wax that sealed them soften, run, melt away as she drew nearer to the fiery orb. She screamed as her wings unraveled. She had been so close. With nothing to bear her up, Sturbridge plummeted away from the jealous sun.

The Koldun staggered back in disbelief as Sturbridge broke from his grip, falling upward, away from the flames. He reached for her again. Too late.

A blaze of incandescent red erupted from the crystal of his upraised fist. With a cry, the sorcerer jerked his head away from the blinding glare. The light pulsed and beckoned like a pillar of fire. It was almost immediately joined by a streak of ethereal silver light. A pillar of smoke.

The Koldun shone like a prism. A dozen searing strands of colored light shone through him. The air was filled with liquid song. It coursed over and through his body.

He could feel heat, worry, responsibility all burning away before the purity of that searing light. He felt the trickling of the chant running through his fingers and puddling on the pavement below. He watched with a strange detachment as the skin of his hands flowed away in pursuit, leaving him staring at the bare, gleaming knucklebones.

He flexed his fingers experimentally. He was unnaturally calm, despite the certainty that these were to be his last moments. The rest of his flesh pooled away, running gently to the ground with a sigh. He had no regrets. He had known he would never leave this place. He had come here—to the Dragon's graveyard—to die.

With great care, he stepped out of his skin. If he had but one gesture left to him, he would step free and dance in his bones. He took a single step and then his bones would bear him up no longer. The earth gathered him in.

Sturbridge settled gently back down to earth. Her splashing feet broke the ghost images gathered in the puddles, scattering reflections on all sides. She took care to avoid the Sabbat's more mundane forces, who still cavorted nearby in the grips of their fire dance.

She did not know how much of the arcane clash they could perceive, but she could pick out a number of them watching now, keeping a respectful distance from the overgrown vacant lot where the Koldun's mound crouched. It was not likely that they would intrude upon the fiend's lair without first being summoned. The Kolduns had a well-deserved reputation for being fiercely territorial.

Sturbridge turned her attention to the novices. She touched each of the tenuous strands of light in turn, assuring herself that everyone was accounted for. Only after the last of the familiar lights had flickered out did she turn to make her own way back to the chantry. Somehow, she could not shake the feeling that something was still amiss. She scanned her immediate surroundings for the slight, telltale visual clues that might herald a new threat. Everything seemed normal enough for the moment.

Well, almost everything. Glancing down, she noted with some puzzlement that she seemed to cast two distinct shadows. A trick of the light? To be sure, she made straight for the nearest functioning streetlight. No doubt about it now. Even under the glare of a bright single light source, she definitely had two separate shadows.

Her first thought was that she was being watched, or worse, followed. She was reluctant to turn back toward the chantry with an unwanted guest literally or figuratively in tow. She assumed the worst. If this new presence were friendly, then why would it not identify itself? Of course it was possible that the shadow did not represent any conscious entity at all. Perhaps it was simply a harmless side effect of the clash of arcane energies. Even old familiar rituals seemed to produce unanticipated results these nights. And the Sabbat sorceries she had faced this evening were an even more volatile element. When dealing with the alien conjurings of the Koldun, it could be difficult to discern between the enchantments themselves and their deadly afterimages.

She regarded the shadow with mingled curiosity and distrust. She half expected it to lunge suddenly ninety degrees to the vertical and go for her throat. After a few minutes of observation, however, she managed to shake free of this apprehension. The shadow seemed to behave normally, if one disregarded the rather obvious fact that it did not appear to react to the presence, direction or intensity of light in the expected manner. And the shape was not quite the same as her normal shadow. It was smaller and its contours were not quite right. The tiny limbs were more gangly, more girlish.

Recognition dawned on Sturbridge, accompanied by a cry of pure animal fury. She stomped angrily in the puddle as if to crush the shifting shadow underfoot. The shadow wavered as the ripples rolled away from the point of impact, but the small fragile figure clung to her tenaciously.

Damn them.

She wheeled angrily as if trying to put, not only the now-familiar shadow, but even the very thought of it behind her.

It was a useless gesture. The little girl's shadow stretched before her on the pavement, taunting her, mocking her loss.

Sturbridge's shoulders knotted beneath the weight of the gathering forces. Her arms snapped forward and down as if hurling a great stone to the pavement. Rage erupted from her hands. The asphalt cracked, smoked, boiled away. Still she did not relent.

She was blinded by the acrid black smoke. Where it touched her skin, it condensed and clung, burning like a liquid fire. She broke off, stumbling backwards, one arm thrown protectively in front of her face. But when she had fought her way back clear of the deadly cloud, the shadow was there before her. Patient, tenacious, reproachful.

Her eyes stung with salt and smoke and her ears burned with the echo of distant laughter.

Nickolai awoke bathed in blood-sweat. A thin red film coated every inch of his body and had already soaked through the silk bedclothes. Ruined.

He peeled away the clinging topsheet and, holding it at arm's length, let it slump to the floor. Blood puddled and lapped over his hands as he pushed himself to his feet. A trail of sticky red footprints followed him down the hall and into the bathroom.

In a matter of days, no doubt, the authorities would discover these macabre signs and begin the search for a corpse that they would never find. But that was nothing to Nickolai. This particular ambulatory corpse would be far away from here long before daybreak.

The shower hissed to life. Nickolai's hand shook as he fumbled with the dial. *Running water*, he thought. *Just what the doctor ordered*. For the first time this evening, he smiled. Running water was the usual folktale prescription for these situations. *Interpose running water between self and pursuing nightmare. Take once per night as needed.*

His kind, however, were traditionally on the receiving end of this particular superstition.

Nonetheless, the scalding water worked as advertised. Its humble magic not only dispelled the physical signs of the previous night's struggle, but some of the terror as well—the terror of waking with the certainty that, while he slept, he had been observed.

It was always the same—the faces of the children, watching him, judging him. He could find no hint of accusation in their glassy, unblinking eyes, nor words of condemnation on their cold, bluish lips. But the very sight of them sufficed to fill Nickolai with a dread, a certainty of condemnation.

For the third night in a row, Nickolai had dreamt of the Children down the Well.

Nickolai closed his eyes. The faces were there still, awaiting him. Round and bright as moons, smiling up at him from just beneath the surface of the still water. Infinitely patient. His gaze was arrested by the face of the nearest youth, a boy of no more than seven years. Nickolai traced the gentle curve of the youth's smooth, unblemished cheek. The boy's icy blue eyes were as large and perfectly round as saucers. His hair fanned out all around the bright face like a fishing net cast out upon the surface of the dark waters. Tangled strands lapped gently at the slick side of the well.

The faces neither moved nor spoke. They had been drowned and their bodies had apparently been some time now in the waters. Although the faces were calm, almost serene, Nickolai knew that their deaths were not the result of some misstep in the dark.

They had *been* drowned. He repeated the phrase a second time with a slight, but significant shift of emphasis. They had been willfully drowned, cast into the well, abandoned to panic, flounder and sink beneath the chill waters. Lost to sight. Lost to memory.

Only they did not stay down (would not stay down!). They had performed that final and miraculous transformation.

They were like the alchemists, struggling for decades in their damp cellars to work the Great Art—to transmute lead into gold—to free themselves from the burden of their leaden physical bodies and achieve the pure gold of spiritual transcendence. But it was the Children who had discovered how the trick was turned.

The waters of the well had swallowed them utterly and completely. But the children, they had worked the Great Reversal, swallowing in turn the waters of the well. They rose, ascending bodily, if not into the heavens, at least to the water's surface. There they hung, suspended like luminous moons, presiding over the benighted waters.

These were his silent accusers, his judges. The lapping waters whispered to him like a lover, promises and gentle reproaches.

Nickolai no longer railed against their rebuke. In a strange way, he had begun to look upon their nocturnal visits as something of a legacy, a birthright.

They were old certainly, those bright, youthful faces. Older by far than Nickolai or any wrong he might have committed. Still, he knew himself to be party to the crime against them—if not against this child who bobbed gently against the slick stones of the well, then certainly against hundreds like him. Souls he had cast suddenly and unprepared into the river of night.

Nickolai had always suspected (but did not know, could never know now) that the well was brimming full of youth, swarming with bright golden eyes, buoyed up ever nearer to the well's lip by the sheer mass of bodies beneath. He imagined that some night soon (very soon now) he might awaken to find that they had spilled out over the brink of the well. He imagined the tide of the drowned washing out over the fields, running like a tangled river through the woodlands, crashing against the heel of the mountains. Nickolai wondered what, if anything, might hope to stand against that great flood—whether any bulwark against the rising tide might hope to endure.

No, they would win in the end, these Children. This flood of shining victims. They had the weight of numbers behind them. They had the advantage of age—of uncounted ages. And they were so very patient.

Nickolai knew that he was to be their victim as surely as they were his own. He had been specially sought out, chosen, marked. When that tide finally rose, when his dream lapped over into the waking world, he would be culled out. Nickolai did not fear death (he had been there at least once already). Nor did he fear oblivion. But he very keenly felt it his duty to remain among the living. This desire did not arise from any overdeveloped sense of self-preservation, nor even of self-interest, nor certainly of self-importance. Nickolai had a very acute sense of what he was. He was the last of his kind. And that was a great and terrible responsibility. He had witnessed what no one should be forced to witness—his brothers, his order, his house, being slaughtered to a man. When Nickolai's death came for him at last, it would obliterate not only his physical form—a debt which was, admittedly, long overdue—but it would also erase forever certain memories, ideas, ideals of which this physical form was the final repository.

With Nickolai's death would pass forever the sight of that ill-fated ritual enacted beneath the streets of Mexico City—the massacre that had destroyed his brethren. With his death would pass the memory of the multiform and varied wonders, the arcana, the passwords, the miracles, the secret sigils, the hidden names of God—the hard-won treasures of centuries. The legacy and birthright of his people.

And with his death would also pass the last living memory of those unforgettable eyes, their terrible brightness undimmed by the weight of death and dark water upon them. In victory, the Children must necessarily die with him and the night tremors—*les tremeres*—at last come to an end.

Nickolai killed the spray of water and walked dripping from the tub, painfully aware that he was one evening closer to that end, and not knowing how to arrest or even delay its coming.

Thursday, 15 July 1999, 1:10 AM
Chantry of the Five Boroughs
New York City, New York

The sensation of the pen's brass nib scratching
across the paper eased Johnston Foley's tension. The
nib grabbed the grain satisfyingly. No slick modern
grade of paper could hope to compare. Craftsman-
ship, tradition—this was the essence of the art. To
Foley, the humble magic of pen and ink was a spiritual rite. Each sheet of hand-pressed parchment, each
individually carved pen was a specially consecrated
ceremonial tool.

His hand moved deftly, confidently, darting in
and among the five oversized illuminated letters that
already graced the left-hand margin. The fruit of his
previous week's labor. Reading from top to bottom,
they spelled out TYLIA—a name to which Foley attached no particular significance.

Foley's scratchings did not pause until he reached
the bottom of the sheet. With a flourish, he generously dusted the wet ink.

Then the waiting.

He let the moment stretch, savored it. A week
of painstaking illumination might have been fulfilled
or ruined in that single minute's mad scribbling. It
was sublime. It was, in many ways, the legacy of his
people, the birthright of the Tremere. The decades
(sometimes centuries) his brothers spent in their patient plotting, their scheming, their jockeying for
position—all leading up to a single night's gamble,
the play for power and prestige. All or naught.

Foley turned the paper on end and tapped it gen-

tly on the desktop. A cascade of fine blue dust settled
to the blotter. With mounting anticipation, he devoured the newly revealed words:

> There is a quiet shadow
> Between pen and page
> The oldest of wards set
> Perhaps to guard the art
> From the casual hand
>
> Yet even now after years
> Of learning the feints, parries,
> Attitudes of approach, I see
> Not one opponent, but hundreds
>
> Living and dead: readers
> Lovers, rivals
> Old works and masters
> And I hesitate
>
> If the pen is truly
> Mightier than the sword, who
> Is cut? Perhaps
> I will write no more
>
> Already the blood
> Of people I will never know
> Has run from the shadow
> Streaking this page
> With words and doubts.

Foley scrutinized each serif, each curve, each of
the eighteen individual 'i'-crowning dots. Perfect.
Opening an upper desk drawer, he withdrew two

pieces of tissue paper and a manila folder. He quickly crossed to an overstuffed file cabinet against one wall and filed the whole—parchment nestled inside paper inside folder—under "T" for "TYLIA."

To anyone else, this filing system might have proved frustrating if not maddening. Foley, however, did not need a "system." His memory was infallible. He could just as easily have filed the piece under "F" or "Q," as the fancy struck him. It made no difference.

But the alphabet was a discipline. An ordered list. Foley appreciated order in all its guises. Over the years, he had become a creature of lists. Initially, the lists had provided him a means of establishing order amidst a world where entropy was only too willing to rush in at the slightest lapse in vigilance. An insane world, a world turned upside-down. A place where the nightmares were real, the dead walked, and the heroes drew pentagrams traced in stolen blood.

Even decades later, long after his faculties had progressed beyond the point that the lists were a necessity, he'd continued and actually redoubled his efforts to tabulate, to enumerate, to impose that perfect order that is a reflection of the truly disciplined mind and spirit. And his unwavering perseverance had not been lost upon his superiors.

Settling himself back at his desk, Foley shifted another sheet of parchment from the pile at his right hand to the blotter in front of him. He considered a moment before selecting a favorite writing implement from the display stand at his left hand. A quill unadorned with any ostentatious plumage. Its former owner, a porcupine.

His hand jabbed rapidly at the page. Words, numbers, formulae began to reveal themselves, rendered almost, it would seem, by pointillism.

Foley took great pride in his attention to detail. His writing table was clear except for blotter, inkwell and paper. His compact study was crammed to capacity with bookshelves, jars of pigment, rare woods, fine specimens of the taxidermist's art, and other curiosities. Nonetheless, it remained distinctly uncluttered.

Each book, each vial, each unseeing glass eye had its place, from which it was removed only when Foley required it, and to which it was invariably returned.

A sharp knock broke the ordered silence of the room.

"Enter," he called, allowing his displeasure to be apparent in his voice. The knock should have come ten minutes earlier.

Jacqueline, Apprentice Tertius, stepped demurely into the small room. She was a mature woman, a former academician whose features continuously betrayed the torment of one accustomed in mortal life to speaking authoritatively to students.

In her new "adopted" family, she had found that she must now accommodate herself to taking instruction and directives from practically every other member of the community. The abrupt disjuncture obviously did not sit well with her.

Her personal contentment—or lack thereof—however, did not concern Foley.

"You are late," he said curtly.

"I was assisting Aaron with…" she began.

"Did I request an explanation?"

"No."

Foley narrowed his eyes. "And that is how you address your superiors?"

Jacqueline stiffened. "No, Secundus."

Foley paused, laying his quill across the inkwell and folding his hands deliberately.

"I mean, no, Regent Secundus," she corrected herself hastily.

Foley sighed in mock exasperation. The novice seemed adequately contrite, though an Initiate of the Third Circle should have been beyond such lapses of decorum.

It was a difficult situation, when an apprentice's capabilities clearly exceeded her understanding of her station. Jacqueline had proven her potential, but the Tremere could ill afford chinks in the armor of discipline that had allowed the clan to survive this long despite determined opposition.

Foley made a mental note to humble the novice publicly at the earliest opportunity. Tonight's ritual should prove a suitable occasion. If the problem persisted, he would be forced to advise Regent Quintus Sturbridge that Jacqueline was simply not working out. And that he had been forced to terminate her.

"I will not abide familiarity in a subordinate," he said at last, then paused again significantly.

"Yes, Regent Secundus."

When Foley was satisfied, he pushed the list across the desk to her.

"Here are the materials I require for a certain ritual next week," he said. "See that they are assembled in my sanctum by dawn of the 22nd."

Jacqueline studied the list. After a moment, Foley held out his hand. Realizing his meaning, she reluctantly returned the paper to him.

eric griffin   29

"That is all." Foley watched as she backed out of the chamber. He was gratified by the brief glint of alarm he'd seen in her eyes as she'd handed back the list. He'd allowed her ample time in which to commit the items to memory. If she'd failed to do so, that was her shortcoming, and she would be held accountable.

Of course, Foley was not about to let her potential incompetence interfere with his upcoming ritual. Dawn of the 22nd would allow him ample time to inspect her work and make any necessary adjustments.

The knowledge that ultimately he would be held responsible for the failings of his underlings was not lost upon Foley.

He rose with the list in his hand and moved into his sanctum. The adjoining room was, if anything, even more packed with oddities than the outer office. The effect was exaggerated as the sanctum was only slightly larger than a broom closet. It was a point of some contention. He realized that the accommodations constituted no personal slight. But the arrangement still rankled.

With open warfare raging between the Camarilla and Sabbat forces—and the battle lines surging back and forth over their very heads—little time and effort had been spared for material comforts. The energy and resources of every Tremere present were required for defense. It had been thus for many years and the situation showed little sign of improving any time in the near future.

Foley supposed he should let the matter drop. After all, his appointment to such a prestigious chantry was not inconsequential. The Chantry of the Five Boroughs—or "C5B" as it was designated in inter-chantry memoranda—was renowned for the unique opportunities it presented. Its name consistently topped the lists of candidates for advancement within the clan. Upon closer examination, however, Foley was forced to concede that most of these promotions were of the battlefield variety.

Five Boroughs was one of the few places in the country where the hawks among the dovecote could openly ply their trade. Foley had endured the posturings of countless self-styled battlemages, pyromancers, astral warriors and other abominations that were so much cannon fodder to be thrown in the path of the advancing Sabbat forces. With the recent Sabbat gains in the Southeast, however, more and more of the clan's hawks were being drawn off toward Washington, D.C. Some of the newcomers to C5B had been enticed by the persistent rumor that the chantry was, due to its somewhat tenuous position, more lenient in enforcing the Third Tradition—the granting of permission to embrace others into the clan.

Ridiculous, Foley thought. He wondered how such an improbable tale was perpetuated. He imagined the formula was one part wishful thinking to two parts never having met Aisling Sturbridge. If the truth were known—and it was not in Foley's nature to distribute a commodity as volatile as the truth without adequate compensation—during his entire tenure at Five Boroughs, not one had ever been granted leave to sire progeny. Not a single one.

Despite this curious—some might say, perverse—tradition, the chantry continued to enjoy a steady influx of new novices by way of transfer from her sister houses all across the U.S.

Foley supposed he should be grateful. It was this very turmoil that necessitated him being here.

Five Boroughs was something of a curiosity, a relic of an earlier age. It always reminded Foley of a medieval monastic house at the height of the order's temporal power—when the abbot of an influential house wielded feudal dominion over the surrounding countryside. C5B enjoyed just such privilege. It was probably the most prestigious chantry in the U.S. that was not the personal haven of some clan dignitary—a great lord or pontifex. Nowhere else in the country could a mere regent exercise such a free hand.

A *mere* regent. Foley snorted. He was a *mere* regent. Never mind that he would be leading any other chantry to which he might be assigned. Five Boroughs was one of the few chantries that supported two regents: himself as the regent secundus and his superior, Aisling Sturbridge. It was not normal clan policy but, as Sturbridge so often pointed out to her superiors— and with such unaccountable and infuriating success—C5B was no normal chantry. Things just worked *differently* here.

It was not such an indignity after all, being a junior regent. Sturbridge herself had been a junior regent at one time. They said that *her* superior had been caught unawares by the Sabbat, just beyond the protection of the chantry defenses. A shame.

There was nothing to say that this same misfortune might not befall Sturbridge herself—some night when she was alone and abroad. Some night like tonight. The possibility that a well-earned promotion might conveniently fall into his own lap was not lost upon Foley. So he tried, if not with complete success, to tuck his resentment back into its appropriate niche. Probably Sturbridge's quarters were no more spacious than his own. He could not speak authoritatively on the matter, of course. He had never been invited into her chambers.

The limited real estate might not have been such an issue if it were not for the increased population pressure. Because of the Sabbat forces pawing at the gate, all of the apprentices, journeymen, masters and adepts attached to the chantry were required to reside on the premises.

Unfortunately, this led to Foley's having to work and exist at uncomfortably close quarters with mere novices like Jacqueline, Aaron, and the others.

The prevalent opinion seemed to be that the chantry, tucked beneath the Camarilla fraction of the city, made up in strategic value what it lacked in acreage.

"There's only so much space between Barnard College and the Harlem River," Sturbridge had told him the one time he'd ventured to mention his cramped quarters to her. Her peculiar summary dismissal of his concerns had dissuaded him from asking why the chantry didn't expand in other directions.

From amidst the tightly packed shelves of curiosities, Foley's hand extracted a modest, wooden chest—no larger than a jewelry box—which held the object of his present obsession.

The preparations he had assigned Jacqueline were only a small part of his ongoing efforts to unlock the secrets of this little enigma. Foley did not like mysteries.

The chest was unadorned save for a tiny mother-of-pearl, fleur-de-lis inlay on the lid. Foley cupped his hands around the box. In the shadow thus created, the design gave off a faint milky radiance.

Excellent, he thought. *It's still active.*

With a steady hand, he opened the lid. Nestled in the felt-lined interior was a semi-precious stone no larger than a marble. It was a finely polished quartz, roughly spherical. Its color was a uniform cloudy red except for two black circles at its poles. The north pole was smooth and flawless. The south pole, slightly jagged. Raised areas on the stone's surface made no special pattern that Foley could discern.

He had never expected the gem to prove of much interest.

Sturbridge had presented him with the stone several years earlier, with the expectation that he would perform experiments on it. The exact nature of these experiments was never specified. The stone had a faint resonance, but then again, so did an amazing number of trinkets, baubles and outright forgeries that found their way into the possession of Clan Tremere.

Foley had done some preliminary experiments, but to little effect. Before long, he'd set the gem aside. He had seldom even thought of it since, and then mostly in disparaging terms—a semi-precious stone taking up precious shelf-space.

All that had changed three weeks ago.

Foley had entered his sanctum and found that the precautionary seal which he had placed on the chest was broken, and the lid thrown open.

The very idea that someone had been *handling* his things! It was unclean. It was a violation. Why, it was an outrage!

Foley had already flogged three novices for their recalcitrance when the event repeated itself the next evening. No one in the chantry would have been foolish enough to so mock him after such a pointed and public a display of displeasure. So he'd been forced into a pattern of watchful waiting. He'd checked the gem several times each night, resealing the chest following each inspection. For weeks, nothing changed, except the normal degradation of the residual energies. Then last night, the gem had suddenly flared to life again and tonight, as indicated by the glowing mother of pearl, it still seethed with power.

To the naked eye, of course, the gem gave no such indication. Foley, however, had come to rely implicitly upon his little box. He had it on good authority that the chest had been brought out of Versailles just days before things had taken an irreversible turn toward the bloody and squalid.

He laid the list he'd shown to Jacqueline across a shallow copper dish on his worktable. He struck a match and held it to the parchment until the edges curled and blackened. Foley needed the list no longer; he'd taken it back merely on principle.

Before the paper was completely consumed, he took a tapering purple candle from a nearby shelf and held the wick to the fire. The candle was another of Foley's creations. To the casual observer, the only visible sign that the candle had been carefully crafted by hand was that its wick ran the entire length of the candle and peeked from its stump.

The flame caught, the melting wax releasing a faint scent of honey. A moment later, the lower end of the wick inexplicably flared to life. Foley rotated the candle slowly, allowing the lower flame to soften the stump end before slamming it down abruptly onto a wicked iron spike that protruded from the northwest corner of the worktable. A mound of hardened wax—the legacy of several nights of vigilant testing—lay sprawled around the spike.

Foley turned back to the chest already uttering the opening syllables of the proper incantation. Reaching into a recessed drawer, he produced a slender silver lancet. Slowly, he passed the fingers of his left hand through the candle's flame. It did not burn him, but he doubted that his handiwork would show the same consideration to anyone else foolish enough to attempt to duplicate the feat.

With a deft motion, he pricked the tip of his middle finger with the silvered needle and watched as a single drop of blood seeped, coalesced, swelled, and finally fell to the sputtering flame below. The fire drank eagerly, releasing a curl of oily black smoke that was heavier than air. The vapor coiled downward, winding languidly about the candle. Tentative tendrils drifted across the worktable and cascaded over its edge.

Foley placed the tiny chest in the precise center of the table and, with his index fingers, drew back the lid.

The candle sputtered and hissed. The flame seemed to arch its back in response to the presence of the lifeless red stone

Foley took a pair of long delicate silver tweezers and gently lifted the gem from its resting-place. With great patience, he moved it closer to the flame.

Twenty inches away. No change. Nineteen. Eighteen. Seventeen. Sixteen.

The flame guttered as if buffeted by a strong wind. But it refused to be snuffed out.

The candle was shrinking visibly, wax pouring down its sides from the heat of its exertion. Fifteen. Fourteen. Thirteen...

There.

Foley had been expecting the candle flame to suddenly surrender the fight with the telltale pop of a small implosion. The same experiment had played itself out for many nights now with nearly identical results. The only variation on the theme was the exact distance at which the stone crushed the fragile flame. That distance, and by association, the gemstone's baleful influence, was increasing nightly.

What Foley was not expecting was for the candle flame to suddenly and inexplicable *rotate* ninety degrees. The tenacious lozenge of flame stretched out lengthwise upon its wick, as if felled by some mighty blow. Lying on its side, the flickering teardrop of flame looked like nothing so much as a tiny smoldering eye. Foley blinked twice in an effort to banish this illusion, but to no avail. Instead, he had the unsettling impression that the flickering orb winked back.

There was a darkness now at the heart of the flame. A shrewd narrowing of pupil. Foley found himself leaning involuntarily closer to the candle. Closer.

The flame no longer shrank from the stone in his hand. On the contrary, it seemed to expand in anticipation of its touch, of their long-frustrated reunion. The yellow eye sizzled, dripping viscous waxen tears. Foley felt as if he were being swallowed, consumed by the baleful stare. He could not wrench his gaze away. His right hand, forgotten, flapped clumsily as if he had lost all feeling in the extremity. It groped, fumbled for pen and parchment.

Finding, as if by chance, the sought-for pen, Foley bore down with a desperate palsied grip. He scribbled wildly. The mad lines staggered off the edge of the page. The delicate brass nib gouged agonizingly into the wood of the worktable.

Sunday, 18 July 1999, 3:45 AM
Morningside Heights
New York City, New York

Sturbridge stormed through the remnants of the dissolving vision. All around her, elaborate arcane constructs streaked and ran like watercolors. The vivid images and incantations that had sustained the ritual fell about her like a gentle rain and puddled at her feet. She clomped angrily through the puddles, each footstep leading her instinctively toward more familiar stomping grounds. The topography of the melting vision gave way to a landscape of streetlit rainbows in oil-streaked puddles.

Through the early morning drizzle, Morningside Heights was quiet except for a low hum of activity from the late-night coffee bars. Sturbridge could feel the tips of delicate and deadly fangs slip down from the roof of her mouth in answer to that hum.

Somewhere within her, hunger raised one sleepy eye, stretched and leaned against its tether. Sturbridge roughly shouldered it aside. She was far more angry than she was hungry.

Far more angry, she repeated, as if to steel her conviction.

It would not be long now. Already she could see the familiar outlines of the residence halls of Barnard College rising out of the misty rain. Soon she would be home. They would, no doubt, be waiting for her.

If only they would not be waiting for her.

She could deal with just about anything else right now except for the looks of concern on their faces. There was a time—yes, she admitted, even a hundred years did little to dim the vividness of the memory—when she had welcomed the look of concern on the faces of her family. When she had *courted* it. Staying out those few extra hours just to see its momentary flicker on her mother's face. Before the expression fused into the harsher lines of anger and indignation.

But that was a very long time ago, she reminded herself. A lifetime ago.

She had a new family now. A family whose "concern" was (quite rightly) feared even in the courts of the immortals. She would not subject herself to that concern.

No, she was their regent. She would be strong. She would be aloof. She would be unassailable.

She would be angry. She thought, *Just have to stay angry.*

Before the door had closed behind her, they were there. The flutter of their words wrapped around her like warm blankets. The flush of their concern pressed upon her like the warmth of a mug of steaming cocoa pressed into her hands. It would have been very easy to sink into the solace of that welcoming concern.

No. Have to focus. Have to stay angry. Those Sabbat bastards. How dare they?!

She waved her arms, scattering novices like a flock of carrion birds.

"Jacqueline, where the hell were you? We've been working on this ritual every night for the last fortnight—ever since we isolated the location of that damned Koldun's nest. And tonight when it comes down to smoking him out, you suddenly recall a prior commitment?

"When we go out to do battle with *that*, we all go. Just because I'm the one out there on the firing line does not mean that you get to take the evening off. Am I understood?"

"Yes, Regentia, but Secundus Foley summoned me to…"

"Foley!"

"Your pardon, Regentia," the secundus pushed his way to the front of the crowd with an air of importance. "It is exactly as she says."

Foley picked uncomfortably at the cuff of his robe. He was irritated, disheveled, distracted. Sturbridge noted that the shirtsleeve peeking from that cuff was soaked to the elbow in smeared ink. His other hand was severely burned, nearly blackened.

"You are unwell." It was not a question.

Foley withdrew his hand into the recesses of his sleeve. "It is nothing. We will speak of it later. There have been…*developments*."

"We will speak of it now. You let novices go into battle alone. You owe them an explanation. You owe *me* an explanation."

"Although I might question whether this were the appropriate time and place to discuss such a delicate—such a *personal*—matter, I remain my regent's good and humble servant. I was in my sanctum, engaged in certain routine activities crucial to the well-being of this house. The novices were hardly alone. Johanus and Helena are certainly more than capable of guiding the novices through the preparatory stages of the ritual until such a time as I could rejoin them. I have the utmost confidence in their abilities. Honestly, my lady, you do coddle them so. They are, after all, *adepti*…."

"Was the chantry under attack?"

Foley's patience grew to match her impatience. "Have no fear on that account, my lady. The premises are…"

"A fire? A cave-in? An earthquake?"

"The *premises* are secure."

"*Something*, then, is unsecure. A spy, perhaps. You have ferreted out a spy in our midst?"

A nervous laugh escaped from somewhere among the assembled novices. Foley half turned, caught an eye, made a mental note.

"Of course not, my lady. All here are unswervingly loyal. To yourself, to this house, to Vienna, to the pyramid. Rest easy," he soothed. "You are fatigued, nothing more. And we keep you here standing in the entryway. For shame."

He turned upon the nearest novice. "For shame. Back to the *domicilium* with you. All of you." He made a broad sweeping gesture, inadvertently revealing his disfigured hand. He hastily withdrew it again.

"Secundus." The edge to Sturbridge's voice brought the retreating novices up short. "What was the nature of the crisis that detained you this evening?"

Foley turned uncomfortably. Pitching his voice low, he replied. "My lady is well aware of the delicate task that consumes my evenings of late. I would hope that she is furthermore aware why it is imperative that we not speak of such matters here."

"I do not recall the nature of this task."

"I beg my regent's pardon. It is a failing of mine. I am always assuming that those around me share my fascination for the mnemonic arts. My lady will recall that she not only authorized my recent investigation into" (his voice fell to a conspiratorial whisper) *"the object we discussed,* but she said the matter was to have the very highest priority."

Foley was quite pleased with himself. He was making Sturbridge's task much easier. The man had a unique talent for being absolutely infuriating. She had seen him ply his trade on several occasions. He could devastate the most carefully constructed plot of a rival in a matter of seconds, by pushing his opponent over the edge at exactly the wrong moment. Sturbridge had recognized this useful talent early in her tenure as regent and Foley had rapidly risen to the lofty position of her second-in-command.

"Did I say that your bauble would take priority over my personal safety, or was that a priority you set on your own?"

Foley stammered, "My lady! I never…I did not mean to imply…"

"We will set aside the issue of endangering my person. For the moment." Even the greenest novice heard in those three words the clear message that there would yet be a reckoning for this failure. A personal and private reckoning.

"My Regent is most generous," Foley replied, head bent in submission.

"The fact remains that you have led this novice astray—a matter which I take very seriously. The Providence Compact is quite specific on the punishment of such infractions."

Members of the chantry were seldom privy to the corpus of the law. Sturbridge doubted that even two of the masters present had heard of the Providence Compact, much less laid eyes upon any of its strictures. Only a regent or a specialized scholar of the law would have had even a passing familiarity with its contents.

She seemed to consider for a moment. "I can see three suitable sentences." There was no discussion of trial, of defense, of appeal—only of punishment. The regent had sole responsibility for interpreting the complex web of bylaws, strictures, compacts and precedents that made up the tangled body of Tremere law. Within the chantry, she dealt swiftly and decisively with any perceived infraction. The regent did not serve the law; she enacted justice.

Sturbridge ticked off the possible fates on the fingers of her left hand. "One, the Atonement of Silence. The secundus shall submit to the removal—by fire—of the tongue which led the novice astray."

She held up a second finger to forestall any interruption.

"Two, the Atonement of Service. The secundus shall undertake the responsibility of training and guiding three new initiates through all seven circles of the novitiate.

"Three, the Atonement of Sacrifice. The secundus shall surrender the object of his obsession, that which led him out of community with his brethren and into solitary peril—the bauble with which this congregation has, perhaps unwisely, entrusted him."

At the mention of the stone, the accused's head jerked up. He could not master himself quickly enough to mask the look of defiance that was plain for all to see. He recovered quickly, mumbling something conciliatory about the wisdom of the regent, and retreated a half step.

"Jacqueline, as the wronged party, it falls to you to decide the matter of the secundus's punishment."

A look close to terror crossed the novice's features. Sturbridge ignored it.

"But, Regentia," Jacqueline stammered, "I am but a novice. How could I presume to judge the secundus?"

"You will pronounce sentence *in loco regentia*, on my behalf." Sturbridge smiled down benignly upon the young novice. *Yes, this little one must also be taught a hard lesson here tonight. A lesson about the chain of command.*

"Silence, service, or sacrifice? Choose."

To her credit, Jacqueline squirmed for only a few moments before gathering her courage. "I...I would like to choose clemency, if it please my most just mistress."

Sturbridge smiled. She would have to keep a close eye on this one. "Nothing would please me more. But lenience will not satisfy the law. You will choose. Now."

Sunday, 23 May 1999, 4:50 AM
Suburban Lodge
Cincinnati, Ohio

Scalded clean and dripping wet, Nickolai
perched on the edge of the bed. He took care to avoid
the blood that still puddled on the mattress. He tried
to force his thoughts to focus on his next move, but
they led him inevitably backwards.

Up to now, his movements had been instinc-
tual—a headlong flight away from the site of the
massacre—away from the blasphemous ruins beneath
Mexico City. Nickolai's sole purpose had been to put
as much distance as possible between himself and the
all-too-recent nightmare. If the truth were known,
he could not say with certainty that it was not already too late.

He did not know how long he had lain pinned
and helpless beneath the ruins. He might have been
unconscious for a few hours or for several evenings.
Nor could he be entirely sure that he had not slipped
into the deeper torpor as his shattered body struggled
to mend itself. If this were the case, the lost time
might be measured, not in nights, but in months or
even years.

Too long, he thought. *Too late*.

Nickolai had awaken to a ravenous hunger, but
he dared not pause even to hunt. He picked his way
back over the U.S. border on foot, avoiding even
incidental contact with the least threatening of hu-
mans. To draw any attention at this point might
have proved his undoing—hastening his detection
and destruction.

Once over the border, he had grown bolder. He allowed himself the risk of preying upon the occasional passing motorist for sustenance and transport. He began to put a slim but critical buffer of blood and distance between himself and the pursuing nightmare.

Ironic, he thought. It was only in the wake of these savage predations that he began to rise above the demands of his purely animal instincts. It was as if only by satisfying these primal, bestial needs, the more rational civilized thought processes could begin to emerge.

Irony. It was a human concept. It was the first time since the catastrophe that his thoughts had risen above the level of flight, of feeding. Nickolai felt as if he were coming home. As if he might somehow survive all this.

Slowly, so as to not provoke the beast, he began to rein in his reckless flight. For the first time, he took note of his surroundings. He was somewhere in the deserts of the southwestern U.S.

As reason gradually returned, Nickolai was horrified to find himself among the familiar touchstones of his unlife. With mounting dismay, he recognized that his footsteps had been drawn to the well-known gathering places, the chantries, the dead drops, the places of power that made up the legacy of his people. It was almost enough to drive him back into the clutches of the beast. Blindly, he fled. Nothing was so dangerous to him now as the familiar. Whatever had destroyed his brethren would surely seek out any survivors. One of the first places it would look would be here, assuming that any stragglers would return home.

After several nights of further flight, always looking over his shoulder for signs of pursuit, Nickolai had felt safe enough to come to ground for the first time. The Cincinnati hotel room was a far cry from the comforts of home, but that might have been the exact reason it appealed to him.

But even here, half a continent away from the source of his flight, it was not far enough. He wondered if it would ever be enough. Shaking his head, he banished such thoughts from his mind. He had to focus on the pragmatic.

The first thing he had to do was to determine exactly who he needed to avoid. Certainly, an encounter with any of the members of House Tremere would be a death sentence. The slaves of the pyramid bore no love for the thaumaturges of House Goratrix.

Nickolai considered. There might still be others, however, that he could reach. Others who were of the blood but not of the pyramid. Refugees, rebels, by-blows, outcasts.

Again, he found his thoughts returning to the legacy of his people. If he could find an apprentice, a successor, then the knowledge of his house might not pass entirely from the earth.

With excruciating care, he began gathering his tools.

Foley's preparations were exacting. He carefully marshaled the eclectic array of instruments on the worktable before him. But his mind would not focus on what his hands were doing.

His thoughts still dwelt on last night's humiliation in the Grande Foyer. Sturbridge's words echoed in his mind. Silence? Service? Sacrifice?

"Reprisal" would be a more apt description. There was nothing quite so infuriating as when your immediate superior failed to back you up—and in such a public venue. His eyes burned at the memory.

It was no matter. He would reestablish discipline swiftly and certainly. The very thought of that novice—a mere novice—presuming to pronounce sentence upon him!

He would see that she learned her place. One way or another.

Three new novices, he thought ruefully. To guide a single neophyte through all seven circles of the novitiate would take him a century at the very least. If the student did not already have a strong background in practical magic, it would be closer to two centuries. And God forbid that he should be saddled with a pupil with a background in the occult—it would take him three centuries just to undo the damage.

Centuries lost, wasted. If Foley took any consolation in his current predicament, it was that he could not recall the last initiate here at the Chantry of the Five Boroughs that had survived long enough to pass through all seven circles of the novitiate and earn the coveted rank of journeyman.

The chief benefit of that lofty position, as Foley saw it, was that a journeyman was immediately assigned to another chantry. The official explanation for this policy was that it afforded every student the benefit of many different teachers along the difficult path to mastery. The unofficial one, Foley suspected, was that it prevented the regent from developing too strong and devoted a local following.

Then a thought occurred to him, a sly and pleasing thought. It was an aspect of his current predicament that he had not previously considered. He cursed himself for a fool for not seeing it sooner.

With three novices placed entirely in his care, he had been given a precious opportunity—the raw materials for forging a faction, a power block. Certainly he already had allies and agents throughout the chantry, but the mentor/novice relationship was a far more formidable bond. It was the closest thing to the mystical tie between a sire and his childe that was permitted within the close confines of the chantry.

Already plans were beginning to decant, to distill, to sublimate. He would begin at once. The first thing tomorrow evening he would petition Sturbridge for the first of his three new pupils. She would not refuse him.

His thoughts immediately returned to Jacqueline. Yes, he thought, she would do nicely. It did not matter that the presumptuous whelp had already been apprenticed to another master for a few decades. Rank, after all, must have its privilege.

He would make certain that his new pupil was well rewarded for the difficult choice she had made.

Foley hummed contentedly to himself as he returned to his preparations.

This evening five candles burned upon the worktable. Another of Foley's double-wicked creations was rammed down onto the iron spike protruding from the table's northwest corner. Each of the four cardinal points boasted a squat votive candle: gold in the east, red in the south, blue in the west, green in the north. At the very center, the fleur-de-lis box lay open, revealing the enigmatic cloudy-red marble.

A black grease pencil lay ready at Foley's right hand. His left hand, carefully wrapped in a pristine white linen bandage, managed to grasp the delicate silver tweezers. Foley was not about to be caught unawares this time. He had played through the memory of the previous night's miscarried ritual a dozen times in excruciating detail.

He had been unprepared. The experiment had run dangerously amok. He was still not entirely certain what had severed the escalating mystical feedback between candle flame and gemstone, banishing the baleful yellow eye he had unwittingly summoned up.

It was possible that the blazing orb had simply run out of fuel. The candle had been consumed right down to the table's surface when he'd come to his senses. The iron spike jutted defiantly from the puddle of yellow-streaked purple wax.

It was also possible that he had blacked out, the link with the eye severed when he lost his grip on the stone. A frantic search had discovered his lost prize beneath the table where it had rolled off the edge and come to a halt against one of the carved lion-footed legs.

Foley was not taking any chances tonight. He had warded the cardinal points with the four elementals. Taking grease pencil in hand, he began the invocation of the four archangelic protectors. As if of its own volition, his hand scrawled out each of the sacred names in turn, rendering them in thin, spidery Arabic letters. In the east, the legend beneath the golden candle revealed *Rapha-el, the healer*. The south bore the name *Micha-el, the guardian*. The west proclaimed *Gabri-el, the herald*. And the north read simply, *Uri-el, the gatherer*.

The epitaph beneath the latter candle specifically did not mention anything about "the angel of death." Foley was just superstitious enough to know that it was a grave misfortune to set the word "death" to paper, much less to use it in a ritual inscription.

His wardings completed, Foley carefully extracted the gem, taking pains to ensure that it did not make contact with his flesh. He began to inch it closer to the candle flame.

Twenty inches. Nineteen. Eighteen. Steady now. Seventeen. No change. Sixteen...

The candle flame sputtered uncertainly and then erupted upwards. Foley staggered backwards a half step. As if sensing weakness, the flame surged forward, cracking like a whip. Foley threw up his left hand to shield his eyes and the gout of flame changed direction midstrike, following the gem.

Realizing the true danger a moment before the two made contact, Foley hurriedly thrust the gem back within the protection of the diagram etched out in candlelight and grease pencil on the worktable.

The viscous yellow flame pulled up just short of the invisible barrier, the air cracking at the sudden reversal. The spout of flame momentarily swayed like a serpent before recoiling to its proper place atop the purple candle.

It curled in upon itself, twisting, churning—resolving into a single burning yellow eye.

They regarded each other across the line of the intervening protective diagram. The eye seethed in frustration. The candle was very nearly expended already by the intensity of the gout of flame. Foley knew he did not have much time.

His right hand found the grease pencil and jerkily—like the hand of a clumsy marionette—began to scratch out sharp Arabic letters.

Suddenly, all five candles went dark.

Foley tensed, awaiting the parting blow.

Nothing. Silence. Darkness.

He forced himself to inhale deeply, exhale. A ritual cleansing. It was many years since he had gained any practical benefit from the habit of respiration. The simple act had been transformed into one of his ceremonial tools.

He summoned up a light by means of the most humble magic he knew. The Zippo chirped, sparked, flared.

In a moment, he would cross to the light switch, gather his tools, methodically erase all signs of the evening's experiment. But not yet.

With growing anticipation he held the lighter over the wicked iron spike in the northwest corner of the table.

There at its base, partially obscured beneath a rapidly coagulating pool of wax, was a single word: *Hazima-el.*

The deceiver.

Monday, 19 July 1999, 1:00 AM
Chantry of the Five Boroughs
New York City, New York

The three matched knocks were softer this time, more subdued, and precisely on time.

"Enter," Foley barked. Jacqueline entered the room with the solemnity of the condemned. She stood in silence before the secundus, her eyes wary, her stance defensive. Foley did not glance up from the official-looking file before him. He allowed the uncomfortable silence to stretch. Occasionally, he attacked the text with a swift marginal note.

Jacqueline found her eyes straining to pick out his notations. She silently cursed herself and assumed a pose of calculated disinterest. Foley was baiting her.

"The Regentia said you wished to speak to me." Sturbridge had said quite a bit more, but Jacqueline saw no reason to make this interview any easier for Foley.

Foley looked up and stared at her blankly as if trying to place her face. "I do not recall addressing you, *novitia*."

"No, Secundus. Regent Secundus," she recovered.

Foley returned to his file. Jacqueline fidgeted uncomfortably. She found herself staring at an uninspired landscape, a turn-of-the-century farmyard scene, hanging behind the secundus's desk. It was the colors that most annoyed her, she discovered after a few moments' reflection. They were all a shade too iridescent for the subject. And the texture was wrong somehow.

Realization dawned upon her and her skin crawled. It was not a painting at all; it was a collage.

The picture was painstakingly assembled from hundreds of individually plucked butterfly wings.

"Is something the matter, *novitia?*" Foley set aside his pen and folded his hands before him on the desk.

Jacqueline wrestled her gaze free of the macabre artwork. "No. Regent Secundus."

"I have been reviewing your progress."

"That is very kind of you. I am certain my meager accomplishments merit no such attention."

"Quite so. It is not your accomplishments, but rather your place within our order which is in question here. I will be brief. I have discussed your case with Regent Sturbridge and she is in full agreement with my assessment. You show great promise, Jacqueline, but without formal discipline and structured training, this potential will lead only to frustration, failure and self-destruction. It is a well-traveled path and one which I would not see you stumble down."

Her tone was strained and formal. "I thank you for your efforts on my behalf."

"Accordingly," he pressed on, ignoring her interruption, "I have offered to take personal responsibility for guiding you safely through the complexities of the Fourth Circle of the Novitiate. Your new course of studies will begin immediately."

"That is quite generous of you, Regent Secundus. But I am sure it is unnecessary to burden one of your status with so humble and unrewarding a chore. Master Ynnis is quite capable of…"

"You will no longer be reporting through Master Ynnis. Make no mistake, however. Your new apprenticeship will in no way excuse you from your existing lessons or responsibilities. You will continue to take rudimentary instruction in the Ars Sanguine with the rest of your peers. Here we will pursue…other masteries. Do we understand one another?"

"I believe so, Regent Secundus."

"Excellent. It is my intention that we should begin at once. You may commence by reciting back to me our conversation thus far."

Jacqueline considered for a moment. "You said you had reviewed my progress and discussed my case with the regent. You said that, without discipline and order, my natural talents would be wasted. Effective immediately, you will be assuming responsibility for my studies toward the Fourth Circle. I will report to you instead of Master Ynnis. I will continue with my normal lessons and responsibilities in the novice hall. Is there anything else?"

Foley's patience was obviously straining. "I will start you off. I said, 'Enter.'"

"You mean you want the entire conversation verbatim? I don't remember it word for word. You said something like, 'Sit down, I have been reviewing your progress.'"

Foley sighed exaggeratedly and began rubbing his temples. "No. Please do not go on. You will only further demonstrate your shortcomings. You do not know. From now on, you have to know. You have to remember. Am I making myself clear? I see we shall have to begin with the mnemonic arts."

Jacqueline's voice was flat, formal. "I must know. I must remember. Are you making yourself clear. You see we will have to begin with the mnemonic arts."

"Better. You are still wrong, but at least you seem to understand what is expected of you. Tell me, where do you think our power arises from?"

"The power is in the blood." Jacqueline automatically shot back the response from the First Circle catechism.

"Ah, I see you can recall something at least of your training. You may yet be redeemable. Tell me, this power, are you certain that it does not arise from the will?"

"The blood looks out on the world through the will."

"And not from the mind?"

"The mind is the conduit of the blood."

"Then you are telling me that the blood flows through the mind?"

"The blood floweth not. Nor doth it fall. It broodeth at the heart of the Father."

"Your blood does not flow? If I cut you, do you not bleed?"

"It is not I who bleeds, but the Father only."

"How is that so?"

"My mind is an opened vein. Through me the Father spills life into the world."

"What form, then, must the mind strive toward? Shall it become a straight and narrow channel? A gutter? A trough?"

"The mind is a pyramid of seven steps. Seven, the number of the Founders. Seven, the number of the Council. Seven, the number of the orders of mystery. Seven, the number of the circles within each order. Seven, the number of the arts that rose from the ashes of those that were lost. Seven the number of the days of the world's making. Seven, the number of completeness."

"Precisely so. The mind is a pyramid of seven steps, Jacqueline, a strictly ordered hierarchy. Just as the Tremere clan is ordered in a pyramid of seven steps. Without that discipline, the center cannot hold. You must order your thoughts, your fears, your desires. This will bring structure to the pyramid of your mind and strength to the pyramid of your clan. Do you understand these things?"

"Yes, Regent Secundus."

"When next we meet, you will recall for me the content of this conversation. The exact content. You will further read and commit to memory a little treatise I have for you here. It is Aquinas's *de Memoria*. No, I don't imagine you would be familiar with the work. It never enjoyed what one might term a common circulation. Can we turn to more practical matters at this point? Excellent."

The secundus closed the file and set it aside.

"Now we will conduct a simple pragmatic test of your progress. This inkwell will do nicely." He placed it squarely before her. "You will use your arts to move it across the desk. I must warn you, however, that this piece was a gift and I have grown quite fond of it. I will not abide your damaging it."

A look of apprehension crossed the novice's features. She began to protest.

"You may begin," he prompted.

Jacqueline caught the look on Foley's face—imperious and spoiling for an argument. She abandoned her objections. Resigning herself, she squared off against the delicate cut-glass antagonist.

The three feet of the worktable between Foley and herself suddenly seemed a vast distance. She took a desperate grip on the table's edge, as if to pin it down, to keep it from stretching away further. Her features furrowed in an expression of intense concentration. She muttered what might have been snatches of verse in broken Greek. Everything about her bearing was rigidly upright. She could feel the wooden slat of the chairback pressing against her spine. It kept her grounded, centered. All other impressions were rapidly receding. There was no longer any thought of Foley, nor of failure, nor of humiliation.

Her austere frame was a fired clay crucible, trembling slightly at the effort of containing the rising energies within. Her eyes glazed, her fixed stare first unfocusing and then turning inward. Even her features seemed to blur, her face growing pale, smooth, brittle— taking on the aspect of cool, implacable porcelain.

Foley, for his part, did not spare a single glance for the inkwell, the alleged object of this experiment. He was instead occupied in studying the lines of Jacqueline's face. He could already pick out the fine cracks in her composure. The faults where the novice's unmastered furies, fears and desires would burst through, shattering the delicate china mask.

He shook his head at the absurdity of it all. The novice clearly lacked discipline, self-knowledge, formal training. She had not even mastered the mnemonic arts. Did she actually hope to move the inkwell by thinking at it very loudly? It was like watching the first clumsy efforts of an infant. Although most infants, Foley acknowledged, were not allowed such volatile playthings.

He had just about made up his mind to intervene when he was distracted by a sound. A wet, turgid, pop.

Glancing down at the inkwell, Foley was just in time to see a second murky bubble rise to the surface and burst, splattering a stray droplet over the lip of the well. The deep red bead clung for a moment, glistening wetly against the crystal. Then the long slow slide.

"Enough!"

Jacqueline recoiled as if struck.

Foley stretched out a hand to snatch away the inkwell, to conceal from her the miscarried results of her efforts. He reconsidered and withdrew.

Calmly he asked, "Shall I measure the distance?"

Jacqueline looked hurriedly to the well. It still rested precisely where Foley had placed it. It had not so much as budged. Her initial disappointment quickly gave way to puzzlement.

The surface of the ink seethed with activity. Viscous streaks of red twisted their way up through the jet-black ink. They burst the skin of its surface and spread out—gasping, seeping, coagulating. She watched layer upon layer of spilled life climb higher up the sides of the well until the sheer weight of it smothered out the new bubbles trying to form. Within moments, all was still once more.

"I don't understand," Jacqueline whispered. "What happened? What went wrong?"

"Do you not? Take it. You have desecrated it with your blood. It can be of no further use to me."

"But how?"

Now Foley was angry. "You must think. And you must question before you act. The power is in the blood. The will is the blood's window into the world. But the mind is the conduit. If the mind is undisciplined, unfocused and untrained, the power of the blood is loosed, but unshaped. It lashes out where it will. The results of such misguided efforts are monstrosities—offenses against not only nature, but against reason.

"Did you think this was magic? These blind, undirected fumblings of the will? *This* has more magic in it than your awkward, infantile efforts." Foley reached out one hand and lifted the inkwell. He held it poised defiantly before her face for a moment before banging it down on the table in front of his own position.

"Power. Will. Focus. Results," he raised a finger to forestall her argument. "That's not magic? Because I lifted the inkwell with something as mundane as muscle, bone, sinew? What precisely do you think magic is? No, spare me further demonstrations of the glaring holes in your understanding. I will tell you. It is reaching out with the will to impose a reflection of that perfect inner order upon the entropy of the external world. From the beginning the earth was without form and void. Magic is the ongoing and continual act of creation."

Jacqueline could restrain herself no longer. "But *this*," she hefted the inkwell and slammed it down in front of herself once more, "is not magic. Is this what we sacrificed so much for? Our lives, our families, our friends?

"Or is that is too abstract for you? After all these years, you get a little jaded, a little tired. Ideals, principles, they never quite penetrate the thickened hide anymore. Well, how about the things that matter, something concrete, something real? The tug of a child's sticky hand? The taste of chocolate? The brilliance of sunlight through stained glass? I didn't give up all of this for you to tell me I could just as easily have picked up the damned inkwell."

"You would do well to remember you are addressing a superior." Foley pushed back his chair and slowly paced around until he was standing precisely behind her. "But, yes, it is far more efficient to move the inkwell with your hand. Nature has provided you with delightfully appropriate tools for the task at hand."

A cool touch brushed her cheek. Her first instinct was to flinch away, but she held her ground. She neither jumped nor turned to acknowledge the unwelcome caress.

"So that's it? Magic is just taking the easy way out? An energy-saving device? A quaint and archaic mechanism?"

"I'm not sure why that should make you so angry. If you would move the inkwell with your hand, you must train up your hand. If you would move it with your mind, you must train up your mind."

What first registered in Jacqueline's mind was the sound of the inkwell sliding away from her across the rough wooden surface. The sight, or perhaps the acceptance of the sight, was slower in coming. It lagged just beyond the sinking sensation in the pit of her stomach.

Foley placed both hands upon her shoulders from behind. It was not a comforting gesture. He leaned down close and whispered into one ear. "Would you learn to move the well with only your mind? I could teach you, you know. Would you like that? For me to teach you?"

She shivered.

"Do you think it would be hard? Arduous? The long nights of study. Months, years perhaps? Would you be willing to make the necessary…sacrifices? Or would you mourn over lost sentimentalities—pudgy fingers, melted chocolate, pretty colors?"

Foley felt her stiffen. He smiled and closed in for the kill. "Would it surprise you, I wonder, to learn that I could teach you to move the inkwell in little more than one hundred hours of concentrated study?

Just about the same time it takes to teach a mortal child to read. Would that surprise you? You yourself were a teacher, once. Surely you've taught a child to read. What could be simpler? What could be more natural? Would you like that? Would you like for me to teach you?"

A change had come over Jacqueline. Her voice was hollow. It sounded as if it came from a great distance. Echoing up from the bottom of a deep well.

"I would...like that."

"Good. I was hoping you would say that. I am certain we shall have great fun together. Yes, I am very much looking forward to the coming years."

"Years? But you said..."

"Oh yes, years. Perhaps decades. But do not worry, we are in no hurry. We quite literally have all the time in the world."

"One hundred hours," she repeated stubbornly. Some of the fire was coming back into her stare. "You said, one hundred hours. Even at only an hour a night, that is scarcely four months."

"I fear you misunderstand. I said I *could* teach you in one hundred hours. Anyone could, really. The power is in you already—in the blood. Despite your enthusiasm, however, I have no intention of loosing that power upon you in such a hurried manner. You would not thank me for it, you may rely upon that.

"You are ambitious, and that is an advantage. But you must temper your ambition with patience. You would have power, yes. That much is obvious. But you would far rather have shortcuts. It is a lack of discipline. It makes you vulnerable."

"But you promised..."

"I promised you nothing, except that I would

teach you. We will not rush through this training. We shall be much more...thorough. The instructing of novices is something in which I take quite an avid interest. Shall we begin with the basics?"

The unexpected offer to begin immediately undermined Jacqueline's objections. She still wanted to argue, to confront Foley with his shadow promises, to throw his transparent manipulations back in his face. But none of his insults, his insinuations carried the weight of that one compelling call—the sound of the inkwell sliding, apparently of its own accord, across the worktable.

"I am ready, Regent Secundus."

Foley gave no sign of reveling in his victory. "The problem is precisely that you are not ready. You lack the proper foundation to grasp even the fundamentals of what I will relate to you. You lack the proper discipline to commit my words to memory, for review when you eventually master the basics. I cannot allow you to take written notes for the obvious reasons, so you must muddle through as best you can.

"There are seven lessons that I teach—the seven great truths of the Tremere pyramid. If you are not prepared to receive them, your efforts here are doomed from the start, relegated to the realm of frustration and failure. The seven lessons of the pyramid are Discontinuity, Hierarchy, Apathy, Favour, Authority, Documentation and Surveillance.

"You will have forgotten all of them, of course, by the next time we meet. So we will only dwell on the first tonight. The first lesson I teach each of my students is discontinuity.

"I barrage them with snatches of astrology, Kabbalism, palmistry, the I Ching, conspiracy theories, Greek myths, Catholic rites, the Tarot, crystals, druids, Gehenna, demonology, evolution, alchemy, the Book of the Dead, Lovecraft, Orphic mysteries, UFOs the Grail cycle, Nostradamus, quantum theory, archangels, the Golden Dawn, radical relativism, neopaganism, the Book of Nod, Catharist heresies, etc.

"Everything I teach is kept uncontaminated by any specific context. Logical progressions—whether they be chronological or conceptual—are harshly suppressed. All theories, even the most tenuously held, are placed on an equal footing. Each is presented as being equally plausible and, in the final reckoning, true.

"If a student should show signs of a developing enthusiasm, we immediately change tack—preferably taking up a tradition that vilifies or is at least openly dismissive of the previous one. But there are ample other distractions to take the novice's mind off the drudgery of any one particular subject.

"The chantry is a symphony of bells and alarms—tolling the hours of study or of service; calling the faithful to meetings or mealtimes; announcing the arrival of emissaries or invaders. In all this frenzied activity, there is an elegant discontinuity—not only of topic, but also of time.

"The benefits of discontinuity are legion. It discourages overspecialization, attachment and sentimentality. It gives the novice the broadest possible base of knowledge. It develops healthy reserves of sophism, cynicism and intellectualism to carry her through the coming struggles.

"But most importantly, it reconciles the novice to her new existence. What use is there for continuity, for interconnectedness, for logical cause and consequence in a world where even the inevitable tie between life and death has been utterly and irrevocably severed?"

Jacqueline listened in growing horror. Surely Foley was just giving vent to a brooding cynicism. Taken at face value, the system he was describing was nothing short of a death sentence. Decades, perhaps centuries, lost for the sake of preserving a crumbling monolithic institution.

If Foley thought that he could shackle her to such an agenda, she would have to disabuse him of that notion.

"Three accomplishments that are well regarded in Ireland," Talbott began, gathering in the crowd like a mother hen. "A clever verse, music on the harp, the art of shaving faces.

"Three smiles that are worse than griefs: the smile of snow melting, the smile of your wife when another man has been with her, the smile of a mastiff about to spring.

"Three scarcities that are better than abundance: a scarcity of fancy talk, a scarcity of cows in a small pasture, a scarcity of friends around the beer.

"So the Triads tell us...ah, thank you," Talbott accepted the proffered cup. "And they are as true today as they were in sainted Padraig's time."

The word 'time' was muffled in the head of the rich brown beer. He drank deeply and with great deliberation.

The anteroom of the Chantry of the Five Boroughs usually had something of the aspect of a luxurious private library about it. The floor-to-ceiling bookcases contained a multitude of scholarly texts rendered in the earthy tones of tooled leather broken only by the sharp contrast of gilt edges.

The arrangement of books was precise if inutile. The volumes were grouped together by the simplest scheme that suggested itself—by color. This approach encouraged a leisurely, disinterested browsing and frustrated any attempts to discover pertinent information. Frequent visitors to the chantry had grown bold enough to remark openly upon the curious and disproportionately heavy representation of the works of a Mr. Z. Grey among the shelves.

At the far end of the anteroom, beyond the ancient oak-paneled double doors—the two faithful and well-loved retainers leaned noticeably together upon sagging hinges—lay the Grande Foyer and Chantry proper. The anteroom, however, was Talbott's private domain. He was the brother porter, the keeper of the gate, the guardian of the way. He had served the chantry faithfully for the better part of forty years.

During his tenure he had been witness to much of the mystery and majesty of the Tremere. Indeed, one could not spend so much time in the close proximity of the tumbledown Great Portal without seeing more than one's fair share of leaky incidental magics.

In all that time, however, of ushering supplicants, mystics, dignitaries and the occasional stray puppy across that formidable threshold, Talbott had never once passed through the great doors in their aspect of the Portal of Initiation.

He had never once tasted of the forbidden fruit. "Never once been tempted," he could be overheard to boast contentedly to a dumbfounded guest. "No sir, never even been tempted."

Tonight, the trappings of the formal waiting room had been rudely shoved aside and relegated to the farthest corners. Talbott held court over an enrapt group of novices, locals, old-timers, and a smattering of the more adventurous students from the college above. All maintained a respectful silence, waiting for Talbott to put down his glass and take up his tale once again.

A hundred slight sounds, however, betrayed their patient waiting. An earthenware mug scraped across a rough-planked table. A chair creaked back on two legs. A match struck, guttered, caught life.

The door to the street swung inward. Moonlight diffused in a lazy twisting cone through the omnipresent smoke. A uniform cloud filled the room from the top down, thick enough at eye level to noticeably darken the interior. A sweet smoke, equal parts peat fire and tobacco.

Smells like moss, Talbott thought. *Green, moist, alive.*

The scent ambushed him with the memory of a favorite hiding spot from his youth—a tiny earthen hollow tucked away beneath the exposed roots of Bent Willow. Gazing out through the tendrilled lattice of root fibers, Talbott had watched afternoons slip downstream pursuing the River of Life as it made its way, in no particular hurry, through the lush green pastures of Meadth. Home.

Talbott shook his head as if to dislodge the dream-image, but gently. The past was tenacious. It clung fast, drew life, drank youth. He passed a gnarled hand through sparse, silvered hair, raking it back from his eyes. *Once golden*, he thought. *Poor wages indeed for a lifetime of service.*

Voices intruded from the opened door to the street. A laugh three levels too loud for the enclosed space cut off abruptly.

"Sorry, lads." Rafferty tried for a whisper, but got hung somewhere midway between his object and a chuckle. He swung the door to, leaning heavily against it as he did so. He descended the three quick steps into the cramped, warmth of the interior.

"Pissed already," came an answering mumble. "And what should his dear mother say to hear of it?"

"She'd say the boy was ever a quick study," came a distinctly matronly voice from somewhere in the vicinity of the fire. "More's the pity he never picked up another subject."

Rafferty slunk toward the fire, head hunched low as if expecting to be cuffed. He ducked, planting a kiss squarely on the woman's cheek and then slipped off to fetch her another pint.

Talbott put down his mug with audible satisfaction and picked up where he had left off as if there had been no intervening pause.

"And they are as true today as they were in sainted Padraig's time. You have, no doubt, heard it told how the Blessed Padraig drove the snakes out of Eire."

Talbott waited for the nods of recognition to make their way around the room.

"Oh, come now Talbott. That's an old saw. Give us something fresh, won't you?" The voice was familiar and perhaps a bit too loud for the close quarters.

Talbott smiled. A smile with a sly edge to it. "All right then, you prancing pagan, if you'll have none of the Blessed Padraig—not that there aren't some present that could stand a nudge in the right direction, mind you—what will you have? The Wooing of Etain is bit less chaste, but I hardly know if I could bring myself to relate the whole of it without falling to blushing and stammering in the present company."

His exaggerated, deferential bow to the nearest group of young ladies was greeted with a chorus of generally unkind remarks which seemed to disparage both the strength and authenticity of his alleged scruples.

Rising to the challenge, Talbott's voice rang briefly above the clamor, giving out the ancient verses in excruciatingly precise meter and anatomic detail. Laughing, he allowed their embarrassed indignation to drown him out.

"Well then. I see you may yet be redeemable," he capitulated. "Some middle ground then, perhaps, between the faultless saint and Etain's immodest exploits. How about…"

"Can you give us Aisling's Tale?" The soft, almost timid, voice cut cleanly through the throng. *One of the novices*. Talbott turned and smiled warmly. *Eva*.

He knew them all by voice as well as by sight. He knew who they were. He knew why they came. He knew what this place did to them.

Others had turned as well. Not all betrayed the same compassion. Some regarded the novice's request with open suspicion and even an edge of hostility. Their thoughts were plain upon their features. *Aisling's Tale. Aisling Sturbridge. The mistress of the house.*

These little gatherings of Talbott's walked a very fine line. In bringing together initiates of the chantry and outsiders, there was always the possibility that something might slip. Something revealing. Something…unfortunate.

"Aisling's Tale? That's a peculiar request, now. Let me think." His eyes probed her face for some hint of what she might be driving at, but he found only a disarmingly childlike curiosity.

"Well, there are, truth be told, not one but many Aisling tales—'Aisling' meaning something after the manner of a 'dream quest' in the old tongue, you understand. The tongue of the bards. No few of the heroes of Erin have stumbled across that wavering line between the waking and the dreaming worlds. And paid dearly for the privilege."

Eva soaked up this revelation eagerly but her thoughts were already rushing ahead. She failed to either hear or heed his warning.

"But is there no tale of a *lady* named Aisling? A lady of Erin? A lady who danced between the worlds?"

Talbott mumbled something noncommittal and regarded the bottom of his mug contemplatively. Already caught up in her enthusiasm, Eva rushed heedlessly onward.

"One who spoke the words of fire and blood? One who made a pact with death and who lost her only daughter down a dark well?"

Talbott raised an eyebrow at her outburst. "It seems it should be you telling this tale, for in truth, you seem to be far closer to it than I."

Eva's face was intent. Her voice was hard. "Is there such a tale?"

An uncomfortable silence had fallen over the room. Talbott let it build, roll slowly like a storm.

"Of course, child," he soothed. "There is always just such a tale. But that does not mean that I have the full telling of it."

Disappointment, frustration and embarrassment vied for control of her features.

"What little I do know," he offered in a conciliatory tone, "I have paid good coin for." *Forty years*, he thought, pushing a weathered hand through his hair. *Silver, gold.* "The knowing has cost me dearly."

Eva's elation made clear she had not heard a word he had said. "I will see to it that you are well rewarded for your efforts."

It was a mistake. She knew it before the words had fallen leadenly into the silent room.

"I think you misunderstand me," Talbott replied a bit sharply. "It was not my intention to barter the price of the tale. We are not fishwives shouting our wares in the marketplace…"

"I'm sorry. I didn't…" Eva began, but was cut off abruptly.

"As I was saying, I know *some* of the telling, but even the slightest knowing has its price. What I do not know is why I should relate it. Why I should put you and these others gathered here at risk."

Her back was to the room. Her voice was hushed, intent, pitched low so as not to carry. "Oh, Talbott. I have to understand. Have to understand her. Have to understand what she has…what *I* have become."

Her face was pressed close to his own. Talbott could see that she was close to tears.

"Be easy, little one," he whispered, touching her cheek. "You will know." Still caressing her cheek, he added pointedly, "But you will pay the knowing for all who are gathered here."

He took her arm and sat her at his feet.

"*The Devil's Toothache,*" he called, breaking the silence of the room. "Aaron, grab an indulgent old fool another mug, there's a good lad."

Upon a time in County Meadth where the River of Life runs toward the Final Shore—that rocky beach whose secret is that it knows only departures and never returns— a girlchild was born in the crook of a willow tree.

Dark as a battle raven she was and straight as a pin. In her mouth was the language of beasts and she could talk before ever she learned to cry. Her eye was milky

with the witchsight and in her thumbs she had wisdom—
wisdom enough to know that a willow tree was no proper
place for a young lady of promise and ambition.

Well, that's where they found her and after she piped
up and greeted them so civilly, they could hardly leave her
there—complaining to the very beasts of the field of the
cruel turn they had played her—so they took her home.
And they called her name Aisling, for it seemed to them
that she must be of the fair folk.

How much trouble, after all, could one small
girlchild be? To her credit, she might well pine away for
her home under the hills until there was nothing left of
her but bare knucklebones. Yes, she did run a bit toward the puny side and wasn't likely to last long enough
to prove much of a bother.

But on the day of Aisling's birth, a ringing began in
the Devil's ear that would give him no peace.

Now they say that Devil, he never sleeps, but a body
still cannot properly enjoy the misfortune of one's neighbor
with a ringing in the head. For the better part of the morning, he stormed about, distracted, neglectful of his duties.
The wailing of the Afflicted went largely unnoticed, much
to their collective chagrin. This further indignity spurred
them to even greater fervor and soon their ill-humor rubbed
off on even the Unrepentant, doing little to improve their
devil-may-care attitude. Even the masses of the Well-In-
tentioned queued up just outside the Gate could sense the
change come over the Infernal City.

Well before midday it became clear that something
must be done. The Major and Minor Calamities took
council and decided to appoint a deputation. With all
appropriate dragging of feet and gnashing of teeth, the

foremost of the Wretched was dispatched to learn what ailed their master.

As might well be expected, what most ailed the master at that very moment was having his well-earned sulk intruded upon. He immediately elevated the poor Wretch to ranks of the Unquestioningly Obedient, conferring upon him all the torments and tribulations associated with that lofty status, and making a rather pointed suggestion as to where his unwelcomed guest might now go. Even so, the master got little satisfaction from the small cruelty.

"Fresh air," he said aloud, for in Hell there is no thought that remains unvoiced. You could always spot the newcomers among the Host of the Damned. Their thoughts tumbled off the tongue, betraying the words muttered in the same breath. They were ever saying things like, "But sir, it was not my fault, you pig-headed spawn of a, damn, I'm for it now. What I mean to say is. Sir. What I mean to say, SIR, is." By that point it was best to just give up and take what was coming to you. You'd get it anyway, in the end. It was the nature of the place. It was Hell. You got used to it.

"That's just the thing to put me right. A walk down pasture. And a drop of drink to clear the head. Ouiskey. Water of Life."

"The very thing, if it please your Underlordship to notice me."

The Sycophants had had quite some time to master the art of seamlessly smoothing word and thought together. All time, in fact.

"Ouiskey. Water of Life," The master mused. "That was one of my own inventions, you know. Still remember as if it were yesterday. So I says to Yourman above, this was back when we were on more civil terms, 'Breath of Life?' says I. 'What're they ever going to do with Breath of Life? You can't very well keep it in the cupboard against chill winter nights, or carry it at your hip to bolster the flagging spirit. And the poor wigglies, what will they do without a decent public house at least, to keep the mind off the fundamental unfairness of it all? No, water's Your man.'"

A babble of earnest voices vied for his attention.

"Would that I could have been there to take part of the, to take part in that glorious achievement."

"Called 'em wigglies to His face! I dare say."

"I'd wager that pitched Him into a right rage. Why it's a wonder He didn't haul back and knock you clear out of...oh dear."

There was the briefest of pauses while the strict hierarchy of the Infernal Court readjusted itself with all the swiftness and subtlety of a sprung bear trap. The next moment it was as if the unfortunate courtier had never been.

"Stupid," chorused the Staters of the Painfully Obvious, making two distinct words of it. "Stew Pit."

"Silence!" yourman the Devil calls. And Silence, she answers his calling. The Host of the Damned kind of edges away sideways, uncomfortable at her passing.

Now they say Sin has an only son and his name is Death. And he is rightful heir to the Kingdom of Man. And all must come at last to pay him homage.

But that Devil, he also has his Pride. A lone daughter, the apple of his eye. And he named her Silence. And when even Death has passed, she follows after.

It was always a terrible moment when Silence entered the Halls of Hell. Pain-wracked visages wordlessly mouthed cries, curses, entreaties. Talon, scourge and hot iron bit soundlessly into yielding flesh. The sound of each *and every shuffling footstep, creaking joint, rasping breath, magnified to the power of countless millions of lost souls crammed into every fissure, niche, and crevice—all gone suddenly, completely, and hauntingly still.*

It was not just the absence of sound; it was its utter negation. All that took place in her presence had an eerie, unreal feel about it. It was as if all the torments of the Legions of the Dead were a sad sort of pantomime. A ritual act whose meaning had become obscure, lost long ago.

The Devil, he smiles warmly. "Take my hand, child. I've a fierce stabbing pain in the head and it's put me in foul temper. I've taken a kenning to have a walk down pasture, take a drop of drink and overlook the wigglies, for I fear they're again up to no good, if this ringing in my ear is any indication. And it usually is. And they usually are."

Silence, she says nothing, just takes her father by the arm and leads him from his hall.

Talbott's listeners were so lost in his strange tale that no one had noticed the silent woman—stern, dark, straight as a pin—who had slipped into the chamber. The Great Portal sighed contentedly closed behind her and she wrapped herself in its familiar, comforting shadow.

Patient as death, she began marshalling her forces—words of fire and of blood. She drew them up into bristly phalanxes, she deployed them in centuries stretching across the field of vision.

She rallied her champions and prepared to defend her home, her past.

"Excellent, Aaron. You have done well. Your preparations are impeccable. Please proceed." Foley gestured absently toward the cleared patch of floor at the room's center and turned away. Until very recently, this space had been as heaped with arcane paraphernalia as the rest of his cramped sanctum.

To all appearances, the room's new arrangement was the result of a fastidious application of blasting powder.

He is insane, Aaron thought. *Dangerously insane.* Cautiously, he gathered up the items he had so carefully arranged on the sideboard for Foley's inspection. *He can't be serious about going through with this.*

For weeks, Aaron had endured the smug glances, the knowing chuckles, the too-familiar touches of his superior. Each of the hundred tiny gestures had been calculated to convey the same unsettling message—*I know your secret.*

Aaron cursed himself for a fool. It had happened that night of the Stalking of the Koldun. The entire chantry had gathered to enact the stalking ritual. At its center, Sturbridge plunged into the very heart of the nightmare, New York's mystic landscape—the Dragon's Graveyard. And they had followed.

He could still recall the vivid towers of pitted steel and sizzling neon rising above him on all sides. He could feel the teasing hint of the familiar behind the rambling procession of bus stops, tenements and yellow police tape. It was almost the city he knew.

But something fundamental had been changed. That was why Sturbridge had brought them there— so that they could see with their own eyes the changes that had been wrought. Ripples from a single stone dropped upwards into the River of Night.

The alterations were subtle but sweeping. The *other* was patiently reshaping the city in its own image. Aaron had thought the anomalous element that had been introduced into his beloved city was the Koldun—the Tzimisce sorcerer. The very word seemed to whisper of blasphemous secrets and unholy predations. It was a breath straight from the grave of the Old Country. It was a word of power, a name to conjure with.

The mere mention of the cult of sorcerous fiends conjured up images of moonless nights centuries distant, nights when Aaron's forbears had hunted (and been hunted in turn) among the blasted crags of the Carpathians. The Tremere had gone to great lengths to distance themselves from such recollections.

Aaron could remember the first caress of the Koldun's dark sorcery. He remembered Sturbridge going down under the enemy assault. He remembered the sick feeling in his withered stomach as he found himself involuntarily rushing to her aid—as if just reaching her would be the culmination of all his decades of unlife, of his strivings, of his sacrifices. Damn her.

And then he was at her side. And she touched him. She knew him. She smiled.

Damn it, he hated that smile. It was a smile she reserved for meetings upon thresholds. She would take your hand and give you that smile and you knew with unshakable certainty that she had contrived this entire improbable gathering just to steal this one sympathetic moment with you. To squeeze a hand, to exchange an exaggerated sigh, and then to be torn away again, becoming everyone's once more.

Aaron was not quite sure how she had pulled them all out, gotten them safely home again. That was the reality, of course, not the damned smile. She didn't need them half as much as they needed her. And they all knew it. Even if it were nice to pretend otherwise, if only for a short while.

But upon her homecoming that evening, she was furious. It was something between Foley and Jacqueline, Aaron was never exactly sure what. Sturbridge was hot, raging on about invaders, earthquakes, traitors.

It was at precisely that instant that Foley had caught his eye. And he saw, damn him. Aaron didn't know how he saw, but in that instant Foley knew everything. Over the last few weeks, he had gone to great pains to let Aaron know that he knew. These wardings—the elemental regalia that Foley had insisted that Aaron gather personally—they were only the latest in a long string of insinuations. Oh, Aaron had followed his superior's instructions to the letter. But he'd thought that would be the end of it. He would present his hard-won treasures before the secundus. He would be humiliated. He would be exposed. He would perhaps even be blackmailed.

But this? Surely Foley wasn't going through with this. From his station in the east of east, Aaron glanced once more uncertainly toward the secundus. But Foley was lost in his preparations.

Aaron stared after him for a long moment, his thoughts racing through the possible scenarios—in-

trigue, threats, blackmail, confession, violence, submission, bribery, reconciliation. He picked up and
examined each in turn like a rare jewel. Just as carefully, he set each aside again, dismissing it. Gradually,
something crystallized within him. His features became hard, angular, sharp.

With the cruel precision of a diamond cutting
through glass, Aaron stooped and marked out true
east on the floor in bone-white chalk. It was not the
east that would read on any manmade compass. Nor
the celestial east of equinoxes or solstices viewed
through menhirs. It was true east, Vienna. The home
of the Council of Seven, the resting place of the Father, the seat of the blood.

Resignedly, Aaron placed his unorthodox ward
over the Eye of the Storm, the diagram's easternmost
point. It was a plank from a gallows, long, thin,
straight as a stave. The wood had the added virtue of
never having touched the earth.

He was now committed. From this point, there
was no turning back from this mad course. Forcing
down any further uncertainties, Aaron paced off the
precise distance to the southernmost point, the Hall
of Fire.

Here he drew forth from his bundle a rusted dag-
ger. The classical lines of the Roman design were
unmistakable, even under the years of wear and cor-
rosion. Aaron placed the knife carefully, its blade
pointing treacherously inward, toward the center.
Toward where Foley must stand to invoke the blood.

Another exact turning brought Aaron to the furthest west, the Waters of Oblivion. Without
ceremony, he deposited the cup of hemlock. He did
not pause to glance into the dark waters at the bot-

tom of the chalice. They would only remind him of those other dark waters and the faces of the Children, round and bright as moons. He hurriedly turned and moved further north.

Pausing to judge his mark, Aaron drew back and cast his final treasure to the ground. It struck, the rotting purse spilling thirteen of its thirty silver coins. A very inauspicious throw. Aaron let it lie.

He turned again upon Foley. Surely, the game was up now. Foley wasn't going through with this. Foley would turn on him, mock him, scorn him. He would bellow something dramatic like, "Now take your proper place at the center of these treacheries that you have brought into my house!"

But no. Foley was composed, hauntingly still. Aaron recognized that stillness. It was the lull, the pregnant pause into which the blood spills.

No, this was foolishness. It had to be stopped. He would ruin everything. What possible use could these assembled barbs and insinuations serve in an actual ritual? An invocation of the blood was a thing of delicacy and no little danger. What kind of madman would knowingly ward himself in these petty treacheries?

Foley's voice was calm. "Aaron?"

"Yes, Secundus."

"Would you be so kind as to send Jacqueline in to me as you go through?"

"Secundus, you can't..."

"Thank you, Aaron."

"No, sir. I'm serious. I'm sorry. It doesn't have to happen like this. I'll...I'll send him away."

Foley smiled. "Send him away? You can't just send him away. I know. I have looked into his eye. There is no turning him aside from his purpose."

Aaron started, catching himself glancing over his shoulder for the dark, silent accomplice that he knew was not yet there.

"But you cannot have looked into his…" Aaron fell silent. It was then he saw the blood. The twisting strands of vitae stretching floorward from Foley's dangling fingertips.

It had already begun.

Foley reached out one trembling hand toward the apprentice. As his palm turned upward, Aaron could see the vicious slashes running in parallel down the secundus's forearm. There was a hole gouged in the center of the upturned palm. A single black and red stone was pressed deeply into the center of the wound. In Aaron's excitable state, the whole resembled nothing more than a single unblinking eye.

"He has shown me all, our dear Hazima-el. I have peered into his eye. His lost eye! Seen into its very depths. Do you think that I do not see it before me when I go to my rest? It is all laid bare before me. You are there, of course, and the other. Your dark shadow. You are conspiring outside the *Exeunt Tertius*. Oh and there are others. Jacqueline is there—that is why you must send her to me."

Aaron could only look on in growing dismay as Foley staggered forward. "But it is not any of these that accomplishes my end." Foley laughed, coughed, barking a fine spray of blood. Fingertips groped for Aaron's cheek. The apprentice braced himself and stood unflinchingly before the ravages of the blood.

Then, as if struck by an entirely different thought, Foley let his hand drop absently to his side. He mumbled something and, turning away, began smoothing the wrinkles from his ceremonial robe. He succeeded only in leaving long smears of blood. A clumsy effort like a child's fingerpainting. Foley looked around the room as if seeing it for the first time. Like a magpie, he turned from one curiosity to another. At times he stumbled. At times, he dashed things from their cubbyholes. At times he tore books from shelves, or pages from books, or words from pages. Some words he brandished at Aaron. Others he ground underfoot. Others still, he ate with great relish, humming to himself.

He's mad, Aaron thought. *He will ruin everything.*

Without a backward glance, Aaron slipped from the sanctum and hurried down toward the *Exeunt Tertius*.

Saturday, 24 July 1999, 11:35 PM
Anteroom of the Chantry of the Five Boroughs
New York City, New York

Talbott fumbled midphrase, and shivered as if someone were walking upon his grave. He covered the lapse in his narrative with a weak fit of coughing, taking the opportunity to gesture for another mug. Someone poked the fire back into a more welcoming blaze, sending shadows scurrying for the corners of the room. Chairs were hastily shifted to make room for the storyteller closer to the hearth.

Talbott was having none of it. When he was again suitably fortified against the chill with a long draught, he waved aside their fussings in mock indignation. "Worry a body to death with all this mothering. Haven't needed anyone to wipe my nose for the past seven decades, close as I can figure. Just had a passing chill." *A premonitory chill.*

Talbott could feel the tale rising up against his approach. This was the trickiest part of the whole endeavor. A story, a real story, had to be coaxed, courted, finessed. He had the uncomfortable suspicion that this story was lying in wait for him.

"*A Spadeful of Earth from Your Grave,*" he called.

"*What's that you see there, child?*" that old fiend he says to his only daughter. "*In the distance. My old eyes have gone rheumy and I can't well mark it. I bid you speak.*"

"*A fire, father,*" came the whisper. *If her stillness cast peril over even the Hosts of Hell, her voice was more terrifying still. It rent the very air. The words she spoke* were softer than an adder's breath, but they fell with the weight of mountains. The voice carried with it a sudden chill as if someone had taken a spadeful of earth from your grave. "Upon the Plain of Adoration."

A hissing invective escaped the Devil's lips, for he had at last figured out what ailed him. "A sign," he said aloud, out of habit. "No mistaking it."

And now he knows. Knows that a child has been born—a babe that might one day stand before the dark well of Cromm Cruaich, the Stooped One—and speak the words of fire and of blood. The fire on the blasted plain marked the child's birth. It beckoned to its own.

That Devil, he finds himself squinting into the distance, trying to pick out the smear of broken ground that marked the boundary of the Plain of Adoration, the place of sacrifice. "Too much blood already," he thinks aloud. "Blood of the firstborn, polishing smooth the crude stone idol. Cromm Cruaich. He was their Moloch, their Kinslayer, a nightmare of an older order. Chidden of God, banished to the dark places of the earth, sheltering from the light of life-giving day. He has had centuries to brood in those shadows, marking time by the spilling of blood into his dark well."

The mere prospect of another soul lost to the Stooped One, well, it makes the Devil's cold heart colder by turns.

So that Devil, he decides to take himself down and see if he can't find this child. And just give him a looking over. Not meaning him any harm, mind you. Not even Old Nick can abide the suffering of children. Oh, he'll get the work done right enough, but it's far beneath him to get any enjoyment from it.

"Leave me," he says kindly and his girl, she is gone as suddenly as she came. A good lass and clever. A great comfort and no small credit to her doting father.

The very stones sighed at her passing.

"Can't imagine how I'd ever get on without her." So down the Fiend goes to that tiny distant smudge of green, just to have a better look.

But the closer that Devil gets to Eire and the newborn child, the louder the ringing gets.

Now, a little discomfort is not going to stop yourman, so he keeps coming. But soon the ringing's grown so loud it's rattling the teeth around in his mouth. He sets his jaw firmly against the riot as he crests the rim of the world, taking seven leagues at a stride. At first nothing of him can be seen but his head, rearing up into view. Ice-blue eyes, bright but opaque, like moonlight through storm clouds. Alien, ambiguous, unreadable.

Then the thin shoulders, tapering to a point behind where they meet the downcurve of the magnificent tracery of wing. By the time the head of his walking stick first rises into view, his own head is already hidden amongst the layers of cloud.

Each time he opens his mouth to draw breath, that ringing it peals out of the cloud like thunder. Fishermen noting the darkening of the sky are already taking in their nets, casting reproachful glances at the sky that has so suddenly betrayed its earlier promise. And the vindictive storm it dogs them all the way back to Eire's fair shores.

That Devil, his head is literally splitting by this point, but still he comes and at last he sets foot firmly upon the edge of the docks at Malehide. The sound of that footstep it thunders as if an entire herd of cattle is clattering up the wooden dock on cloven hooves. The fishermen they look up apprehensively and return to hurriedly lashing tight their moorings and stowage. The looming storm it promises to be a visitation from the very gates of Hell.

Well, yourman the Devil, he's close enough at this point that if he merely falls forward he'll hit Irish soil. But he can come no closer. So there he just sits himself down, cradling his aching head and moaning quietly to himself. A low, forlorn sound, like a storm gathering, rolling shoreward.

And as he rocks himself slowly back and forth, he seems to spiral inward upon himself. Like a snake swallowing its tail. Soon the cloud-crowned giant is no bigger than a mere mountain. Then he's a proud ship, rising just above the crest of the world. Now he's a noble house, overlooking the town. Now a bear, standing head and shoulders above the startled hunter.

And soon he's no larger than a man and a small, sad man at that. And yourman, he's still curling inward at his edges.

"Here now," Corraig shouted above the rising maelstrom. "You'll catch your very death out here, with that monster of a storm breaking. Here's a hand. There's a good man. Are you hurt? I say, are you hurt?" That Devil, he just sort of scowls up at the fisherman and waves him off. With each flat gesture of his hand, the waves crash higher over the docks. Corraig shrugs and mouths something that is torn away by the wind. He readjusts the net draped over one shoulder. Then he stoops down and clasping yourman's forearm, hauls him upright.

When it's clear yourman has his land legs once again, Corraig looses him, clapping him once on the shoulder for good measure. Then, setting his back to the howling wind, he makes his way up the dock.

He is no more than half its length when he glances back and sees yourman still standing just where he was left. Casting eyes heavenward, Corraig fights his way back toward him and throwing the man's arm across his shoulders sets the pair of them toward home.

Talbott jumped as the hand closed over his shoulder. There was no reassurance in that grip, no warmth of human contact. No pulse of circulation belied its death-cold grip.

"My lady…" he stammered. "We are honored. Please, join us." He cleared the bench nearest him with an exaggerated shooing motion.

Sturbridge neither loosened her grasp nor moved to accept his invitation.

Talbott hurried on. "It seems you are just in time. I was just relating the tale of…"

"I have some passing familiarity with the story."

"My lady, we meant no offense." His voice fell to the whisper of a confidante. "These young ones, they are devoted to you. Their greatest desire is to please their mistress. They only want to know, to understand, to draw closer."

In stark contrast to his hushed tones, her voice clearly carried over the crowd. "It is not your place, Brother Porter, to promote familiarity between the instructors and pupils here." Her grip was ice and steel.

"No, no. You are quite right, my lady."

"Who do you think will be left to pay the price for this lapse in judgment?"

Behind her, Eva stood up.

"Regentia, I asked Talbott for the tale. He is not responsible. He tried to dissuade me, but I insisted. I will pay the price of its telling."

Sturbridge looked hard at Talbott. "The price of its telling. Those words ring of your voice, brother porter, not hers. Have you told her, as well, exactly what the price of that telling would be? And in what coin it must be paid?"

Once golden, he thought. Talbott began to explain, but Eva cut him off. "Regentia, if I have trespassed in some way, I will pay the price."

Sturbridge turned and regarded her levelly, sizing her up as if truly seeing the novice for the first time. She nodded gravely.

"From your mouth to the Devil's ear, child. It shall be as you say."

Foley came to an abrupt halt as he careened into the worktable. He patted the table apologetically, already spinning off in another direction. Then he stopped and took a step back. He surveyed the paraphernalia assembled on the table in open wonder. Then he bent low, studying the peculiar implements with a critical eye.

With satisfaction, he took the measure of the two eight-inch-tall, four-inch-wide oval mirrors. He ran a finger over their perfectly polished silver rims, admiring the smooth glass, the silver backings. One, he noted distractedly, now bore a hairline crack running the mirror's length from upper right to lower left. The bar sinister.

Dimly a recollection intruded upon him. *Jacqueline*. Yes, these were the objects he had instructed Jacqueline to prepare. He could see the list before him now, with all the clarity of his advanced mnemonic powers. It was a perfect image, a flawless reflection.

Carefully replacing the ruined mirror, his fingers fumbled among six sticks of smoothly sanded pine. Each was carved to about the size of a schoolchild's chunky pencil. They had once been carefully arranged upon a flat silver tray engraved with a familiar fleur-de-lis inlay—a companion piece to the chest that had, until recently, housed his little gem. His eye. His eye to the Eye. *That Eye is like unto this eye*, he thought. *But in a low place, not in a high place*.

Now the pieces of pine lay jumbled like pickup sticks in the wake of his precipitous collision with the worktable. Foley picked up first one stick, then another. He stared at them intently, as if to wrest their secrets from them. With a patience exceeded only by the uncontrollable shaking of his hands, he set about arranging the sticks.

He stood them on end and leaned them together like drowsy soldiers. They tumbled down again.

His hand slipped. One of the sticks snapped sharply in two against the tabletop. It was not sap, but blood that flowed from the break. It slid effortlessly, languidly, across the fine silver of the tray.

A distant part of Foley's mind was aware that something was wrong. Terribly wrong. It was the blood—the way it flowed, its consistency. It was too thin; it was too lithe.

The apprentice should have infused the sticks with her own blood—the blood of the Tremere, the blood of the Seven. *The power was in the blood.*

Foley opened himself to the Sight. His gaze became fixed on an imaginary point in the middle distance. His eyes unfocused. He opened his hand, revealing the blazing red eye embedded in his palm. And he saw.

A lithe shadow slipped between the pine sticks, winding about them, rubbing its side up against them. Purring.

A black cat, Foley thought. *The blood of a black cat.*

All was becoming clear now. It would be unnecessary for Aaron to send Jacqueline to him after all. He now understood why the Eye had shown her to him and the part she would play.

Foley looked around absently for Aaron, but could not see the apprentice anywhere. It was no matter. He would return soon. He had to return. That much was clear.

With great deliberation, Foley reached out and took up a second stick. He broke it and let the blood rejoin that already spilled on the tray. He took up another.

At the snap of the sixth and final stick, seven red candles flamed to life. *More of Jacqueline's handiwork*, Foley mused. His judge, his apprentice, his would-be murderer. He smiled.

His instructions had been precise. Each of the candles were to be painstakingly melded with entrails of wild owl. To speed the thoughts winging out across the night. To give piercing insight through the veils of darkness.

Several of the candles had already taken flight when Foley careened into the table. They were scattered across the floor when the bough broke. They burst merrily aflame. Their merriment quickly spread. The smoke that rose on all sides pulsed redly—taking its lead from the blazing red stone embedded in Foley's palm.

There was the unmistakable odor of blood that had been left out in the sun.

But the candles too, were wrong. Foley could already pick out the afterimage, not of the snowy owl, but of a black cockerel, preening and strutting among the flames.

Blood of black cat, heart of black cockerel. *Company's coming*, Foley thought. Instinctively, he found himself judging the distance between himself and the protective circle. Too far.

Sunday, 25 July 1999, 12:14 AM
Barnard College
New York City, New York

It was the fourth night of his vigil outside Milbank Hall. The campus administrative building was silent. From his vantage point, concealed within the shadow of the adjacent science building, Anwar kept his attention fixed upon a particular disused side door.

For the first time since he had begun his surveillance, the door had opened. Instantly, he was totally alert, transcending even his normally high level of vigilance and entering into that hypersensitive state where duty and faith merged and were one.

The man who slipped from the doorway appeared nervous, agitated. He was young, fair, clean-shaven and dressed casually, after the manner of these western *kafir*. He might have passed among the faculty of the college without question.

If Anwar had half expected a gnarled old gnome—bearded, robed, a silver skullcap perched precariously atop bald pate—he did not let his disappointment to show. Instead, he allowed his expectations to align themselves with the reality before him.

With the appearance of the nervous man, the field of possibilities before Anwar had just narrowed to two. Either this was his contact, or this was someone who had discovered the clandestine arrangement, removed the contact from the picture, and unwisely decided to keep the appointment himself.

Anwar held his ground and awaited the prearranged sign.

The newcomer scrutinized his surroundings, peering intently into the crisscrossing shadows formed by the trees and academic buildings. Anwar drew more deeply into his concealment, the shadows both common and preternatural that cloaked him.

He is looking for me, Anwar thought. *But if he is the one, why does he delay? Why doesn't he give the sign?* There were no witnesses or other obstacles that might justify his hesitation. Anwar, however, had the advantage of having been secreted in that spot for several nights. Perhaps the thin man was merely being cautious.

Or perhaps he had failed to extract this one crucial detail from the original contact.

The newcomer continued his fidgeting. He paced. He stopped suddenly to peer intently into the shadows and then went back to his pacing. He wiped perspiration from his forehead. He rubbed his eyes. He muttered to himself.

The man's unease was contagious. Anwar instinctively palmed a knifeblade.

The man wheeled. His gaze stopped on Anwar—stopped and *saw*. Anwar was sure of it. Their gazes locked for a moment before the newcomer spun away and resumed his distracted pacing.

There was more than nervous agitation in the other's eyes. Was it madness? His gaze seemed filled with blood and fire. Anwar shook his head to clear the impression. Romantic foolishness. It was only the result of the blood-sweat that dotted the nervous man's forehead, that he kept smearing into his eyes with the back of his hand. Nothing more.

Anwar watched the newcomer even more intently. The other gave no outward indication that he had picked out the lurker in the dark. He checked his watch, muttering under his breath. With a scooping motion, he cupped his hands before him. Inside the hollow formed by his hands, a low flame leapt to life. He'd struck no match, raised no lighter, yet a flame danced upon his open palm. He raised his hands to his mouth as if lighting a cigarette. Anwar could see the light flickering momentarily through the lattice of the other's fingers. Then, as quickly as it had appeared, the flame puffed out.

Anwar knew that anyone else observing the brief glint of flame would doubt what he had seen, would convince himself that he had been mistaken. Anwar himself would have doubted the evidence of his eyes, were it not for the fact that the flame was the very sign he had been awaiting. Even now, after the time for action had clearly arrived, Anwar held back a moment. His impulse was to cling to the sheltering shadows and skirt the open area between the buildings as much as possible. He suppressed it.

If his contact had not kept his end of the bargain—by making the proper arrangements to ensure the success of the mission—there was little Anwar could do about it at this late date. Little, save meet his end with dignity.

Now that the long nights of inactivity were at an end, the indirect approach would consume vital seconds. Anwar strode purposefully across the open ground.

He watched his contact's hands carefully as he approached. They betrayed impatience. Anwar knew it was not yet too late to escape should the *kafir* prove untrustworthy. Once he was within the chantry proper, however, he would be completely under the warlocks' power. Escape might well prove impossible. He pressed the concealed blade of the knife more tightly against the line of his forearm.

To his credit, the nervous man did not jump as Anwar broke from the sheltering shadow. Instead, he checked his watch a second time and cursed.

"I am Aaron." The voice was level, curt, as if he had been the one kept waiting. At close quarters, the skin of his fingers and face betrayed his youthful appearance. His flesh was too tight-fitting. It crackled like parchment about the eyes.

Anwar inclined his head in greeting, his eyes never leaving the warlock's. In those blood-dimmed eyes, Anwar had expected to see the hard edge of cunning, ruthlessness, opportunism—traits for which the warlocks were infamous. Perhaps he had even hoped to glimpse some hint of the traitor's motive— the heat of avarice, the sideways cast of guilt, the pure luster of vengeance.

Instead he saw only desperation, impatience and abandon. It was an unhealthy combination and one which Anwar was accustomed to giving a wide berth. His partner in this evening's endeavor was quite obviously beginning to unravel about the seams.

"May Haqim guide your hand and speed your purpose, Aaron Light-bringer. This evening we are of a single will. May the blood that falls between us belong only to strangers. All is in readiness within?"

"Not here," came the low-pitched reply. Aaron turned his back and fumbled at the doorknob. Anwar was acutely aware of the cold edge of the knifeblade pressed against his forearm. He held the blow, awaited bigger prey.

The door gave inward revealing only darkness beyond. Aaron slipped within. If he realized the danger he had so narrowly avoided, he gave no outward sign.

Anwar followed. Crossing the threshold, he was painfully aware that he was now at the mercy of his enemies. But he was not without resources. He found himself wondering how it was that the elders had come to hold power over this warlock—how one of the hated Tremere had become indebted to the children of Haqim. Rumors abounded regarding the fanatical loyalty of the warlocks. Whispers of the unbreakable bonds of blood among the Tremere—bonds that should have made this type of casual betrayal all but impossible—had reached even the remote mountain refuge of Alamut.

Like all of his people, Anwar could personally attest to the potency of the Tremere mastery over the blood. And of their power to enslave others with it. The memory of the centuries his people had suffered as blood thralls to the Tremere curse was not likely to soon fade—not until the blood of the last of the oppressors had been reclaimed.

But the elders, Haqim be praised, had discovered a way to turn the tables upon the Tremere and break free of the dark power of the warlocks' tainted blood. And if the elders could lift the Great Curse that bound the people, what was the bloodbond of one solitary Tremere novice?

Anwar must have snorted aloud. The sound could not have been louder than a whisper, but his guide turned sharply and motioned him to silence. It was evident that he feared discovery. Good.

Anwar lingered upon the thought of a world in which warlock turned against warlock. He pictured the children of Haqim, as numerous and inevitable as the sands of the desert, rising up to engulf the Tremere pyramid. They would dance *hadd*, vengeance, atop its ruins. Their pounding feet would drive even the last memory of the warlocks down beneath the shifting sands. Oblivion.

Yes, the fortress of vengeance was rising even now from the swirling sands, its vast walls climbing, one grain at a time, above the desert wastes. Each grain was mortared to its brother with the blood of their enemies—the blood that had been so long denied them. Surely some great reckoning was at hand. The blood that Anwar would shed tonight would bring his people that much closer—precisely one grain of sand closer—to that fortress of final vengeance.

What more did Anwar need to know in preparation for this night's undertaking? He was merely a tool of vengeance. It was not given to him to know the mind of the builders. He was not privy to the secrets of the elders. His duty was merely to strike true. And to avoid, at all costs, twisting or breaking in the master's guiding hand.

He had not been instructed in the details behind the *kafir*'s betrayal of his own foul kind. Anwar had no reason beyond idle curiosity to possess such information. This did not, however, keep him from wondering. Surely the warlock knew the end that awaited them at the termination of this path.

Anwar grew wary. He was not at all pleased with the arrangement that left him relying upon a *kafir*—especially one who had given himself up to despair and betrayal. How could such a one be trusted? How could such a one hope to survive his treachery?

"Follow me," Aaron whispered. "Stay close."

Anwar did so. He placed each step precisely in the space Aaron's foot had recently abandoned. He suspected that they were already within the perimeter of the chantry's arcane defenses. There would be no room for misstep.

A narrow corridor ran from the side door into deeper darkness. The hallway led past a heavy oak door with frosted glass and the painted words: ASSOCIATE DEAN OF INTERDEPARTMENTAL ACADEMIC DISCIPLINARY REVIEW. Anwar memorized each letter and its exact position in the sequence.

He wondered at the meaning of the strange words, but, respecting his guide's admonition to strict silence, Anwar did not press him to read the inscription. The lettering looked bureaucratic and daunting. The effect was calculated, no doubt, to turn away the merely curious—an epithet that encompassed the vast majority of those who haunted these western "universities."

Aaron was not put off by the inscription. He inserted a normal-enough looking key into the lock and led Anwar inside.

The assassin expected to step from the drab, collegiate environment into a stronghold of splendor and debauchery befitting the excesses for which Clan Tremere was renowned. Instead, the office beyond the forbidding door was as nondescript as the corridor without. A desk, filing cabinets and a few chairs were its only furnishings.

Aaron locked the door behind them and exhaled audibly. "Here we can talk. But we've got to hurry. He's going to ruin everything." He crossed to the desk and picked up one of two gray robes that lay draped across it. He tossed it toward Anwar.

"Who's going to ruin everything?" Anwar caught the robe. He did not don it right away, but waited patiently until Aaron had his head and arms entangled in his own robe. Only then did Anwar follow suit.

"Foley. The target." The Tremere stumbled guiltily over the word.

"Johnston Foley," Anwar recited, checking his facts. Regent Secundus, second-in-command, Chantry of the Five Boroughs, New York City, New York. Height: 177 cm. Weight: 80 kg. Hair: dark, graying. Eyes: brown. Mustache, beard: full, graying. Apparent age: late forties. Actual age: circa two hundred years, American antebellum period."

"Yes, yes. Foley. That's very impressive. But the problem is..."

"Known threats—Thaumaturgist: blood magic manifesting through the written word, drawings, glyphs, wardings, ritual diagrams. Firearms: passable shot with pistol, usually unarmed. Poisons: suspected involvement in deaths of two fellow novices, Atlanta chantry. Reassigned, high-risk posting to C5B. Political: high-level connections with..."

"He's gone mad."

This brought Anwar up short. Another mad warlock. Things were becoming complicated. "Please explain."

"I can't believe he's actually going through with it. If we don't get to him soon... Look, when I left

Foley, he had already started the ritual, a very stupid and dangerous ritual. It's going to kill him. If we don't get there first."

Anwar considered. "I do not understand your sudden concern for the target's safety."

"Look, I don't know what your hidden masters will do to you if you return without killing Foley. But I know what...I know it's important that Foley is assassinated. Here. Tonight."

"And it shall be so. Is he alone?"

"Yes. He was. But he kept saying something about others coming. I think he might have been talking about you."

All right, Anwar thought. *Two mad warlocks, and the target has been forewarned.*

"May I ask you a further question, Aaron Light-bringer? A personal question?"

Aaron looked impatient, but motioned for him to continue.

"Why is it important that Foley be assassinated? And tonight? And within the walls of the chantry? Why are you doing this?"

Surely you can see how this must end.

Aaron returned his stare, unflinching. Slowly, pronouncing each syllable distinctly, he replied, "Why are you doing this?"

Anwar was taken aback to hear his own question parroted back at him. Then, at last, he understood. Anwar bowed deeply, formally, to his guide. "Let us do, then, what is needful. Shall we go?"

"Let's get this over with." Aaron turned toward what was apparently a coat closet. He placed a hand upon the knob.

"I do not think we shall speak again. Beyond this point, it will not be safe. I will see you safely to Foley's sanctum. If you succeed, I will see you safely out again. More than that, I cannot do. If we are intercepted en route..."

Anwar nodded. "Say nothing more. It is sufficient, Aaron Light-bringer. We shall do what is needful."

The warlock turned his attention back to the doorknob and muttered a few words beneath his breath. Anwar could not be sure if it were an incantation or a desperate prayer.

Anwar felt his skin tingle momentarily as the words were spoken, whether due to some sorcerous incantation or merely the power of suggestion. He silently berated himself for the shiver.

The door opened to reveal plain concrete walls and a narrow metal stairway leading downward. The confined space was cool, damp. Something about the view put Anwar in mind of gazing down a well. Anwar dutifully recorded every detail of their descent—the precise number of steps to each turning (seven); the total number of landings (fifty-two); the number of doors they passed in their downward spiral (four); the number of times Aaron stopped completely (twelve), apparently listening for sounds of pursuit, or perhaps catching the distant hint of trickling water, or timing the return of the echoes of their footfalls clanging back up at them from the depths.

Aaron's impatience was obvious, so Anwar did not question his frequent stops. He knew if they were not necessary precautions, Aaron would have dismissed them out of hand. It might have had something to do with the chantry's defenses. Whatever wards they might have passed through thus far, however, were of such a subtle nature that Anwar could not detect them. Perhaps his elders in their wisdom, hearing his exacting description of what he had seen, could unravel mysteries that were hidden to him.

He kept close to Aaron and turned a deaf ear to the voices rising up at him from the depths of the central well. He was well aware that it was merely a trick of the acoustics that rendered the lull of trickling water into plaintive voices. Children's voices.

Hadd, the Children whispered to him. *Vengeance*.

Sturbridge regarded Eva levelly, sizing her up as if truly seeing her young protégée for the first time. So much was riding on her. So much she could not hope to understand.

Sturbridge nodded gravely.

"From your mouth to the Devil's ear, child. The price of the tale is yours alone to pay."

Turning her attention back to Talbott, Sturbridge took the storyteller by the crook of his elbow and half-lifted him to his feet.

"Cede the stump, old bard."

"My lady?"

"Have done. Take a pint and a seat by the hearth, you've earned it. The night has grown deep and the tale has passed on to other hands. And don't argue with your elders," she added in afterthought to pre-empt further objections.

"My elders," he scoffed nervously. "Well you know that if I were to turn down such an offer—a pint of brown beer and a seat of honor at the hearth—the order would revoke my poetic license. I yield. It is, after all, your tale to tell and none other's."

Sturbridge squeezed his shoulder in parting, and settled in comfortably. Her voice carried over the room with authority. "*A Strange Catch to Show for Your Day's Labor.*"

Emer was waiting in the doorway, her face full of concern. Seeing the pair of them, she turned, scattering a flock of children back into the house. By the time they arrived, there were dry clothes and warm blankets ready to hand. The chairs had been pulled over to the fire.

The children tore about on their various hastily appointed tasks. One, two...four of them? Only Emer stood unmoved in the middle of the whirlwind of activity, her arms folded across her chest.

"Corraig ap Culain." Emer pronounced the name dispassionately, like a lord passing sentence. "Sometimes I think you haven't the sense the good Lord gave a goat. Did you not see this storm boiling up? Worry a good woman half to death." She threw a towel over his head.

"And what a strange catch to show for your day's labor." She took the stranger by the arm and led him to the fire. "You must forgive my dear husband. He's a fairly stable sort most days. And to think he came with such high references. Of course, you'd never know it to look at him. 'Puny,' my poor mother always said, 'Won't last long.'"

"And proven wrong on that count as well," called Corraig peeking from beneath the towel he was still rubbing over his head. "A man could do quite well for himself by consulting her religiously and then taking the other path."

"My, how you will go on. I'm sure Father would be glad to avail himself of your expertise on the subject of divination. I will make sure to mention it to him on Sunday. In the meantime, you might pour our guest a drop to put the warmth back in him. Poor soul's soaked through. And trembling."

"Mustn't let her frighten you," Corraig called over his shoulder. "I've seldom seen her actually talk the ears off a body."

"Pay him no mind." She scowled after her husband. "Dropped on his head as a child, poor innocent. His mother never forgave herself. Here, wrap up in this. Thank you Padraig. There's a useful lad. A wonder where he gets it from. Brigid, dear, ladle out a bowl of stew for our guest. And yes, you might as well get one for that man there as well."

Corraig recrossed the room with a cup in each hand. "There now. Your health."

The ouiskey coursed through the veins like liquid gold—the warm welcome of an old friend. The mind-numbing agony in the Devil's head receded a pace. The pain, it was still there, but yourman is no stranger to pain.

"My thanks to you and your lovely lady for the kindness you have shown a stranger. I do not know what came over me. But the spell has passed and I'll be on my way."

"We'll hear nothing of it," said Emer firmly, her eyes fixed on her husband.

"Of course not. With that storm blowing out there? Well, I'd as soon give a man up to the Devil himself. Small credit to me should I send a man to such a fate."

"No, put the thought far from you," Emer soothed, pressing the bowl of soup into his hand. "Thank you, Brigid. And even if you should venture forth, where would you go? You are clearly a stranger to these parts, you'll pardon my saying, and even the inn's door will be shut tight by now. No, we'll keep you well enough this night. Make up a place for you here by the fire."

"You are too kind to an old fiend." The Devil lowered the half-empty bowl from his lips and wiped his mouth with the back of his hand. He drew up short, seeing young Columcille eyeing him from the far side of the room.

"My manners." he said apologetically. "It's been some time since I've dined in such company. Mostly I take what meals I can get alone." Then, more confidently,

"The stew is excellent. And I suspect you are harboring more than one fine cook beneath your roof." He peeked around to where Brigid leaned against the table, watching the newcomer with undisguised curiosity. She retreated behind her mother's skirts.

The Devil finished the fish stew more carefully. One spoonful at a time. By the time he had finished, he had the worst of the cold and pain at bay. The small thatched cottage was cozy enough. A single room. To one side a table, various pots and pans hanging above it, and a pantry. Against the back wall, fireplace and sitting area. On the other side, a curtain of sailcloth separated the bed from the rest of the room and hid a cradle as well, from the sound of it.

"That'll be Brendan," Emer said, already heading in that direction. "You'll excuse me."

"Of course, of course."

She vanished behind the curtain and the Devil he waves Corraig closer.

"A fine woman, you're lucky to have landed her."

"She reminds me daily. But tell me, now that you have your breath back, what brought you to these parts? Do you have kin here, or just down Dublin-way perhaps? I'm surprised you didn't put ashore there. We don't see many but our own fishing boats dock here."

The Devil, he wasn't inclined to point out his host's mistaken impression. "My people are scattered to the four corners of the globe." It was not an idle boast. "I would be surprised if I didn't find some long-forgotten kinsman right here amongst your own. But I was turned about and forced ashore here by the storm. We were indeed making for Dublin town. And I must be away again shortly."

"Rest easy, your mates will not be putting out to sea again this day. Nor tomorrow, likely. We can send word round to them in the morning. Let them know you're well and will rejoin them soon. Are you a trader, then?"

"No. Myself, just a traveler, a self-imposed exile far from the comforts of home and family." And truer words were never spoke.

"But I would like to think that there are one or two in these parts who might yet have cause to remember me fondly." At this, the Devil he grows thoughtful. "There was a young lady of my acquaintance, a lady of Baerne. A clever lass with a rare knack for finding things that were lost. Everyone for miles about remarked it. But that would have been many a year now since last I darked her door."

"The Hag of Baerne?" Corraig laughed. "Why I'd be willing to bet no one's called the Wise Woman a "lass" since long before you or I were born. I only wish she could be here to hear you say it herself. I can see why she was fond on you, old silver-tongue." Corraig's face became somber. "She was a good woman for all her divining and charms and philtres. She will be missed."

"What? Do you tell me..."

Corraig raised his glass. "To the Wise Woman of Baerne. May she be in heaven half an hour before the Devil knows she's dead."

Part of Foley's mind was vaguely aware that a disjoint had taken place. That time was proceeding without him.

His eyes opened but, due to the perversity of time, there was a discrepancy between the physical act and the arrival of light waves that normally followed it. The portion of his mind that was still attending to such external details received stimuli that seemed already several minutes old.

His lips were moving as if of their own accord. They chanted words in a dead language. But the time-sense of his speech was different from that of his vision. Words that would only find voice an hour hence mingled with sights that were already lost to the past.

A ripple obscured the time-sense, shifted relationships. Foley saw now the way in which his hands would grasp (had grasped?) the pine sticks. His eyes recorded how he would snap each stick, and how not sap but blood would drain into the silver tray—the blood of a black cat. That was significant somehow.

Of course, Jacqueline! The cat had a child's face, a little girl. It smiled up at him, baring vestigial fangs. Foley let the face age in his mind. Its lines hardened, twisted into middle age, revealing the familiar features of his apprentice, his judge, his would-be murderer. Of course. Again he heard his mother telling him that a cat in the house would steal a baby's breath.

Foley was unsure of the passage of time in the outer world and he feared he was collapsing dangerously inward. But there was something more here. Something he had missed. He was very near the center now, the *Interiora Terrae*. If answers were to be found anywhere, they would be here. If only he could...

Suddenly, a light flared in the darkness of the labyrinth. A blazing yellow orb. The eye regarded him suspiciously. "Who's there?" The voice seemed to come from somewhere beyond the eye. "I know there is someone there, but I can't make him out. You see him? In the shadows, there, between the Witch's Shins."

A second voice soothed, "Be easy, dearest. It is nothing. A trick of the light. There is no one here who can harm you."

Foley warily circled the eye, peering intently into the shadows it splashed upon the labyrinth walls. He thought he could pick out the outline of an opening of sorts, a dark gap where two pillars leaned noticeably together. He moved closer.

"There! It moved again. Catch it. Bind it. Send it away. It cannot be allowed to interfere."

The second voice tried another tack. "Leopold, look who is here. It is our friend, Foley. Foley has come to visit you. Isn't that lovely? Leopold, you remember Foley."

Leopold dropped his chisel. It clattered to the cave's floor. He refused to turn. "I do not."

"Foley, come here, into the light, dear. Let me look at you. That's better. Here is your cousin Leopold. We were just talking about you, weren't we Leopold?"

Foley still could not pick out the second speaker

in the shadowy vastness of the cave. There was a glimmer of something just beyond a turning in the cavern. Something just beyond the edge of his vision. When he squinted his eyes, he had a vague impression of something vast. Something coaxed from the shadows and given form only by the ambiguous magic of reflected light. Something that gleamed dully, with a flat luster like that of beaten gold.

"Foley? Foley. Don't know any Foley. Oh, send him away."

"Now, that is no way to treat your cousin. And he's come such a long way to see you. To see your *work*."

At this Leopold turned. He took a quick step toward Foley and then drew up short as if struck. "It's not finished. Can't see it yet. Come back later."

"Leopold!"

The cave itself seemed to reverberate with the force of the gentle scolding. Somewhere behind Foley, the eye flared. Leopold shrank back before its intensity.

"All right. He can wait then for all I care. But not a word out of him or…"

"Now, there will be no threats here, Leopold. There can be no threats between cousins, dearest."

"Or it's back down the well with him."

With growing horror, Foley felt his lips moving, as if of their own accord, forming the dead words begun hours before. He watched the syllables tumble out into blackness.

"*Visita Interiora Terrae, Rectificando Invenies Occultum Lapidem.*"

"What's that?" Leopold pressed very close to Foley, pawing at him, shaking him. "What's that you say? *Occultum Lapidem?* The stone? The secret stone? Give it to me!"

Foley raised one hand to ward him off, revealing the baleful red gemstone embedded deep in his bloody palm. Too late, Foley realized his mistake. He felt a quickening of interest from the darkness, felt the eye press closer.

But Leopold turned away in disgust. "He knows nothing. Nothing! Oh, make him go away." He turned upon Foley. "Did you think to tempt me, to dazzle me with your pretty little gemstone? I have called the fire from the slumbering rock. I have molded it in my hands, felt it stream between my fingers. But it is not enough. It is not the medium I was promised.

"Where is your *Occultum Lapidem?* Your living rock? Bring me the stone that breathes life! Now that would be a worthy gift to set before your cousin. But instead...no. It is enough. You were a fool to come. Take him away."

"Leopold," the voice cajoled. "Will you get the pretty red stone for me?"

Foley felt the air temperature drop dramatically. He began to cast about for the way he had come.

"No. Damn the stone. Just go away. Can't you all just go away? I've got so much work to do."

There. Foley saw two stalagmites that seemed to lean toward one another. He began backing slowly in their direction.

"Leopold..."

The artist fidgeted, picked up his chisel.

"LEOPOLD..."

The voice reverberated, its cry tearing from dozens of separate mouths. Foley, brought up short by the shrieking chorus, stopped, turned. Another mistake.

There, just around a turning in the rock, the cavern opened out and Foley found himself face to face with the enormity of Leopold's blasphemous, gibbering masterwork.

Foley's last memory of the cave was of clawing frantically at the stone floor, trying to bury himself from sight.

In the absence of any conscious direction, Foley's fingers had turned to the familiar comforts of quill and ink. Instinctively, they had scratched out the ravings their master was vainly gouging into the cave floor.

A black cat with the face of a child. A radiant yellow orb. A knock-kneed witch. A golden calf. A one-eyed sculptor. A secret stone. And finally, the faint hint of something vast with a dozen distinct gibbering maws.

Punctuating the macabre illustrations in a shaky script were the words, "Hazima-el, Leopold, *Occultum Lapidem. Down the Well*." The bottom of the sheet bore the strange legend, "Leopold = *Lapidem*(?)"

Foley felt as if he were drowning in stone. Slowly, painfully, he tried to resurface. He seemed lost without the scratching of the quill to guide him. His lips still moved, forming words of power, but no sound disturbed the air.

It was then he felt the impact of a blade. With one precise, forceful jab, it severed his spinal cord. He felt his face crash against the surface of the table.

The collapse of the vision pained him far more than the physical attack. The mystical energies he had ridden to the Cave of Lamentations turned upon him. They exacted their due.

April 23, 1890
House of Corraig ap Culain
Malehide, Ireland

An Even-Handed Warrior.

"What?!" that Devil cries aloud. "How can this be so? I've had no word of it. Surely if the Hag were dead I would be the first to know. Unless…no, surely not."

The Devil trailed off into a distracted mumbling. Corraig eyed him curiously, suspecting the fever was upon him. Every once in a while, a phrase would leap out of the stream of murmurs: "Don't care HOW you find out," or "deal with him myself," or "cleaning up after Kerberos until Hell freezes over."

Corraig had gone off in some haste and returned with the jug. He poured generously, sloppily, and pushed an overfull cup toward his distraught guest to replace the spilt one.

"Come, friend, a drink to the memory of the Wise Woman of Baerne," Corraig says again, straightening and again adding the prayer, "If it please our Lord, may she be in heaven half an hour before the Devil knows she's dead."

The Devil, he just looks at him, cool-like. The glass untouched at his side. "Corraig," he says at last, "I thank you for your hospitality, but I have to be going." He waved aside the man's protest. "My trip here is all for naught, and I have to away home with all haste. Here now, I'll have no argument. You've been more than generous and I'll not burden you further."

His voice pitched lower, "No, not a word. I know how poor a catch the sea yielded today and no fault of your own. There will be little enough to go around these next few days until the storm breaks. I will not have your little ones do without on my account."

This approach allowed no room for argument. "That's settled then," the Devil said. "But I would like to repay your kindness in some way." He thought for a moment.

"Hard times lie ahead, Corraig. You may rely upon it. Listen well. Else, when the time comes when your children cry out to you in hunger, and your kinsmen's children, and your neighbors' children, you will try in vain to remember my words.

"There will be a child come into your life, Corraig. A foundling, may she ever give you as much peace of mind as she's given me this day. And as long as you can keep her safe, no harm will come to you or yours. But you must keep her well clear of the Plain of Adoration where the Stooped One broods alone over his dark hungers. An ocean between the two might not go amiss, if you take my meaning."

Corraig looked up at the Devil uncomprehendingly.

"Remember, Corraig. How will you face them if you cannot remember?" The Devil stepped from the doorway, wings unfurling above him. The rain fell away hissing, sputtering.

Corraig looked on, a forgotten ouiskey glass dangling from the end of one arm.

Somewhere behind him, a baby was crying.

No sooner was that Devil outside than the ringing pain in his head returns stronger than ever. Oh yes, a full foul temper was upon him.

"'Before the Devil knows you're dead,'" he says aloud and with dripping malice.

Well, blasphemy is never far from the Devil's lips

and with a curse, he turns away from Eire's fair shores,
already plotting mischief. And as he turns, one bead of
sweat from his brow falls upon the water.

Up come the fish, boiling to the surface and the
waters frothed red and would yield no catch for another
season, and many starved and many more went hun-
gry. Some among you may remember the Spring of the
Red Tide and will say whether these things are true.

And then the Devil, Chiefest of Calamities and most
even-handed of warriors, was gone.

The warlock, deep in trance, had no opportunity to save himself. Anwar's ferocious thrust-wrench with the *katar* was one fluid motion, and the *kafir* struck the table like a fallen timber. Anwar was on his victim and drinking deeply before the eyelids ceased their fluttering.

Hadd. Vengeance.

For five centuries, the children of Haqim had languished under the curse of the Tremere, had been unable to partake fully of the ways of the blood prescribed by the elders' elder. But now the second fortress, *Tajdid*, was reclaimed; there would be payment in full for each hour of servitude. Anwar had struck but a single blow—a small step along the road of the *hijra*.

But there was little time to bask in the deed. New strength flowing through his veins, Anwar glanced at Aaron. The Tremere, his discomfort apparent, gawked at the body of his clansman. *Have you no stomach for blood?* Anwar wondered. Or perhaps it was the focused brutality of the act that unnerved his guide. But surely he had known.

Slowly, methodically, Anwar began to search the victim. Aaron half turned away. "Is this really necessary?"

Anwar prised open the warlock's clenched fist. He removed something from the dead man's grasp. "It is done. We go."

He wrapped the bloody stone in a cloth and tucked it within his sash.

Aaron wavered for a moment. Then, decisively, he snatched up a piece of parchment from the floor and stuffed it into the sleeve of his robe.

"A memento?" Anwar teased.

"Incriminating evidence."

Anwar bowed slightly. "Lead on."

They retraced their steps, Anwar following close on the warlock's heels. As they ascended the whispering stairwell, Anwar found himself again on his guard. It was not too late for some devious trap to be sprung, for a horde of warlocks to swoop down upon him and drag him back into the depths of the chantry.

But no hidden assailants materialized. They passed through the upper office and down the short corridor to freedom. Anwar felt the cool night air on his face.

"You should not have spoken to me in Fol...in the warlock's sanctum." Aaron accused. "It was dangerous and unprofessional."

"You are displeased with the manner in which I have fulfilled the contract?"

"And you missed the sketch."

"Mad scribblings. I noted them. They were of no relevance. I disregarded them."

"I was in that sketch. If I were implicated in this, you don't think that would be relevant?!"

"I intended no slight, Aaron, Light-bringer. But it will not be relevant."

"What do you..."

"Your superiors will be displeased."

"Yes," Aaron replied guardedly, "I suppose they..."

With one graceful step, Anwar looped the garrote over the Tremere's head. The wire dug into the warlock's neck, slicing through trachea and jugular. A sharp jerk, and the head and body fell separately to the floor.

"This is likely a mercy compared to the fate your clansmen would have devised for you. Rest well, Aaron, Light-bringer. In peerless service, there is both glory and redemption."

Three sharp knocks. Sturbridge rolled over, slapping at the bedside terminal. At her touch, the monitor blinked in surprise, coming abruptly out of sleep mode. A man's voice, grumpy, and with a decidedly Cork singsong to its accent, issued from the tinny speakers: "Early-morning guests. / Raiders, famine, boils or fleas / Would be more welcome."

Sturbridge ignored the disgruntled computer and keyed the visual. The camera just outside the chamber door revealed Eva, paused uncertainly at the threshold.

She was dressed not in the normal robes of the novitiate, but in a blouse and long black skirt. Civilian clothes. She stood awkwardly with one hand raised, as if debating the wisdom of knocking a second time.

A gesture from Sturbridge retracted the hydraulic bolts securing the vault door. Eva stepped back suddenly from the reptilian hissing, then, as the door swung back, she took three determined steps into the room and then stopped. Eva stood unspeaking and unmoving, her head and shoulders bent as if under a great burden.

Sturbridge pushed herself to her feet, scooping up a robe that lay draped over a nearby chair. "Come in, Eva. Thank you for coming to see me. Please, sit down."

The novice continued standing, head bent, refusing to meet the regent's eyes. "If it please my mistress, I will stand."

Sturbridge pulled tight the sash around her waist, regarding the girl with curiosity. "I see. Very well then, tell me, what's on your mind?"

Eva gathered her courage. "I have come to submit myself to your judgment, Regentia. Talbott's story, he said it would have a price. I am here to settle my account."

"Ah, yes. The price." An uneasy silence fell between them.

"I would have thought," Sturbridge mused aloud, "that a novice coming to lay such weighty concerns before her regent would come formally attired in her robes of office."

"I have returned my robes to the vestry." The admission cost her dearly. "I have broken trust with my regent. I have placed myself out of communion with this chantry. I submit to your judgment."

"Hmm? Oh, yes. Yes, you are quite right to do so. Well then," Sturbridge turned her back upon the novice and picked her way toward the tumbledown throne of books, "I suppose the question now becomes, What are we to do with you? You don't mind if I sit down? Thank you."

Sturbridge settled into the high seat and raised her voice as if addressing a courtroom.

"Disciplinary action record. Case before the regent: FitzGerald, Eva. Novice of the First Circle."

The bedside terminal gave off a series of reluctant grumblings, thinly veiled as efforts to access the hard-drive, and then began a running transcription of Sturbridge's words.

"The novice comes before us self-accused and confessed of, how did you put it again, dear?"

"Breaking trust with my regent," Eva recited, "and placing…"

"Oh yes, breaking trust with her regent and placing herself out of communion with the chantry. Nicely put.

"The novice is also delinquent in her account with Brother Porter, in the amount of the price of the telling of one tale. The record will note that the tale in question was, after the brother's usual fashion, a bit rambling and thus its price might similarly be expected to be quite large. If one were to take into account the exorbitant amount of interest the novice seemed intent on paying the storyteller and his tall tale, the bill might well be presumed to have grown exponentially. Have you got all that?"

The computer began to read back the transcript.

"Regentia, please! This is quite serious. I've been up all…thinking about leaving the…and you're…"

Sturbridge crossed the intervening space and put an arm around the novice. "I know, child. It's all right."

She rocked Eva gently back and forth. "You wanted to know more. About me, about where I came from, about who I am, about *what* I am. About how I got this way and what I'm supposed to do about it now. Yes?"

Eva nodded, unable to master her voice. She buried her face in Sturbridge's shoulder.

"It's all right. It's all right to wonder. It's all right to ask questions. It's all right to doubt. I'm only sorry," she continued after a pause, "that you did not feel like you could come to me and ask me these questions."

"What right do I have to demand explanations from you?" Eva's reply was quick, with a note of bitterness behind it.

Sturbridge held the girl's shoulders out at arm's length. "You don't have any right to demand explanations. But you can come to me. You can ask questions, even the hard questions. And if I can, I will answer them. Do you understand? That is a promise. If I can, I will answer them."

Eva nodded past her tears.

"Now you sit down right here and wipe your face. You're a regular fright with all that blood streaking down your cheeks, a regular little monster."

She was rewarded with a choking laugh that quickly dissolved back into broken sobs.

"That's better, settle down here next to me and I will tell you more of the story you so dreadfully needed to hear. It's a story of magic and immortality. Of devils and witches. Of blood and fire.

"It's your story. Did you know that? You've already paid its price. You pay it every evening when you—against all reason and logic—rise again. You pay it every night when you hunt, drink life, endure. You pay it every morning when you surrender once again to the little death.

"Already, you can recognize hints of the familiar in the tale, snatches of dream, shards of song. Things you knew before their knowing. Yes? Good. They are our heritage. The legacy of the Pyramid. The Blood of the Seven that runs through all of our veins. Connecting us, drawing us closer together, uniting us.

"It doesn't matter how far away you go, little one. You reach out one hand. You touch the thrumming strand of blood that stretches between us, and I can feel your touch. Right now, I can tap my sire. Watch. Closer. You can almost see the shiver running up the nape of his neck. Just like someone walking on his grave.

"Ah, now he's found us out." Sturbridge's eyes closed at the answering caress, lost for a moment in memory before breaking contact.

"We are of a blood. Nothing can take that away. Nothing can change that. Not even death. Do you understand? Quiet now, child. Quiet now."

Eva was silent a long while. Then she asked tentatively, "Regentia, what Talbott said, is it true? About your having a daughter, I mean?"

The lines of Sturbridge's face grew hard. Just a moment before she had found herself calling this little one "child." She fought to master herself before she spoke. "Yes. I had a daughter once. A beautiful little girl. A magical living child. I know such a thing is hard to imagine here."

She found herself thinking, not for the first time, how much alike they were—her young novice and her lost daughter. They were of an age and there was even a hint of resemblance between them. She knew she had felt instinctively protective of her newest novice from the day she had arrived at Five Boroughs.

Eva's voice broke in upon her musings. "I think I should have liked to have had a daughter."

Sturbridge gathered in her young novice and buried her tears.

part two:
interiora terrae

Tuesday, July 27 1999, 3:16 AM
Chantry of the Five Boroughs
New York City, New York

"All of them, Regentia?" the overwhelmed novice asked.

"All of them," Sturbridge replied. "And I want all of his papers: his notes, his letters—his grocery lists for that matter. All of these books that are not in their proper places, I want them. If they are lying open, mark the pages. If they're not open, scan them for marginalia and mark those pages. Give the whole room—make that the room and the entire way down to the *Exeunt Tertius*—a good going-over for any resonances. Anything you find, I want that too. That ought to get me started. What do you know about the ritual he was enacting when he was...interrupted?"

The novice's eyes kept involuntarily straying to the desiccated body at the room's center. "I don't...I mean, it's a questing, obviously, looking at the *diagramma hermetica* but... Surely Jacqueline would be better able to answer these questions. She assisted in preparing for..." The novice broke off, but recovered herself quickly. "I'll send her along too," she added hastily, forestalling the next order.

Sturbridge paused, then dropped the finger that was raised to instruct Eva on this very point. She smiled. "Better. Tell me, how would you say he died?"

"Something went wrong, Regentia. The protective circle has been effaced in places, the candles overturned. We're lucky the whole room didn't go up in flames...."

"It can't, but go on," Sturbridge interjected.

Eva looked questioningly at the regent, but as no further information seemed forthcoming, she continued her speculation. "The ritual went wrong. Something...stepped through. It killed him and fled. That way, toward the *Exeunt Tertius* and out. Aaron tried to block its escape and was killed as well."

Sturbridge shook her head slowly. "You're rushing ahead. But perhaps you do not appreciate the danger. We're dealing with death here—the Final Death. Do you understand? When you hunt mortals, you can be ravenous. If you would contest with Death, however, you must be dispassionate. You must be disciplined. You must be patient. Death is so very...patient."

She drew out the last word like a caress. But there was no warmth in it. "You proceed from too many assumptions. For starters, how did the ritual go wrong? Foley was a regent secundus. He was assisted by two apprentices, one of the Third Circle, one of the Seventh, either of whom could have pulled off a simple questing by himself. It simply does not hold together."

Eva began to protest, but was cut off.

"Two. You can't 'step through' a questing. Nor can any of the denizens from the 'other side'. That's an old wives' tale, fit only for frightening neophytes. A questing is not like throwing wide the postern gate. It's more like putting an eye to the keyhole. A seeing, rather than a going. Or, as a *diligent* novice would say, a scrying rather than..."

"An apportation," Eva finished quickly, ducking a rather longish lecture implicit in the regent's glare. "But what if it wasn't just a questing? What if it was a full-blown summoning? I know the standard precautions aren't in place—there are none of the names of the archangelic protectors, no proper warding of the cardinal points, nothing more efficacious than chalk and candlelight and quill and parchment. But maybe he didn't want anyone to *know* it was a summoning."

The regent gave her a look of stern reproach. "You know full well that it is forbidden to perform any summoning within the *domicilium*. Even to assist in such an ill-conceived venture would be to invite my extreme displeasure."

The tone of this last pronouncement carried a far greater threat than the words themselves. Eva, however, was too caught up in fitting together the pieces of her theory to take the hint.

"All the more reason for him to conceal the true nature of the ritual! Any of the protective *diagramma* would have given him away. His assistants would have divined his purpose and," she paused triumphantly— and then suddenly remembered herself. "And dissuaded him from such a disobedient course of action," she finished, somewhat lamely.

"Yes, the assistants," Sturbridge resumed the narrative. "Whom Foley had decided to include in his 'secret' ritual for what purpose? It seems to me that not even druids, Satanists and Templars go to such great lengths to ensure that their secret rites are so well-attended."

"If I might speak frankly, Regentia," Eva began meekly, "There are those within our chantry who do not feel as fervently about the *interdicti* as you and I do."

Sturbridge raised herself up to her full height and seemed for a moment as if she might strike the novice. Eva, for her part, scrutinized some detail of the complex pattern of floor tiles, her head bent in submission.

Sturbridge exhaled audibly. "The *interdicti* exist precisely to keep foolish novices from indulging their folly unto self-destruction. Whether you realize it or not, we are besieged here. Do you know what lies beyond these walls?"

A slight smile stole over Eva's features before she could suppress it. She was thinking about the relatively cloistered campus of Barnard College upon which the chantry was situated. She wisely did not give voice to these thoughts.

"Beyond these walls," Sturbridge continued, "lies enemy territory. New York is a Sabbat stronghold. *The* Sabbat stronghold. Notwithstanding anything you might hear to the contrary from the self-styled Ventrue 'prince' of the city. Thus far, you have been carefully shielded from this harsh and uncompromising reality. But surely, even from within the safety of this chantry, you realize what is at stake here."

"Yes, Regentia." Eva's tone was submissive.

Sturbridge raised the novice's downcast face. "We can hold the ravening Sabbat at bay. We *will* hold them at bay. But we will do it the right way. We will not resort to high-risk rituals—especially those that dispense with proper wardings—within the confines of the chantry. We will not endanger our sisters in our search for better weapons to bring to bear upon our enemies. We will not embroil other powers—particularly those from beyond this terrestrial sphere—in our struggle.

"What is most important in fighting monsters is to ensure that one does not…"

"Become a monster," Eva finished quoting the philosopher. He was a countryman of hers, part of the complex intellectual and mystic tradition that was her birthright. Eva could not help but call to mind, however, that the catchy phrases of the philosopher were also a part of the birthright of the Reich. How often had his aphorisms been used to defend and expound a pogrom of genocide that humbled even the worst excesses of the undying?

Words too, it seemed, could become desperate and monstrous.

Sturbridge put a hand on the novice's shoulder and steered her toward the doorway. "But you look weary. Go to the refectory. Get some nourishment into your system. When you are quite certain you can hold something down, then—and only then—may you return here and gather the things I have requested."

As Sturbridge closed the chamber door behind them, Eva visibly sagged as if the immediacy of the corpse was the only thing that had been keeping her upright. She staggered down the corridor toward the refectory. A somnambulist.

Sturbridge watched the receding figure until it reached the bend in the passage, as if to make certain that it would not stumble and fall before then. Satisfied, she called after her, "Eva…"

The figure turned with apparent effort.

"Be wary. Not all monsters come from beyond these walls."

Sturbridge strode off purposefully toward her sanctum. The few novices she passed along the way, catching sight of their regent's demeanor, pressed back into doorways and side corridors to let her pass.

Sturbridge batted absently at something before her face as if trying to clear away a cobweb or persistent insect. She purposefully triggered no fewer than three defensive systems (two silent and one very much audible) which she left for the security team to disarm in her wake. She was none too pleased with the demonstration of their obvious shortcomings two nights earlier, and was not inclined to make their work enjoyable tonight. She even went so far as to collar a particularly perverse guardian spirit and dispatch it to convince the chantry's autonomic defenses that the *domicilium* was ablaze. That particular impossibility ought to keep them occupied for some time. They would probably have to take the "malfunctioning" system oh-so-carefully offline, dismantling and reassembling the complex series of mystic, electronic, biochemical and geomechanical wardings one by one.

It was, perhaps, a small cruelty. But not one of which Sturbridge repented. The punishment was, if anything, overly lenient compared to the bloodprice she might have exacted for their recent failure—a failure that resulted in the murder of her second-in-command in the sanctuary of his own workshop.

As she passed into her own sanctum, she noted with satisfaction that the door sealed itself behind her with the hiss of hydraulics and the singing of steel bolts ramming home. She called for the status of the chantry's exits and found them all secured. She crossed to the desk and keyed a gimmel-level override, unbarring one of the exits (the *Exeunt Tertius*, just to rub their noses in it a bit). A few quick gestures and she set a ward—a screamer, and a loud one—to go off when the door was resecured, crying the exact response time.

Only then did she allow herself to collapse into the overstuffed armchair in the room's farthest corner. This chair was the only concession to comfort in the austere study. Even so, there was something imposing, almost throne-like, about it. The chair seemed to rise from a dais of piled books. Jumbled stacks of tomes rose to well above shoulder-level in places, swaying precariously. Not infrequently, an entire wing of the edifice would break away and cascade to the floor in an avalanche of illuminated manuscripts, fashion magazines, papyrus scrolls, advertising circulars, penciled manuscripts, clay tablets, and loose-leaf paper.

Sturbridge sank into the voluminous chair. She wrapped herself in the enfolding wall of books, pulling it tightly about her. She felt its reassuring proximity, its warmth, its protection. Slowly, the dark wings that buffeted about her face began to recede.

She was more than casually acquainted with their shadowy touch—the flurry of blows that neither cut nor bruised but rather seemed to smother. Her ears rang with the cry of carrion birds. She could feel their weight above her, hovering oppressively like the noonday sun, waiting. One among them, bolder than its fellows, picked experimentally at the hem of one sleeve.

She snatched back her hand to within the shelter of the cocoon of books. Her first instinct was to lash out, to strike, to shriek, to frighten and scatter the murder of crows. With effort, she suppressed this instinctive animal response.

She knew better. There was no point in expending her energies in avenging herself upon mere messengers, upon these harbingers of the end. She withheld her scorn, reserved it for their master, the one true nemesis.

So he is come among us once again. Sturbridge found herself unconsciously gathering her defenses about her, sketching the outlines of cunning wards, beckoning to unseen allies. She harbored no illusion as to the eventual outcome of the life-long confrontation. Even her (not inconsiderable) powers would avail little against her unwelcome guest.

Sturbridge was no legendary beauty, to compel suitors and rivals to overcome intervening oceans and generations. Her particular suitor, however, possessed an inhuman patience and persistence.

It was not the first time that Death had come to call upon her. On his last visit, he had robbed her of not only her mortal life, but also of her humanity, her art, and her only child.

She only hoped that, this time, he would not be inclined to linger.

Tuesday, July 27 1999, 5:04 AM
Chantry of the Five Boroughs
New York City, New York

The rattle of the teletype broke in upon Sturbridge's morbid reverie. She checked a start that nearly precipitated another avalanche of books and papers. From her perch atop the precarious throne of books, she could see the leading edge of the tickertape probe the air experimentally, like the tongue of an asp.

Even here, within her *sanctum sanctorum*, there were implicit perils and poisons. With exaggerated care, she descended. Despite her precautions, a small wave of papers and bindings broke in her wake. She seemed for the moment a classical figure emerging from the sea and shrugging off a mantle of foam. Before the cascade of papers had subsided, Sturbridge was struck with more than a vague premonition that the news was not good. From long habit, she braced herself for the worst.

It is Washington, she thought. *Washington has fallen.*

It was not the city itself she feared for. She knew it to be lost already, damned—a casualty of the ongoing massacre that raged the entire length of the eastern seaboard. The Sabbat was crashing over the bulkhead, as inevitable as the tide. There was hardly any point in denying that they were, even now, firmly in control of the nation's capital.

It was not a reassuring thought.

The patter of the tickertape fell suddenly silent.

What instruments we have agree
The day of his death was a dark, cold day.

Sturbridge placed one hand atop the smoky glass of the bell jar to steady it as she tore free the ribbon of parchment. A dim illumination played just below the surface of the arc of glass. It broiled like a distant thunderhead, pregnant with the promise of lightning. A smear of light and color stained the glass, spreading out from the point where her hand contacted the opaque surface.

Sturbridge resisted the temptation to delve more deeply into the play of images forming and dissolving within the bell jar. It was a humble, almost reflexive magic—this peering into crystal, this seeing through a glass darkly.

The art was her birthright, a legacy that had come down to her through generations of fortune tellers, wise women, hedge witches, oracles, scryers, diviners, priestesses and soothsayers. Sturbridge was the end product of several hundred, perhaps several thousand, years of occult experimentation, spiritual searching and fervent prayer.

The crystal responded eagerly to her familiar touch.

It would be very easy for Sturbridge to lose herself in the dance of light and form that beckoned from within the crystal. But it was an indulgence. And she could ill afford indulgences right now.

Instead, she turned her back upon the arcane device and turned her attention to the ominous scrap of tickertape. She read with growing agitation.

Begin
Baltimore comma 27 July 99
period

To Sturbridge comma Regentia comma
C5B period From Dorfman comma
Pontifex comma WDC period Greetings
etc period comma Disturbing news
from Camarilla council period
Xaviar comma Gangrel justicar comma
storms out period Threatens to pull
clan out of Camarilla period
Sturbridge comma Regentia comma C5B
to report to Baltimore immediately
period Gather intelligence comma
damage control period Briefing en
route period

Keep your head down comma
Dorfman
end

Damn. Pull the Gangrel out of the Camarilla altogether? Could he do that? There must be some mistake.
Perhaps the message meant to say that the justicar
threatened to pull the Gangrel out of the defense council meetings in Baltimore. Surely that was it. Xaviar was
undoubtedly one of the most prominent Gangrel war-
lords. But the members of his clan prided themselves
on an almost rabid independence. Sturbridge doubted

that even the respected justicar could presume to speak authoritatively for his entire clan.

She found herself wondering what offense might have been so grave as to drive the justicar not only out of the council in Baltimore, but perhaps out of the Camarilla entirely. It just didn't add up.

Sturbridge read the note over a second time, scouring it for hidden meanings. *Keep your head down.* Sound advice. Things in Baltimore seemed to have taken a decidedly unhealthy turn of late.

Sturbridge's thoughts kept returning to Maria Chin, her predecessor on the council. Chin was dead. Assassinated, she corrected herself. Sturbridge had run through the scenario over and over again in her mind, realizing how easily it might have been her instead of Chin on the receiving end of that garrote. Sturbridge tried to think who would have any reason for wanting Chin dead. She performed a quick mental calculation and sighed. As was all too often the case among her fellow Tremere, it would be far easier to answer instead the question, Who did not have a reason for wanting her dead?

Sturbridge would be the first to admit that she was an ambitious regent. One did not arrive at such a position without bloodying a few noses. And one certainly did not hold such a controversial posting for any length of time without attracting the unwanted attentions of a few equally ambitious rivals.

It was not only one's peers that a regent had to take preemptive maneuvers against. There was a flicker of covetousness in the heart of even the most modest novice, and a dangerous flashfire of jealousy behind the cool exterior of even the most aloof superior.

Eric Griffin

Chin's death might well have been politically motivated. Sturbridge knew very little of the details surrounding her fellow regent's demise. The official reports had called it an "assassination," which clearly implied politics. But this was no reason to assume that it meant *clan* politics.

Chin was among the founding members of the impromptu Camarilla council that had convened in Baltimore. In some respects, calling the gathering a "council" was something of a euphemism. It was more like a natural puddling in the stream of refugees fleeing the devastation in the Southeast as Atlanta, Charleston, Raleigh, Richmond, Washington and who-knew-what other traditional Camarilla strongholds fell in rapid succession to the ravages of the Sabbat. Sturbridge could not begin to imagine what strange alliances of convenience Chin might have run afoul of among the floodtide of refugees.

And all these speculations ignored perhaps the most obvious suspect—the slavering horde of Sabbat that had surrounded, cut off and besieged Chin's chantry in Washington, D.C. The Sabbat certainly would not mind seeing one of the D.C. chantry's major players carried bodily from the field. That the plot had succeeded boded ill for the D.C. chantry— the last knot of Camarilla resistance within the nation's capital. The pattern was unambiguous and none too reassuring. Sturbridge could not help but notice that every Tremere who had dared lift her head up above the trenches of late, had had it summarily removed for her trouble.

And now this summons. She had quite enough to worry about at present without being dragged away to Baltimore. Didn't they know there was a war on, right here in the streets of New York? She could not coordinate the defense of even her own chantry from Baltimore—much less the defense of the city or the region. The most recent reports hinted at a stepped-up Sabbat presence upstate. And she couldn't even spare the manpower to preempt that little incursion at present.

Damn it. This could not have come at a worse possible time. But it appeared that all had already been decided from further up the chain of command. She had no choice but to shore up the defenses as best she could here, and jet down to Baltimore to size up the situation.

There was always opportunity in such high-profile assignments. The trick was, of course, to avoid an equally high-profile demise.

Damn them. "Keep your head down." She snorted indignantly.

Laying both hands upon the bell jar, she made a few languid, prescribed passes and began to dictate:

```
Begin
New York comma 27 July 99 period
To Dorfman comma Pontifex comma WDC
period From Sturbridge comma Regentia
comma C5B period Dorfman comma Dire
omens indeed period Will be honored
to serve period Looking forward to
seeing you upon arrival etc period
comma
Sturbridge
end
```

It would have been smarter just to go to ground.
Nickolai let the feeling of self-reproach crash over
him like a wave. *To give up, to go down.* He felt himself borne under, felt acutely the weight of water upon
him. It was the sheer enormity of the past that held
him under—the voracious flood that had already
swallowed three-fourths of the earth's surface and still
was not sated.

Nickolai knew from personal experience that this
flood could never be sated. Not until it had encompassed the entire world. Its pull was unrelenting and,
in the end, irresistible. Already, the deep had claimed
the unlives of his entire people. It had singled them
out, marked them, stalked them, tapped them. It had
gathered them in and now he was the last. By de-
fault, he had become the embodiment, the end
product, of the Great Experiment. He was the sole
receptacle of the accumulated knowledge, ambitions,
lore, strivings, rites, disappointments, schemes, hungers, ideals, tragedy, devotion and pathos of a proud
people. Of all those that bore the name of House
Goratrix, he was the last.

And he was little more than a drowning man.

No, far better just to let the waters close above
him and rest. Finally, to rest.

There was something seductive in the watery
embrace of the past, in its oblivion. It would have
been very easy to surrender himself to that floodtide.
Even if it were to mean being brought face-to-face
with all the indiscretions of a lifetime, or more precisely, of several lifetimes.

Nickolai was strong. He knew he could bear the accumulated indiscretions, even the inhumanity, that had been his constant companions these many nights.

He turned the new recrimination over on his tongue. Inhumanity. It had a more wicked edge to it than his original thought, *indiscretion*. The salt water stung his throat, but he swallowed it. Yes, he could endure even the renewed acquaintance with inhumanity.

But new images were rising toward him through the murky waters. They worried away at his rationalizations, eroding them, carrying them away upon the tide. The images spoke to him of a greater reckoning. They tugged at the gauzy concept he was sheltering behind, this "inhumanity," and tore it away, exposing the red, raw skin beneath. They left him with a far less comforting reproach to cling to. Bloodshed.

The waters ran red about him. *In blood, there is life. In blood, there is magic. In blood, there is power.*

Nickolai knew himself to be a creature, a construct of the blood—a flashing dynamo distilling energy from vitae. It was blood that gave him his longevity. It was blood that gave him his power over the mortal world. It was blood that fueled the rites and rituals of his people.

If there were a single common element to the seemingly endless procession of nights, it was the insatiable need for blood. There was no advantage in contesting the fact. He resigned himself to this latest condemnation. He inhaled deeply and allowed his lungs to fill with the blood which surrounded him and sought to drown him.

His body was racked with sudden screaming pain. Where Nickolai had thought to swallow only his bloodshed, he found himself filled with a far harsher realization. It was not mere bloodshed on his lips, but killings. Murder.

An unending maelstrom of murder. The sheer monstrosity of his crimes—of not only what he had done, but what he had become—surged through him. It tore at him from the inside. He bent double, vomited up blood. Years of blood. It streamed from his eyes, his nose, his ears. Nickolai could feel himself withering away at the extremities. His fingers dried, cracked, curled. His arms withered, wrists and elbows drawn in at improbable angles. He felt his cheeks draw taut and then part, exposing bone. A hint of laughing skull.

No!

I am the last.

Nickolai flung the credo into the face of the voracious past. A howl of pure self against its inevitable ravages.

I am the last. I will endure.

He could feel the wave break and begin to roll back before him, retreating. Leaving him gasping for the life-giving present.

I am the last. Though the entire world be drowned beneath this flood, I will remain.

Nickolai spat the last of the mingled blood and bile and salt water from his mouth. He was a mountain rising from the sea.

Perhaps I am the last of only a race of monsters, a people of depredations.

The mountain contorted, revealing twisted crags, cruel sea cliffs.

Perhaps I am a creature of blood and death, murder and cruelty, unholy rites and blasphemous hungers.

The mountaintop shook, crumbled, slid away

into the waiting sea below. At the mountain's summit all that remained was a blasted jumble of rock and desolation.

Perhaps my very existence is a continual curse upon the earth.

Stunted black trees sprang up, dotting the mountainside. Dark shapes slipped through the undergrowth.

But I will stand firm against the oblivion.

The sea gathered its might, surged against the palisade of sea cliffs, and was thrown back in disarray.

I will build myself a monument, a lasting remembrance of my people.

A dark cloud passed over the summit like the hand of an angry god. In its shadow, something was gathering, rolling stormlike beneath it.

A thing of terror and of beauty. And all who look upon it will tremble and remember.

Far below him, the waves scratched tentatively at the foot of the cliffs. Yes, in time, they would have their way. Of that there could be little doubt.

Soon the waters of the past would cover the entire earth. In those final days, the only remaining line of retreat would be inward—to sink into the very heart of the earth.

To give up, to go down.

To go down. Soon, now. Patience.

Already Nickolai could hear the madness of the lapping waters against that Final Shore.

Eva noisily deposited another armload of books upon the floor. Already it was getting difficult to see Sturbridge, half-buried as she was amidst the tumble of the dead man's books and papers. She was oblivious to the clamor of falling books, barely glancing up from the text she was scrutinizing as Eva muttered her hasty apologies.

The formulae that the present tome described had something to do with an ink made from an extract of owl's blood. Eva's sticky note that marked the page read:

Shelved.
Sealed (bound by sigil, familiar. Variant of Foley's makers markt) but not warded
Resonance: recent use.
Ingredients corroborate Jacqueline's shopping list

There were at least fifty books just like it already patiently awaiting Sturbridge's attention. Many of them boasted no fewer than a dozen tell-tale pink sticky notes peeking surreptitiously from the edges of their pages. Sturbridge closed the book with a sigh of resignation. This was exaggerated by the sudden inrush of air as the book sealed itself, as if from old habit. The simple enchantment was oblivious to the fact that its master no longer required its services.

Something was bothering Sturbridge. She pushed herself slowly to her feet, rising from the clutter of Foley's books and papers. She braced herself against the numbing tingle of circulation returning to her cramped legs and then chided herself for her foolishness.

Another senseless old habit refusing to acknowledge the death of its master. It had been several lifetimes since Sturbridge had needed to concern herself with such distracting biological inconveniences as circulation.

This line of inquiry was getting them nowhere.

"All right. Three nights of cataloguing Foley's books, papers, curiosities, and we've got no clearer picture of the events of that night than when we started. Perhaps we're on the wrong track."

Eva, glad for the reprieve, flopped down on the floor beside her. "The secundus was such a packrat—if you'll excuse my saying so, Regentia; I intended no disrespect to the deceased—it would be easier to compile a list of things he *hadn't* crammed into that study."

"Fair enough," Sturbridge replied, playing along, "What wasn't in Foley's sanctum? Or, more precisely, what was *missing* from the room?"

"Oh, that's easy enough. How about a slavering demon? Or maybe a Sabbat raiding party. At this point, I would even settle for a shadowy assassin lurking in the corner...."

"It just doesn't sit right with me," Sturbridge mused. "I keep thinking the answer must be here, among his papers. I know Foley. I knew Foley. Whatever he was up to, he wrote it down somewhere. He was never quite at ease without pen and paper in front of him. Look at all these scribblings, the lists, the marginalia. It's obsessive."

"I don't know why he ever bothered," the overwhelmed novice replied. "To write anything down, I mean. It's not like he ever forgot anything. Do you remember my first day here, at the chantry? I was so flustered I can only remember a few scattered impressions—the tiny savage faces etched into the fountain in the Grande Foyer, the singing of the bolts on this door when it opened to admit me for my first audience, the unexpected weight of the novice's robes, their coarseness. It's silly, really, the things you remember.

"But the secundus, he could recite the exact details. He could tell you who was there when you arrived, where they stood, what they said. He could call to mind each of the small cruelties, the platitudes, the seemingly friendly overtures and the subtle strings attached. It was uncanny. It was uncomfortable."

"Yes. It seems Foley had that effect on people."

They sat in silence for a time, each pursuing her own memories of their fallen comrade.

"Which people?" It was Eva that broke the silence.

"I'm sorry?"

"I said, 'Which people?' He had that effect on which people?"

"Oh I see. Yes. Well, just about everyone, I imagine."

"You?"

Sturbridge smiled. "Certainly. But I didn't kill him, if that's what you mean."

"No. I suppose not. Things won't be any easier around here. Now that the secundus is gone. And Aaron. And with Jacqueline…" she broke off.

"I haven't decided what to do about Jacqueline yet. Even if she is innocent of any wrongdoing in this matter—and I remain unconvinced on that point—she still let this ill-considered ritual go way too far. That's irresponsible. And I won't tolerate that. Can't tolerate it. Damn it, there's too much at stake here."

"It's the petty intrigues," Eva replied after a pause. "I mean, that's what it all comes down to in the end, isn't it? Sure it's hard to see it when you're right up close to it, face to face. You're holding the body in your arms and all you can see are the bullet holes; your head is full of the smell of blood and spent powder. And you think, chalk up another one for the Sabbat."

Three nights of shock and horror continued to tumble from her lips. "Only it wasn't the Sabbat, if you follow me. Sure, some Tzimisce shovel-head pulled the trigger, but you've been shot before. *I've* been shot before. Why are we still here when folks like Foley are gone? Because it wasn't the Sabbat that got him. It wasn't the bullet that killed him either. It was the damn intrigues.

"Foley gets himself killed in some damnfool high-risk ritual. Jacqueline is supposed to be assisting him. Only she doesn't assist him. She doesn't *stop* him. I don't know why. But I can make a guess. How about resentment? Foley's been gloating about his latest little conquest for a week. And Foley wouldn't have had any new apprentice to gloat over except that Jacqueline saddled him with that obligation of service. And Jacqueline wouldn't have been backed into making that stupid choice if she hadn't been trying to draw attention to Foley's little sideline project by failing to return to the stalking ritual. And it just keeps going like that. Layer upon layer. It is all so absolutely senseless and self-destructive and hateful. I hate it. I just hate it."

Sturbridge put a hand on the novice's shoulder. "It's all right, Eva. It will be all right."

She gazed down at her newest novice. Her young protégée. She was their best hope. Sturbridge's features drew taut. Yet she was unmistakably a product of this house. She bore the signs already—this young woman who was more afraid of her own sisters than of the Sabbat.

"Jacqueline did not kill Foley," Sturbridge said. The phrase seemed incongruous, but at the moment, it was the most comforting thing she could think to say. "No one here killed him. Do you understand?"

Eva wiped her eyes and nodded.

"We failed him. There's no denying that. We all failed him. But we don't kill our own."

Sturbridge trailed off. Her thoughts were not on Foley, but on Jacqueline, who still awaited judgment for her role in this unpleasant affair.

"We do not kill our own."

"Oh Regentia. I am sorry. It's all just so…"

"I know, child. I know."

"Jacqueline told me she tried to warn him, to make him stop, but he only…" she pushed the details of the unsettling encounter aside. "He wouldn't listen to her. You know how he was when he had gotten his mind set on something. He'd just assume anything you said was an attempt to sabotage him. It was like that with that box of his. Obsessive. Wouldn't let anyone else near it. Why, one night he found it lying open and he had three novices flogged to within an inch of…"

"I am aware of the incident in question." Sturbridge's disapproval was evident in her tone.

"Oh, Regentia. You should have just taken that box back from him. You should have…"

Sturbridge turned the novice to face her. Eva's eyes went wide.

"Forgive me, Regentia! I did not mean to imply that this was all your fault. I only meant that I wished…"

"You don't know what was in the chest," Sturbridge realized aloud. Eva looked confused.

"But I thought the box *was* the… It was very old and very beautiful. And it had a strong resonance about it—a sense of history. But not a pleasant history, I think. If it is all the same to you, I would prefer not to have to handle it again."

That was an interesting impression. Sturbridge filed it away for later consideration.

"There was a stone, a gemstone. Small, spherical. Cloudy red with black spirals about the poles. It wasn't there when we found the body. I know, because I looked for it. I had assumed you would know what to look for, too. Never mind, I need you to think carefully. Have you come across such a stone, anytime in the last three days? Not just in Foley's quarters, anywhere."

Eva considered. "No, I think I should have remembered anything like that."

Sturbridge cursed herself. If she were overlooking such obvious details, what else might have slipped by her?

"All right. Let's go over the obvious. The body intact? All parts present and accounted for?"

Eva wrinkled her nose. "Yes."

"The box. I've got a pretty clear recollection of this one, but let's check it against yours. Nearby?"

"On the floor. Beside the worktable."

"Open or closed?"

"Lying open, and face down. As if it had fallen."

"Any contents?"

"Empty. The lining was black felt. It was singed."

"Cause?"

"The fire around the base of table. Some candles overturned. Seven candles. A scattering of papers were burned, damaged or destroyed. Incidental damage to floor and table legs."

"Well, we seem to have papers aplenty. But so far, nothing that looks like notes, preparations, formulae, description or transcription of the actual ritual in progress."

"Chalk that up to his blasted memory."

"So nothing from his papers, books. We've been over all that. At great length." Sturbridge looked ruefully at the small mountain of books they had not yet gone through.

"Did he have a pen out? A quill? A stylus, anything?"

"A quill, yes. On the worktable. It was broken in two."

"Where?"

"Sorry?"

"The quill, it was broken where? Midway? At the tip?"

"I wouldn't say 'midway'. About an inch from the tip. Why?"

"Right at the point where he would have been bearing down on it. It suggests he was writing something *sometime* during that ritual. If he were just breaking a quill as some ceremonial act, he would have broken it in half, in the middle. How about an inkwell?"

Eva paused and thought a moment.

"Yes," she replied uncertainly. "There was an inkwell. On the floor, not too far from the box, I think."

"Another fall from the worktable. Was it broken?"

"No. It was overturned, though. It must have been nearly empty. I don't recall any ink stain on the floor."

"Inconclusive. It might have overturned before falling to the floor. Or it may have fallen onto one of the scattered sheets of paper."

"More missing papers."

"What do you mean?"

Eva took a moment before replying. "I mean, if the ink spilled onto a piece of paper, where's the paper? Sure, it could have been one of the ones that burned, but how about whatever it was that Foley was writing? You said he had to have been writing *something*. Was he signing his name to some dark compact? Transcribing the formulae to a forbidden rite? Trying desperately to leave us a warning? A confession? A suicide note? Where's the missing paper?"

"It's not in the room. We've been over the room."

"Maybe the murderer took the evidence with him."

Sturbridge shook her head. "No, that's still no good. We haven't got a murderer. All we have is a victim."

"No." Eva's voice was steady, confident, despite her rising excitement. "All we have is two victims."

"Well, I'll be damned." Sturbridge was on her feet and pulling the novice after her.

"Probably."

Sturbridge, in the doorway, half turned but then thought better of it. Eva caught only the briefest glimpse of a smile. "If there is one thing I cannot abide in a novice, Ms. FitzGerald…"

Eva quickly fell in behind her mistress, matching her long, purposeful stride only with some effort. "Yes, Regentia. Familiarity."

"No really. It wouldn't be any trouble. I don't mind searching his room." Eva's voice faltered. The rough-hewn walls snatched it away from her, hopelessly muddling her words with the distant plish of falling water and gruffly passing the result from hand to hand down the tangle of winding tunnels.

"The papers aren't in his room." Sturbridge explained patiently. "The papers are on the body."

"Yes. Well. Not meaning to introduce any unnecessary complications, but how are we supposed to find the body?"

"What could be easier than finding a body in a mausoleum? Watch your step."

Without warning, the space to Eva's right suddenly opened out onto abyss. She hastily scrambled back from the edge, dislodging a fistful of knucklebones that clattered over the precipice.

"All these old galleries," Sturbridge continued as if nothing untoward had happened, "wind about that central well. You only occasionally catch a glimpse of it, but you always know it's there. You can tell the walls that back up onto the abyss because they are cooler, and damp."

"What's at the bottom?"

Sturbridge shrugged. "More bones. At least one of my predecessors was so averse to the place that he was in the habit of making more room in the upper corridors by sweeping the previous tenants over the edge."

Eva quickly changed the subject. "You didn't answer my question. How are we supposed to find the body we are looking for? As opposed to say, that one. Or that one. Or…"

"Those are just decoration, dear. Here we are." She drew to a halt in front of a niche carved into the wall. It was identical, so far as Eva could determine, to any of a hundred others they had passed already.

Sturbridge began rummaging around in the dark recess. Her efforts were accompanied by the occasionally musical sound of bone clattering over bone.

At last, she extracted a carefully folded robe from the niche. It was covered with a powdery white dust. "Can't imagine why they should have put this in first," Sturbridge complained, shaking out the robe.

Eva recognized the markings of a novice of the seventh and final circle. *Almost free*, she thought.

"Let's see what we have here. Pockets, empty. Cuffs. Lining. Carefully now. We don't want to tear it."

She drew a fingernail down across the seam and the material parted without resistance.

"Now let's see what Foley wanted us to know, and Aaron did not."

Sturbridge extracted a single sheet of parchment. She studied the page a moment, the curious illustrations, the enigmatic inscriptions. She clucked her tongue in disapproval and passed the sheet to Eva.

"Shall we go? Something about the air down here, it always puts me in mind of someplace else I should be."

"Professor...Professor Sturbridge!"

A flicker of surprise or annoyance crossed Sturbridge's features as she turned. She tried to pick out the source of the voice from amidst the press of— distractingly warm—bodies. Angrily, she forced such thoughts aside. There would be time enough to feed later, once she had reached the relative safety of Baltimore. Here, at the very doorstep of Sabbat-torn Washington, she was vulnerable, exposed.

She must remain vigilant not only against overt threats—and a fifteen-foot-tall, gibbering Tzimisce war ghoul was not entirely outside the realm of possibility here, she reminded herself ruefully—but especially against the more subtle dangers: impatience, indulgence, indiscretion. These three deadly sisters would kill as surely, if not as swiftly, as any fiend.

The surge of human bodies parted midstream, breaking against her rock-sharp gaze. Falling back, the river of humanity regrouped and then swept around her on both sides. Sturbridge could not seem to focus on the individual faces streaming past, no more than she could pick out the individual heartbeats. But someone in this crowd had recognized her, or worse, anticipated her.

She needed to find that person and quickly.

Sturbridge's first reaction had been to wheel and confront this unknown presence head-on. As she scanned the crowd, however, she began to gain an appreciation for just how many dangers this sea of blood might conceal. Cautiously, she retreated a step, hoping it was not already too late, and allowed herself to be borne slowly backwards by the crowd.

An arm clutching a mass-market paperback thrust into view above the throng. It waved back and forth in an exaggerated manner, pages fanning and flapping. "Professor Sturbridge!"

The arm seemed to be attached to a baggy gray sweatshirt (proclaiming, "GEORGETOWN") and a headlight-white grin. Shifting pocketbook and paperback to the same hand, a slight young lady plowed forward. She clasped Sturbridge's hand and squeezed. She shook hands with her whole body, straight-armed, from the shoulder, pumping up and down repeatedly as if for emphasis.

"Professor, I am so delighted to finally meet you." Again the beaming smile eclipsed her entire face. "Francesca Lyon, anthro department, call me Chessie. I am a *major* fan."

"Miss Lyon," Sturbridge replied, holding the girl's hand at arm's length. She regarded the newcomer skeptically.

She was in her early twenties, slight, her dark hair unkempt. Her glasses were probably the main perpetrators in giving her the air of being somewhat bookish. Her jeans, however, were muddy about the knees. To all appearances, Sturbridge's accoster was exactly what she presented herself to be—a grad student dropped by to pick up a visiting professor at the airport.

Sturbridge's suspicions, however, were not allayed. Perhaps because, for starters, she knew just how deadly a mistake it would be to assume that she, herself, was merely a "visiting professor."

But there was something more disturbing here. Sturbridge had gone to some pains not to advertise her itinerary. She was not certain who (if anyone) outside the Tremere hierarchy might know of her new "appointment" to the *ad hoc* Camarilla council in Baltimore. Reflexively, she ran down the possible suspects in her mind.

Pieterzoon would know to expect her, of course. As *de facto* leader of the council, he would have been informed that she was to serve as the new Tremere representative. He might even have a rough idea of when to expect her.

But he could not have anticipated that she would come from the south, from war-torn D.C., from the very heart of the Sabbat threat. Sturbridge had relied upon that particular piece of misdirection—and willingly submitted herself to the additional risks— to buy her safe passage into Baltimore.

From the moment she had first heard that voice calling her name, however, Sturbridge had known that her safe conduct had been summarily cancelled. She was now alone, on the ground, in enemy territory.

For all Sturbridge knew, Pieterzoon might have announced her pending arrival to his fellow councilors. He might have been so incautious as to speak of it before a full assembly—including not only all the Baltimore Kindred but the uncounted swarm of refugees fleeing the Sabbat occupation in the South.

Too many people, she concluded. Too damned many people. Too many damned people.

Chessie's voice broke in upon her calculations. "Dr. Dorfman was so sorry he could not be here to meet you in person. But he's still out of the country. Vienna! Lucky bastard, couldn't you just kill him?"

"There is no need to apologize." Sturbridge's gaze bore into the girl, trying to wrestle her meaning from behind the screen of ambiguous commentary and that infuriating grin.

Dorfman. That was something concrete. Pontifex Peter Dorfman. In Tremere circles, *that* was a name to conjure with. The mere mention of that name would throw open doors against which the last three centuries most concerted advances of money, power and privilege had availed nothing. Dorfman was what the novices back at the Chantry of the Five Boroughs unguardedly referred to as a "Ramses"—a major figure in the Tremere Pyramid.

It was no secret that Dorfman headed up the clan's political operations on the North American continent. Nor was it any surprise that he made his base of operations in Washington, D.C. Outside of these two critical bits of trivia, however, there was very little obvious about Peter Dorfman.

Dorfman had taken the Tremere proclivity for casual subterfuges and intrigues and turned it into an art as precise, beautiful and deadly as a clockwork cobra. He was a da Vinci of deadly machinations.

He was also the man responsible for drafting her to this ambiguous honor—representing the Tremere to the besieged Camarilla forces in Baltimore. The thought did little to comfort her.

It was not a glamorous assignment. Her fellow councilors would, no doubt, want to know when they could expect some concrete assistance from the Tremere. By "concrete" they would mean "arcane." By "arcane" they would mean something along the lines of raining fire down upon the Sabbat war parties or psychically assassinating their leaders, or perhaps merely reversing the flow of time so that their homes had never been sacked, plundered, razed in the first place.

Sturbridge did not come with miracles in hand. She didn't even have the answers they wanted. She expected resentment. She anticipated feelings of betrayal. She would not be surprised by accusations of treachery.

"I'm sorry to have missed him," Sturbridge replied. "But it was kind of you to come in his stead."

"Wouldn't have missed it for the world. Things have been a bit hectic since Dr. Dorfman left, but we do what we can. I have a car waiting outside and Dr. Dorfman has left you some material on the conference in Baltimore. I would love to drop in and hear you speak. What will you be presenting?"

"A little piece about the Evil Eye in New England folk custom. Give me your address and I'll send you a copy. When did Dr. Dorfman say he'd be returning?"

Chessie laughed. "It's always so hard to tell. But I'll tell you this, if they were to fly me to Vienna, I don't know if I would ever come back."

Friday, 27 August 1999, 11:52 PM
McHenry Auditorium, Lord Baltimore Inn
Baltimore, Maryland

Sturbridge paused outside the double doors, weighing her options. It was not too late just to turn around now. The doorman would even hail a cab for her. She could be at the airport in half an hour and back in New York in time to frustrate any of a half-dozen petty intrigues that would have hatched in her brief absence.

No. Better to go in and get it over with. She braced herself and entered the auditorium expecting the worst. It seemed the festivities were already in full swing.

"*What in the nine hells were you thinking?*" The voice, which Sturbridge instantly recognized as belonging to her dear neighbor, Prince Lladislas—most recently of Buffalo—resounded from the rafters. The fact that the party he was addressing—a dignified man matching the briefing description of her host, Prince Garlotte—stood a mere two paces away from him in no way moderated the volume of Lladislas's outburst.

Garlotte weathered this fresh insult with visibly fraying patience.

Sturbridge performed a hurried calculation as she slipped into a seat in the front row. Lladislas and his remaining entourage could not have been in Baltimore for much more than a week now. Judging from Garlotte's expression, it had been a very full week.

"Since embracing a bunch of know-nothing neonates worked so damned well in Buffalo, you're planning on doing it again in Hartford? What the hell! I might have expected this kind of stunt from you, Garlotte. But Theo—"

The Brujah archon calmly and gently placed a restraining hand on Lladislas's shoulder. The displaced prince shook him off with a snort, but abandoned his tirade. His voice was pitched low, but his accusation carried.

"I trusted you."

Bell regarded him levelly. "Good. That and a dollar gets me a cup of coffee." He smiled broadly and clapped Lladislas on the shoulder. "Buffalo was a deathtrap. You know that; I know that. Sorry if it's hard to hear. There wasn't anything more you could have done there but go down swinging. But I'll tell you this, there will be other fights, real fights, fights that mean something. And I want to have you there for them. Do we understand one another?"

Lladislas threw up his hands. It seemed he was still adjusting to the humbling role of prince-in-exile. Sturbridge could follow his tortured thoughts in the lines of his face as Lladislas struggled to gauge exactly how far he might push his host.

Garlotte's voice broke in upon her musings.

"...Our privilege to have with us Regent Aisling Sturbridge of the Chantry of the Five Boroughs in New York. May I say that it is a great honor to have such a seasoned and steadfast opponent of the Sabbat advances here among us, Ms. Sturbridge."

Sturbridge composed herself, rising to her feet to address the gathering. She nodded in turn to the principals on the council, matching names to the few unfamiliar faces: "Prince Garlotte, Archon Bell, Prince Vitel, Prince Lladislas, Mr. Pieterzoon."

Her tone was carefully dispassionate, formal. She might just as easily have been lecturing a group of school children, or giving directions to a lost motorist, as addressing the remnant of the pride of the East Coast Camarilla.

"Three weeks ago, Prince Garlotte informed the Tremere office in Washington of the assertions that Justicar Xaviar of Clan Gangrel made before this body. Speaking officially, on behalf of Clan Tremere, we can lend no credence to the wild claims that have been reported to us.

"We have no reason to doubt the justicar's veracity. He has ever been a tower of strength and a pillar of integrity. We deeply sympathize with his unsettling loss. We mourn our fallen comrades. We cannot, however, accept at face value the justicar's assessment of the situation. There are monsters enough slavering at the very gates of this city. There is little need to conjure up mythical Antediluvians to further distract and demoralize our forces. We can ill afford to draw off much-needed resources from the present conflict to avenge the personal loss of Xaviar's warband.

"Make no mistake, their loss is a tragedy. They will be sorely missed in the troubled nights ahead. But the Tremere will not be swayed, nor driven to petty vengeance by the justicar's less-than-veiled threats to this council."

Sturbridge looked to each of her fellow councilors in turn. She saw her sentiments echoed silently in the stoic looks, the downcast eyes, the averted faces of her peers.

"What troubles me," Pieterzoon broke the uncomfortable silence, "is what could have *frightened* someone like Xaviar that badly. If I were to come back raving about Antediluvians," he gave a self-depreciating smile, "We could have all just laughed it off. But Xaviar, he just doesn't seem the excitable type."

"Whatever they ran into up there," Garlotte said, "it's best given a very wide berth. It may sound callous, but my feeling is that whatever it is, it's the Sabbat's problem now. Sorry, but that's how I feel."

"Just like New York." Sturbridge's words fell heavily into the silence.

"Beg pardon?"

"New York. It's the Sabbat's problem now. Buffalo, Albany, the Bronx. What's one more nightmare loose upstate?"

"Ms. Sturbridge, I have been a poor host. I did not mean to offend. Nor did I mean to rush you straight into council session before you could rest and recover from your voyage. I hope you will allow me to make amends."

"That will not be necessary, Prince. I spoke out of anger. The comment was not representative of my clan's position. I withdraw it.

"It is not my intention to dismiss the justicar's concerns out of hand," Sturbridge continued. "We have uncovered further evidence that I hope may shed light on just what exactly Xaviar and his band ran afoul of in those mountains."

She placed a leather attaché case on the table and removed a plain manila envelope containing a single piece of parchment. She handed it to Jan, who opened it.

Staring up at him was a single unblinking eye. Further illustrations and annotations crowded the sheet, all rendered in the same sprawling, desperate hand. The parchment seemed to writhe in his grasp. Jan shivered involuntarily. "What's this supposed to be?" he asked, quickly passing the parchment to Vitel at his right.

"Well, that is what I had hoped you would help me determine, Mr. Pieterzoon. The page was discovered on the body of one of my associates," Sturbridge rushed through the half-truths, "who was killed during the execution of a rather…unorthodox ritual."

The sheet of parchment continued clockwise around the table to Gainesmil, Garlotte's steward and right-hand man. He let out a low whistle. "Some piece of work, whoever thought this stuff up. A real headcase." He passed the paper to Victoria Ash, his hand lingering a moment too long at the point of contact.

"The reason I wanted to place this sketch before the council is that illustration in the lower left—the one-eyed man surrounded by what looks to be a mound of splintered bones. The sketch put me in mind of…"

"Yes, I see." Vitel had one hand on the paper, but Victoria seemed reluctant to surrender it. "Xaviar's description. The monster with the blazing eye."

"The circumstances surrounding the creation of this picture are still a bit muddled, but the timing coincides almost exactly with the confrontation described by the justicar."

Despite Sturbridge's low-key delivery, her words were having an effect. Jan shifted uncomfortably in his seat. "What the hell *is* that thing?"

"A reasonable question," said Sturbridge. If she had any reasonable answer, she did not offer it.

"May I?" For the second time, Vitel attempted to take the paper from the unusually withdrawn Ms. Ash. Her grip on the parchment was white-knuckled.

What do the Tremere hope to gain from this? Jan wondered. Did they think they could divert attention away from themselves and their pointed non-involvement

in the current crisis by feeding this council such ambiguous information? What he needed was solid
intelligence—enemy positions, troop compositions, supply points. Not marginalia and pointless speculations.

"Leopold."

Victoria's voice came to them as from a great distance. A hollow plish from the depths of a well.

"Beg pardon?" Garlotte turned toward her.

"It's Leopold," she said quietly, her eyes never
leaving the parchment.

"Yes, I think that's one of the inscriptions here."
Vitel leaned over the parchment. "*Leopold*. And this
one looks like *Hazima-el*. And this one, *Occultum*..."

"No, this. This is Leopold," Victoria's fingers were
so knotted around the edges of the page, it seemed
she would surely tear it.

"You know him?" Gainesmil asked incredulously.

"Who," Prince Garlotte asked, "is Leopold?"

Victoria stared at the picture without acknowl-
edging the prince. Her hands shook. She seemed to
recede before their eyes.

"Can someone tell me, who the hell is Leopold?"
Lladislas was on his feet.

"No one," Victoria said simply. "A sculptor. A
Toreador. From Atlanta."

Everyone spoke at once.

"I don't believe this. What you're trying to tell
us is..."

"Are you quite sure you recognize him? It is just
a penciled..."

"This is ridiculous. I've had quite enough of..."

Sturbridge could feel the dark wings closing in
about her. Angrily she waved them away. "I'm sorry.
Did you say 'Atlanta', Ms. Ash?"

TREMERE

Victoria just nodded, but Garlotte was already racing down that line of speculation.

"It seems a bit of a coincidence, does it not? A Tremere regent assassinated. The first of the Sabbat assaults. Your own...narrow escape. And now, you would have us believe, this creature..."

Lladislas was struck suddenly by the absurdity of it all. "You're not suggesting that a lone Toreador destroyed a small army of Gangrel?!"

Now Victoria did look up. She looked directly at Jan, silently entreating his belief. "I'm only saying that this is Leopold." She pushed the sheet away from her and folded her arms.

"It's all right," Sturbridge soothed briskly. "It's not your fault." She looked pointedly at Lladislas, as if daring him to contradict her. "It's not your fault."

"All right," Garlotte was regaining his composure. "So what do we do now? Send someone after Xaviar? Tell him it's all been some big mistake? That the thing he ran into out there was just..."

"Oh, that will go over well!"

"I'm afraid there is little you could say to our proud justicar at this juncture." Vitel's voice was calm, reasonable. "I'm not entirely sure that there is any practical benefit to be gained from this information. No offense intended toward the Tremere representative." He inclined his head in Sturbridge's direction.

Sturbridge turned to face this subtle attack from an unexpected quarter. "None taken, my Prince."

"I'll go." Victoria said in a quiet voice.

Vitel continued to muse aloud, almost absently. "Tell me, Ms. Sturbridge, did you say you had come through Washington? How is..."

My city. Sturbridge could hear the words as clearly as if he had spoken them aloud.

"How is the effort to reclaim the capitol progressing?"

There was a groan from across the table and Lladislas threw up his hands in exasperation.

"Not that old song again!"

Sturbridge ignored him. "The chantry still stands, my Prince. And while it does, there is still hope."

"To Atlanta. To find Leopold. Someone's got to go." Victoria seemed unaware that the conversation had already taken another turn.

"Out of the question," Garlotte said. "Dangerous. Pointless. Let's hear nothing more about it."

"Don't you think we should hear her out?"

Sturbridge spun upon Jan, stunned at his casual betrayal. His features were impassive. Smoothly, almost effortlessly, he had completely redefined Victoria. Where once she had been a peer, a fellow councilor, perhaps even a rival, she was now just another expendable to be thrown into the teeth of the Sabbat forces. It was unsettling.

"You are quite sure you want to do this?" Gainesmil's concern was tempered with an all-too-apparent desire to distance himself from any unfortunate entanglements with the sinking Ms. Ash.

"I'll leave at once." She pushed back her chair, almost toppling it to the floor. "Mr. Gainesmil, my Prince. Jan." She all but fled the table.

Vitel nodded distractedly, seeming to take no note of the Toreador's hasty departure. "Still hope. Of course. Of course. But tell me, Ms. Sturbridge, what word of my old friend, Peter Dorfman? I must confess to being...saddened by his silence. Since I have gone into exile here."

Sturbridge felt a chasm opening up beneath her. Dorfman. Vitel. Damn. How had she missed that connection previously?

She tried to push back the rising insinuation. "The pontifex has been out of the country for some time, my Prince. The motherhouse. Vienna."

The words turned cold and heavy upon her lips. Lies, she realized too late. Transparent lies.

"Vienna," Vitel repeated absently. "I see. So he has not been involved in the resistance, the defense of the city? He might, even now, be unaware of the cruel card that fate has played his old friend?"

Sturbridge saw the horns of the dilemma bearing down upon her. She tried to beat back the insinuation. "It is my understanding that he has been there since before…"

"The surprise attack? A fortunate man. A very fortunate man. There is no taking that away from him. I am sure he will do well for himself. In Vienna." He added pointedly.

"What is it you're getting at, Vitel?" Garlotte broke in gruffly. He more than anyone seemed rattled by Victoria's abrupt departure. "You're not trying to imply that the pontifex had some advance warning of…"

"No, no. Nothing of the sort. How could you even suggest such a thing? Why, to know of a Sabbat attack upon your own city and fail to warn your prince, why it would be…"

"Preposterous. Baseless suspicions. Really, Vitel, this is unworthy of you."

"It would be almost as bad," Vitel continued in a quiet voice, "as actively courting such an attack."

Sturbridge paused, one hand on the antique oak-paneled door that stood vigil before her suite at the Lord Baltimore. The entire wing was silent. A welcome change from the uproar of the council chambers. Given the fate that had befallen the last Tremere that had been the guest of this establishment, Sturbridge had had little trouble convincing her host of the necessity of setting aside this entire floor for her personal use.

She was in no mood for company.

Events in the council chamber had taken a dramatic and unexpected turn for the worse. She had been caught badly unprepared. She had not anticipated such concerted opposition from the former Prince of Washington, D.C. With a few carefully chosen insinuations, Vitel might have systematically destroyed what credibility she—and by extension, the Tremere—had with the council.

Immersed in the nightly struggle for survival in New York, Sturbridge had been isolated from what she imagined must have been a truly epic and ruthless rivalry being played out behind closed doors in the nation's capital. Dorfman and Vitel. In hindsight, Sturbridge was surprised the city had managed to contain two such ambitious and unscrupulous powermongers for so long.

Vitel's claims were patently ridiculous, of course. Dorfman was a keystone in the Tremere Pyramid. One simply did not rise to that level of influence without learning some hard lessons—prominent among them, that you don't bankroll private grudges with clan credibility.

Sturbridge had been there, so she knew what it was like. She had a chantry of her own to look after. The very thought of putting all that on the line—the decades of careful planning, the hard choices, the sacrifices—just to settle some personal vendetta... It was unthinkable. It was monstrous. It was...

It was, she realized, exactly what the others might expect of such an influential and unscrupulous Tremere powerbroker. Vitel's claim struck so dangerously close to exactly what they wanted to believe, that they accepted it instinctively. Her efforts here had been utterly undermined before she had properly begun.

Sturbridge leaned heavily into the weathered door to her suite. It looked as if it had come through a shipwreck, long ago, in the days when the tall ships still dominated the harbor.

Perhaps that was what stopped her. The sense of age—of history—about it. Sturbridge scrutinized the lines and knots of the old wood like a palmist, trying to divine the meandering threads of its past and future.

She could pick out the tracery of gangly masts and flapping sails that once swooped in and out of the harbor like exotic birds. They skimmed the surface, snatching a glistening cargo, and fluttered away again.

She laid bare the door's story with her fingertips, feeling its grain, its warmth, its solidity. The telltale remainders of a distant life. Some distant part of her—an ancient, weathered, wrecked part of her—stirred in answer.

Maeve.

She forced the thought down and away. Far away. Back down into the furthest recesses of pain and loss.

But even this instinctive defense hurt her. In some inexplicable way, banishing the memory felt like banishing Maeve, herself. It was a betrayal. As she shoved the recollection back down into the well of memory, it was Maeve's face that she forced down beneath the surface of the dark waters. She held it there until it stopped struggling.

After a few moments, the memory had sunk beneath the depths and Sturbridge again mastered herself. *You would think that after all these years—all these lifetimes of training!* Sturbridge raged against herself, against her own weakness, against her lack of discipline. It gave her focus. It was worth being angry at herself if only to have something concrete to be mad at. She could not rage against memories and regrets. There was no substance to push back against there. And, she realized, she was as helpless to prevent these onslaughts as she was powerless to strike back against them.

Still chastising herself for her frailties, Sturbridge turned her attentions back toward the door. There was something about the ancient wood, something in its slumbering pulse of life, that had reminded her of…that reminded her. Hesitantly, Sturbridge reached out for that something.

She wrapped her awareness tightly around the old wood and felt it slowly warm to her touch. She slipped between the bars of its grain. Her footfalls echoed deep within the labyrinth of wood fibers. The corridors and galleries were draped in dangling pulpy tendrils. She turned each damp coarse thread over in turn, separating, scrutinizing.

There. She pounced upon a single strand and held fast. Triumphantly, she squeezed down upon the tremulous pulse. A vein. A lifeline.

It tried to flee her, to escape deeper into the labyrinth. But Sturbridge only clung the tighter. She rode the dim pulse of life back to its source, to the very heart of the wood.

It was a fragile thing, the wood's heart. A crystalline skein woven entirely of rope fibers. It was lustrous with life.

Sturbridge breathed deeply of the aroma of green growing things, of loam, of life. She drank in the delicate pattern ravenously. She traced every twisting, searching for the resonance of the living crystal, its still point, the very crux between its growing and its dying. She tapped once, her finger falling with the surety and grace of a jeweler's hammer.

She felt the crystal crack, cleave. The fibers groaned, twisted and popped as the elaborate knot began to unravel violently.

Sturbridge retreated back up the coarse, fibrous corridors, fighting off the flailing and groping tendrils, each as big around as a ship's anchor line. With a final heave, she broke free and staggered back a step away from the door.

A single bloody palmprint showed clearly on the ancient surface.

The wood creaked, buckled, split. New green shoots broke from the cracked surface. The entire doorframe seemed to shudder, to draw breath. The ancient wood festooned itself with new life.

Sturbridge took a step closer to the unfolding wonder. Reaching out gingerly, she felt the emerging knobs of new buds beneath her fingertips. The newborn shoots drew toward her instinctively, as toward sunlight. They coiled about her fingers, caressing, intertwining. Enrapt, Sturbridge watched as leaves appeared. They slithered forth from the living wood and unfolded like the mouths of serpents. Each gaping maw revealed veins of sickly red and black that pulsed slightly. The barbed leaves snapped at her fingertips as Sturbridge recoiled, tearing out a fistful of questing greenery in her hurry to free herself.

The shoots hardened into twigs and then quickly into wicked thorns that glistened wetly with some dark, viscous substance. As she staggered backwards, Sturbridge saw that a red, slightly phosphorescent fungus had already engulfed the upper portion of the door.

The entire surface creaked and writhed. It strained toward her, its creator, its life-giver, its mother. Her first reaction was to shrink back from it, to withdraw.

Maeve. Somewhere, not far away, (although whether separated by an intervening space of distance or time, she was not certain), she heard the cry of a child. Her child. To her shame, her first reaction had been to withdraw.

Her first reaction had always been to withdraw. *Damn it. Not again!*

Sturbridge fought to force the rising tide of memory back down, to drown it in the black waters of oblivion. But it was stronger now. Fed by the strength of new life. New life given and new life scorned. She could feel its undeniable hunger, its need. It was overwhelming. It was dragging her upwards by the heels, toward the surface, toward the light of recollection.

The first touch burned like the noonday sun. Sturbridge screamed.

Behind her a child was crying, an infant. Before her the works of Aesclepius lay open amidst a clutter of candles, chalk diagrams, elemental regalia. She tried to ignore the crying. The hunger, the incessant need. She tried to focus on the discipline of the Great Work, on the calm grandeur of the Mysteries.

Sturbridge could feel her flesh begin to blacken and crack beneath the relentless sun. Blood began to well from the split skin.

Angrily, she slammed the book shut and snatched the child from its cradle.

A beautiful little girl. My Maeve. My beautiful little angel.

The evaporating blood felt cool upon the surface of her parched skin. Slowly, tortuously, the life-giving liquid boiled away into the parched air. Rippling waves of rising heat drifted lazily skyward before her eyes. It would not be long now.

She bounced the baby up and down gently, in a distracted attempt to calm it. "Mom-my's. Lit-tle. An-gel. Mom-my's. Lit-tle. An-gel." This only seemed to increase the wailing.

It's the blood. Sturbridge heard her own voice as if from a great distance. *The sun, it doesn't want me, it just wants the blood. Once that is gone, it will leave me alone. Leave me in peace. Soon now. Peace.*

"All right, all right. Hush. Mommy knows what you want." She returned to her worktable, swept aside the trappings of the arcane and sat down, putting the baby to her breast. It latched on readily and a contented silence descended once more over the tiny garret.

Sturbridge came to herself before the heavy oak-paneled door that stood vigil before her suite at the Lord Baltimore. One hand rested gently against the cracked, weathered surface. She felt its grain, its warmth, its solidity. The coarse red fungus beneath her hand did not disconcert her. Nor did the sting of the thorns cause her to draw back. Nor did the pricking of the ravenous leaves make her withdraw the flow of life-giving blood.

All around her, digging through the walls and furnishings of the suite just beyond, tendriling roots were spreading, searching, taking hold.

She could see them, follow the intricacies of their twistings and turnings. She could see where the latch of one shutter had been recently forced. She could see the listening devices concealed in the chandelier and in the vase of flowers on the nightstand. She could see an envelope that had been hastily pushed under the door.

The snaking tendrils started to retrieve the letter for her, but she dismissed their concern. There would be time enough—for reading, for letters, for plots and intrigues, for veiled threats and promises—later.

Nickolai held the beaten copper bowl before him at arm's length. The severed digit drifted lazily atop the coagulating liquid. He squinted one eye and sighted along the line of the finger's point. North by northeast. Deeper into the mountains.

Like a hawk catching sight of its prey, Nickolai dove headfirst into the questing. The luxurious hotel room fell away forgotten behind him. The spurting pain in his hand—the rhythmic backbone of the ritual—was all that anchored him to his physical form.

So far he had little to show for his efforts. A series of frustrating attempts to reestablish contact with his own kind had led him here, to New York City. It was like starting over from scratch. House Goratrix was an insular order; Nickolai had few close ties outside his brethren. He knew that attempting to contact anyone who knew him too well might quickly turn into a death sentence for everyone concerned.

In the end, he had called an old business partner, someone who could be persuaded to help him. But afterward, Benito Giovanni, too, had gone missing. Nickolai should have been able to find him, but the trail had grown suddenly and ominously cold. Nickolai feared the worst. The very possibility that the enemy might have taken Benito made it absolutely imperative that Nickolai find the one Kindred who bound them together.

He must be close now. The blood did not lie. He slipped deeper into vision. The very light on this remote mountainside had taken on an unhealthy

aspect. It was far too white, too glaring for the reflected glow of moonlight. It reminded Nickolai of
the piercing white of hospital or sanitarium—an obvious and futile attempt to hold back the encroaching
darkness of death and madness.

He could feel the weight of that light pressing
down upon him, slowing his ascent up the
mountainside. It was like walking underwater. The
membrane of light shifted to anticipate and resist his
every movement.

Still he struggled up the exposed rockface. He
tried to keep to the infrequent trees, if only for the
brief moments of shade and respite they offered. But
the light seemed to come at him from all directions
at once, as if the mountain were blanketed in a lumi-
nescent fog. It seemed to Nickolai that the glare
brightened near the mountain's peak. There was no
hint of the ruddy glow of sunrise catching the summit. Rather, the light grew paler, harsher, white-hot.
Nickolai found himself thinking of the desert wastes
near the Mexican border, of shallow roadside graves,
of moonlight on bleached bones.

Nickolai stumbled, but retained his balance. The
ground here was broken, craggy. Jagged shards of rock
seemed to rise up suddenly to block his path. He gingerly picked his way over and around these obstacles,
wondering at the cataclysmic forces that had, in ages
past, so violently thrown these mountains heavenwards. Judging from the jumble of boulders littering
the rock face, many of these throws must have fallen
a bit short of their mark.

Perhaps it was a trick of this infuriating light,
but as he struggled toward the summit, Nickolai began to think that the tumble of granite was taking

on more recognizable shapes. Here was surely a great obelisk toppled from its pedestal. There, a collapsed bridge spanned a dizzying fall into the luminous mist below. There again, a great flat table of granite, large enough to feast several score of guests.

Nickolai found himself absently wondering where the guests had rushed off to in such a hurry and why they were so long away from their feast. Many of their seats were overturned and their food had grown stone cold.

As he progressed, the tumble of rock littering the mountainside seemed to grow more regular, as if some hidden pattern were struggling to assert itself over the landscape. Nickolai could not help noticing and then admiring the artful arrangement of the stones. There was a hand at work here, an artistic eye. He could plainly read the devotion of some unseen groundskeeper.

Without any hint of apprehension or distaste, Nickolai now realized he was among the precisely ordered headstones of some forgotten cemetery. He paused, head cocked to one side, listening for the telltale whispers among the tombstones—the litany of the dead, repeating to themselves endlessly their same discourse: names, dates, deeds.

But the stones were strangely silent. They held their peace.

Saturday, 28 August 1999, 1:52 AM
Lord Baltimore Inn
Baltimore, Maryland

Sturbridge secured the door with a casual gesture. Gnarled tendrils of blackened wood snaked down from the overgrown network of vines that hid the ceiling from view. They lovingly embraced the ancient portal, bolstering it, reinforcing it. Sturbridge nodded her approval. Anyone foolish enough to attempt to force entry would have better luck tearing through the wall. That would delay them a few moments. Time enough to muster her defenses.

Satisfied, she crossed to the roll-top desk at the room's center. A latticed arbor rose up behind her chair without visible means of support. It craned over her shoulder, forming a makeshift canopy over the desk.

She clicked on the banker's lamp and picked up the first envelope. The engraved golden letters read, "Councilor Aisling Sturbridge." She flipped the envelope over and sliced it open with a single motion. A card, similarly engraved in gold, fell to the desk— an invitation to dine privately with Prince Garlotte that very evening.

Councilor Sturbridge,

The prince begs the honor of your company this evening, that he might personally welcome you to our beautiful and historic city.

My lord will call upon you himself, at your apartments at three, to escort you on a tour of our renowned harbor.

Light repast to follow in the Master Library of the Lord Baltimore.

The invitation was concluded with Garlotte's seal, the three ships riding at anchor beneath the crossed Keys of the Kingdom.

Sturbridge held the invitation at arm's length, as if clutching an asp. She was far from convinced that the prince was the doting old gentleman he represented himself to be. She had seen some of the other councilors, Ms. Ash in particular, buy into that persona. It struck Sturbridge as a particularly dangerous miscalculation.

Her thoughts kept returning to Maria Chin, her unfortunate predecessor on this council. If the prince wanted to remove the Tremere presence from the gathering, or even from his entire city, nothing would have been easier. Chin had been his guest; she had placed herself entirely in Garlotte's hands. Like all the other councilors (not to mention the horde of refugees), she had submitted to his rules, his curfews. She spent her days—her time of greatest vulnerability—under his roof. At night, Garlotte's feeding restrictions dictated exactly when and where each of his "subjects" could hunt.

Sturbridge had been briefed on these "precautionary measures" on the way up to her suite. The bellhop had been both thorough and polite. Sturbridge was already getting a feel for the peculiar political climate in the besieged city.

Yes, it would be a simple gesture for Garlotte to reach out and pluck the unlife from any within his domain. He knew precisely when and where each of them would be when her defenses were down.

Sturbridge cautiously returned the invitation to its envelope. Withdrawing a sheet of stationary and a fountain pen from the desk, she dashed off a quick and elegant apology. She had no intention of spending a single day within this city. Baltimore was a city under siege—not only from the Sabbat forces slavering at the gates, but also from within. An entire city of kindred placed under siege by its prince.

Sturbridge could see that already many powerful players had fallen into the labyrinth that was Baltimore, this city of dead ends and false turnings—this elaborate trap. Jan Pieterzoon. Marcus Vitel. Theo Bell. All powers to be reckoned with in their own right. But each of them had been uprooted from his native soil and hastily transplanted here, to feed and serve the doomed city. Already, their roots were lost among the city's roots. And, when the time came, the city would sacrifice them, willingly, readily, to preserve itself.

Sturbridge was not entirely sure that she herself would be allowed to walk away from this tangled city. But she would make the attempt this very evening. By morning she would either be safely back within the walls of her own chantry, or Garlotte would be explaining the latest calamity to a rather unsympathetic Tremere pontifex.

To lose one Tremere ambassador might be considered a tragedy; to lose two smacked of carelessness.

Jacqueline closed her eyes, counted to three, and tentatively pushed open the little door.

Nothing. The room beyond was silent and pitch dark. From the tiny square of her field of vision, her eyes—long accustomed to nocturnal hunting—could pick out the shadowy outline of some of the room's more dominant furnishings. She quickly identified the leonine supports of the ponderous worktable, the lower drawers of two overfull file cabinets, the gangly legs of a stuffed ibis, and a number of books, curiosities and other obstacles scattered haphazardly about the floor. There was a stillness hanging over these objects, a stagnation that was more than simply the musty air of a room that had been closed off for several weeks.

Jacqueline crawled forward on all fours, ducking her head to avoid hitting it on the lip of the cupboard. As she emerged, breaking the plane of the low doorway, the vertigo slammed into her like a physical blow to the pit of her stomach. Both of her ears popped at once and she felt a tiny trickle of blood begin to trail down her left cheek. The floor lurched up at her and was only narrowly warded off by a sharp, if unintended, blow from her forehead. It was probably as well that she had not been standing. Jacqueline shook her head to clear the ringing pain and crawled fully from the low cupboard into Foley's sanctum.

She did not close the little door behind her, lest she sever the link back to the vestry—the tenuous connection that she had so painstakingly constructed over the past two weeks. She was discovering that the actual use of this particular ritual was more taxing than its preparation.

Master Ynnis, her former mentor, had made it all seem so effortless. She vividly recalled the first time she had seen him absently fumble open a drawer of his rolltop desk and extract a cleaver—one she knew very well to be in the stainless steel drawer just below the washbasin in the refectory. (Jacqueline was more than casually acquainted with a wide range of mundane tasks necessary to the maintaining of the chantry.) The blade had still had drops of water clinging to it.

Ynnis was an undisputed master of translocation. He could work the trick on just about anything that opened and closed. He maintained a regular correspondence with an associate in the London chantry by means of an ornate bamboo bird cage and a particularly threadbare stuffed carrier pigeon. She had seen him drive Foley into an apoplectic rage by "accidentally" removing papers from the secundus's jealously guarded file cabinets and then apologetically returning them to him. There was always a feeling of trepidation when putting your hand to a door handle in his presence. One was never quite certain where an ordinarily reliable door might lead.

Jacqueline did not recall, however, ever experiencing this disorientation, dizziness, nausea. She tried to ignore the unexpected side effects and push herself to her feet. A bad idea. She found herself unceremoniously returned to the floor.

She forced her eyes to focus on the small square of floorboard directly in front of her. The dizziness receded a pace. From this proximity, she could pick out even the grain of the wood through the faint smear of chalk and dust, scuffed by the passing of feet.

Foley would not have tolerated it, of course—were he still around to object. To leave the residual traces of ritual wardings, even until the next morning, would have ensured a harsh reprimand from the secundus.

Jacqueline was particularly interested in the wardings, after the rumors she had heard whispered in the novice hall. Experimentally, she lifted her head to follow the line of the hermetic *diagramma*. Seeing that the vertigo did not lash out at her for this presumption, she made so bold as to creep forward along the line on all fours. Yes, it was as she thought. The *diagramma* had been purposefully obscured, erased. But why?

The junior novices were full of tales of unwarded summonings and dark rites and devils. Jacqueline blamed that fool storyteller Talbott for fanning their wild speculations. The first thing to do to forestall further talk of the dark arts—a discussion that might lead to a closer examination of the ceremonial tools employed in the ritual and certain suspicious ingredients used in their creation—would be to let it become known that the proper wardings had been in place. That the ritual was perfectly normal and perhaps even mundane. But—that the wardings had been purposefully obscured by Foley's murderer.

It would not be prudent for Jacqueline to point this fact out herself, but there were ways in any tight community to ensure that certain things were spoken of.

Jacqueline raised herself to one knee, leaning heavily upon the nearest file cabinet. Better. Another long pause, and she felt confident enough to regain her feet. She had some things to gather and, even with the thought of another wrenching translocation before her, the less time she had to spend here, the better.

Looking around the room, Jacqueline discovered

that there was, as she had suspected, at least one other warding in the room. This later addition was quite obviously installed after the discovery of the murder. It adorned the near side of the room's only door—the one leading to the adjoining office. It was not difficult to extrapolate the existence of a similar warding upon the outer door of Foley's apartments.

It was her anticipation of these wardings that had led Jacqueline to the avoid the standard means of ingress altogether. Her ritual had cost her two weeks' time—a small price to pay under normal circumstances, but time was dear because there was much more at stake here. Jacqueline lived those weeks in constant dread of a summons to appear before the regent for judgment.

But that summons had never come. Jacqueline had weathered the initial interview by adopting the time-honored persona of the terrified novice. She had blathered, she had fumbled, she had begged forgiveness for each time she had thought ill of the secundus. She had steadfastly maintained the ludicrous assertion that she was personally responsible for Foley's demise because deep down she had wished him dead.

It was entirely possible, of course, that her efforts had not been convincing, that she had not escaped judgment at all, that her sentence of Final Death was only a bit delayed in arriving. If Jacqueline could remain patient through those agonizing weeks, certainly Sturbridge could as well.

Now, even with the regent away in Baltimore, Jacqueline knew her very presence in Foley's rooms put her at grave risk. The warding on the door would certainly bring a full security team down on her, should she inadvertently trigger it. And this was assuming, of course, that it was not efficiently designed to neutralize any intruders by itself.

With agonizing care, Jacqueline crossed the room to the worktable. She stooped and studied something lying neglected on the floor. A red candle. Satisfied, she nodded. From the voluminous folds of her robes, she extracted a bundle and unrolled it flat upon the table. It contained precisely seven red candles and seven wooden sticks. She removed one glove and, lifting the first pristine candle, traced a line down its edge with her fingernail. Where she touched it, the wax melted and ran. She judged the length of the candle and then of the wick, pinching it off neatly and noting the clean, black, seared edge. She cracked the candle at precisely the same point where the other had been broken in its fall, and then examined her efforts with a critical eye. That would do.

She swapped her less-incriminating replica with its twin on the floor, taking a moment to get the positioning just right before beginning her hunt for the next of the scattered candles.

In the end, she only recovered five candles and six pine sticks. She would have to hope that the rest had been consumed in the fire. She did not care to dwell on the alternative—that they had been removed from the scene.

She carefully repacked her bundle, pulled on her glove and turned back toward the low cupboard. There was a reassuring faint crackle of energy from the arcane membrane that remained stretched taut across the opening.

Jacqueline froze. The sound had nearly, but not entirely, masked a faint noise from the outer room. The unmistakable sound of a doorknob turning.

Saturday, 28 August 1999, 3:00 AM
Lord Baltimore Inn
Baltimore, Maryland

"Ready to go already, Professor?" Francesca Lyon hovered in the doorway as if unwilling to intrude.

"Very nearly, Miss Lyon. Please come in. It was kind of you to come on such short notice." She gestured toward the seating arrangement near the fireplace and returned to her packing.

"Thanks. Can't I give you a hand?"

"No, just finishing up now. Please, sit down. Make yourself comfortable."

Sturbridge crossed to an intricately carved oak cabinet along one wall. The twin doors were decorated with a knotted design resembling a wreath woven of dried twigs. Her audience had the distinct impression that the cabinet door swung open a fraction of a second before Sturbridge's hand found the latch. She withdrew a decanter and two crystal goblets from the shadowed recess.

It was not until that moment that Sturbridge committed herself to this course of action. Perhaps it was her unsettling experience earlier with drawing life from the ancient wood that had put her in mind of it. Perhaps it was the all-too-fresh memories of her own daughter. Perhaps it was only the frustration of the prospect of having this entire trip to Baltimore prove to be a waste.

As she recrossed the room, she studied her guest's features for any sign of recognition, of apprehension. In this she was disappointed. Chessie's demeanor remained friendly, personal, at ease.

Sturbridge began to fill both goblets.

Chessie raised a hand in polite refusal. "No, not

for me. I'm driving. But thank you."

"But I insist. We will toast Dean Dorfman, so you can put it down to official university business."

"Dean Dorfman warned me about drinking with any of his colleagues," she said with subdued conviction.

"This is a particular vintage that I keep on hand for just such occasions. It has weathered the scrutiny of the most exacting of palates. I think you will enjoy it."

Slowly, some idea of what she was being offered seemed to dawn upon Chessie. She regarded the proffered glass as she might a cup of hemlock.

"It is an old family recipe, handed down to me by my sire, and by his sire before him. There are many generations to its noble lineage." Sturbridge swirled her chalice reverently, inhaling the heady aroma.

"It sounds delightful. But I can't ask you to share such a family treasure with me. Dean Dorfman…"

"I will be frank, Miss Lyon. I am concerned for Dean Dorfman's safety. He has been gone overlong in a time when he can scarcely afford to be absent at all. If he does not return quickly, you will find yourself in need of a new advisor. I would like to help you. Do not be nervous. This is how we sit down to discuss business in my house. Do you understand? First, there is blood between us. Then there is business."

"I did not know that you trafficked in trust, Professor."

"I don't. I trade in blood, Miss Lyon. Only in blood. Everything else is fleeting, treacherous, and, in the end, inconsequential."

"To blood." Chessie raised the glass to her lips, closed her eyes and drank. Immediately, she slipped sideways into the whisperings.

"To business," Sturbridge countered, savoring the heady vintage.

Chessie was surrounded by hushed voices. A landscape composed solely of wisps of night and hushed voices. The whispers were pitched low, just beyond the range of her understanding. The words seemed to lose their way in the darkness; she could pick out only the symphony of tones. They tugged at her, poked and prodded. The voices seemed to be alternately urging her to action, consoling her, passing judgment, haggling, hinting at the forbidden, barking commands, reciting elegies, giving patient instruction—but all of them were quite clear on this one point. They all wanted something from her. Expected something. Something she could not quite make out from the incessant and hopelessly intermingled mutterings.

She was buffeted by the maelstrom of their expectation, drawn in, borne down. Her consciousness flickered dangerously on the edge of being extinguished. Each new gust threatened to snuff out the delicate flame utterly. She clung to life, to its broken fragments, like a person floundering amidst the wreckage of a sinking ship.

Chessie broke the surface, gasping, not for air, but for awareness. Her grasp found and latched on to some jettisoned piece of flotsam. It writhed in her grasp, but she held firm. Clawing the hair from her eyes with her free hand, she saw that which she clung to, and her hope failed her. A great eel, its lustrous skin gleaming redly, wound its way free of the wreckage and out into the open sea. Chessie watched in horror as her lifeline twisted, arced, and then plunged into the deep. She clawed at the slippery flank with both hands as it bore her under for the final time.

The eel was a streak of red cutting through the deep. As awareness faded to a dim glimmer of light far above her, Chessie found herself musing that the back of the great red eel resembled nothing more than a stringy tendril of blood suspended in the murky water.

Awareness flickered one last time and was gone. Blotted out by the weight of dark water above it.

Then there was only the blood.

The blood bore the broken shell down, down deep to the very heart of the sea. It buried it there in the powdery and ever-shifting sand.

Miserere nobis.

Miserere nobis.

Dona nobis pacem.

The ocean floor was a vast hourglass. Years passed, their number measured out in the shifting of a given number of grains of sand.

Years later.

The bottom of the ocean.

The scratching of the grains of sand. Sliding slowly. Slowly sliding.

The sound intruded upon the welcome oblivion. Like a soft scratching at the coffin lid. The sound of years passing.

Scrape. Scrape. Scrape.

A drifting of three years.

Scrape. Scrape. Scrape.

The sound rose in pitch and immediacy. It fell with the regularity of a spade.

Strike, scrape, slough.

A shovelful of years.

Strike, scrape, slough.

There was an urgency in the song of the spade. A compulsion. And a note of something familiar.

Fran. Ces. Ca.

Fran. Ces. Ca.

The alien syllables meant nothing to the dead and broken shell buried at the ocean's heart. But the sounds echoed and rebounded within the hollow of that shell—redoubling in meaning and intensity— until something deep within stirred at the sound of that summons.

Francesca.

Awareness came flooding back in an excruciating rush. She curled in upon herself, tumbling, kicking. She tried to burrow deeper into the sands, into the warm oblivion.

Still the voice would not let her rest.

Francesca.

She knew that voice. Sturbridge. Professor Sturbridge.

Francesca oriented herself by that voice and kicked out desperately for the surface.

The first thing to return to her was light. Slowly it resolved itself into distinct shapes, patterns, vision. Soon she could not shut out the swarm of wriggling shadows that surrounded her.

The sea was filled with hundreds of drowning bodies, all fighting for the surface. The blue and bloated limbs of those who had already succumbed to the struggle snatched at her, clung to her, bore her down. Back down toward the ocean floor and the waiting arms of oblivion.

"Aisling!"

A swollen face pressed close to her own. It bobbed gently, aimlessly, from side to side, its hair fanning out in the current. It regarded her with a clinical, almost serene detachment. Thick, sausage-like fingers experimentally probed and prodded her. Chessie batted at the corpse, trying to dislodge it.

"Fear not. I am here." The voice was small and distant.

The drowned body was much more immediate. Draped languidly in fetters of clinging seaweed, it embraced Chessie, entangling her flailing limbs as the pair tumbled over and over. From somewhere amidst the tangle, a glint of metal, the kiss of scalpel-sharp blade, and a viscous trail of blood extending out like a lifeline from an incision in Chessie's chest. Lost beneath her own howl, Chessie thought she could pick out Sturbridge's calm voice, plodding on with patience and reverence as if reciting some ancient tale or scripture.

"He was the serpent in the Garden of Hermes. Our beloved oracular serpent. The end product of hundreds of years of devotion to the Great Work."

The apparition clutched its prize tightly within one oversized fist. With a deft motion, he snared the end of the trailing strand of blood, still uncoiling from the gaping wound in Chessie's chest, and looped it three times about its fist.

He tested its pull. She bent like a bow.

"He was the object of our devotion, the meaning behind the sacrifice of uncounted lives—Pythagoreans, Catharists, Masons, alchemists—all struggling in darkness so that one day, generations hence, one man could hold in his hand the forbidden fruit, the Philosopher's Stone, the elixir of life everlasting. His name was called Goratrix, our light-bearer, our Prometheus, our Lucifer."

The bloated face leered over her in a mocking half-bow. It reeled Chessie in slowly, pressing uncomfortably close, a lover bent on confiding a dark secret. Its chill lips brushed her ear.

Helpless in that grasp, Chessie felt more than heard the words:

Visita Interiora Terrae, Rectificando Invenies Occultum Lapidem.

"Visit the center of the Earth," she haltingly translated. "And by...purifying?...you will find the secret stone."

A grotesquely swollen blue hand slapped her heartily on the back. The corpse's head rolled back slowly in a laugh that Chessie thought might dislodge head from body altogether. In this, she was disappointed.

Shouldering Chessie's lifeline, the drowned man turned and plodded off downwards toward the ocean's floor. His captive had little choice save to flounder along in his wake.

Chessie felt the darkness closing in once again. Consciousness slipping from her. Seeping away through the hole in her chest.

Sturbridge's voice was the sussurant lull of the ocean currents.

"It was in the blood, of course. The power was in the blood. But Goratrix did not partake of the dark gift. Not right away. Instead he returned to his House and sought out his master, laying before him the forbidden fruit."

Chessie could not focus upon the words. She could no longer discern where she ended and the expanse of dark waters began. She drifted unhurriedly toward a murky hole in the ocean's floor, following a distant bobbing light. The elusive light seemed to sneak past the tin shutter of an upraised lantern. The lamp was held aloft by a solitary laborer making his way home after dark, and struggling under a heavy burden.

As the laborer shifted the load to his other shoulder, Chessie perceived that the light was not separate from the lantern but attached, intrinsic to it. The light streamed out behind it—red, coiling, restless.

It is in the blood, of course, Chessie thought, a dark almost hysterical laugh welling up inside her. *The light is in the blood*.

My blood.

She was very close now. Close to the reckless abandon of hysteria. Close to the point of surrender, of returning to oblivion. Close to the dark hole at the center of the ocean's floor.

Visita interiora terrae.

The center of the earth. The forbidden place. The dark region at the very center of herself that she dared not go (could not go). The place where she kept, carefully guarded, her secrets from herself.

It was a place denied her. Beyond the comforting walls of self-deceit, of self-delusion. She knew there was a still point, a place of searing clarity where all the justifications, all the rationalization, of a lifetime of inhuman hungers burned away. Leaving her alone with her sins, her shortcomings, her selfishness—her self.

It was a dwelling place of truths so dark they had to be forced down, chained to the bedrock, lest they rise up to assail her in the dark hours.

Visita interiora mea.

There was a movement in the deepest recesses of the dark hole at the ocean's heart. A stirring.

Chessie twisted, thrashed against her tether. Trying in vain to avert her gaze from the presence rising up from the depths.

There was a swirling of sand, resolving itself slowly into a twisting funnel. A looming mass taking form, becoming.

The rising maelstrom howled with the grinding of sand and water. Chessie shielded her eyes. She could distinctly feel the impact of each grain of sand slicing into her exposed lifeline. The shadowy form that dragged her onward was already lost amidst the turbulent waters.

The only evidence that her predecessor had not already been utterly destroyed was the continued pull upon her yoke. Drawing her directly into the heart of the maelstrom. A great rushing of sand and water buffeted her, blinded her, snatched her up. She spun wildly, spinning end over end, dragging against her anchor line.

She could not quite shake the feeling that there was something behind the roiling waters, a presence stirring up the fury of the deep, a will. Chessie clawed sand from her eyes and squinted against the weight of the water.

There, at the very center of the maelstrom, a vast shape was rising, patiently, layer upon layer. She strained to catch a glimpse of it through the swirling sand that gouged at her eyes. She had to know. Had to understand. If only for this brief moment before her vision was taken from her.

Deliberately, she steeled herself and kicked forward into the depths.

Suddenly, there was still water all about her. Buffeted, bleeding, half-blind, she had flailed her way through the maelstrom. She now floated, suspended, inverted, at the very eye of the undersea storm—the still point at the heart of the swirling confusion of sensual perceptions.

Bracing herself, Chessie forced her eyes open, and she saw.

A gargantuan form loomed over her, filling her blood-glazed field of vision. Its feet were lost in the unguessed depths of the hole in the ocean's floor. Chessie had the unsettling impression that its roots burrowed into the very core of the earth itself.

Visita Interiora Terrae.

Its stony visage glared down at her from high above. Its crown, exalted, streamed toward the surface—toward the world of light. In between these two extremes stretched the vast expanse of wall, its once-sculpted surface worn smooth with passage of water and years. Chessie's gaze raced the length of that wall, fighting the feeling of vertigo as she struggled to orient herself.

The wall did not, as she first thought, stand fully erect. Rather, it leaned ponderously toward its fellows. Its two fellows, she realized with dawning clarity. A vast pyramid.

As the feeling of vertigo passed, she realized that it was she and not the pyramid that was moving. She sliced through the depths, plummeting toward the base of the great wall.

There was an answering motion, far below her, at the point that the pyramid had so violently pierced the ocean's floor. Chessie thought she could pick out a familiar figure there, going through the motions of some elaborate ritual. She recognized the bloated corpse she had wrestled with earlier—her captor, the drowned man. Sturbridge's voice echoed in her thoughts, confiding a name. Goratrix. The Tremere's beloved serpent. Our Prometheus, our Lucifer.

Light streamed from the mage's upraised fist as he hammered three times on the unyielding door of the pyramid. Chessie felt the repercussion of each of those blows within the hollow of her breast. She tumbled in her downward plunge and nearly smashed against the side of the pyramid.

From within an answering voice:

Who dares demand admission....

"It is I." Goratrix raised his fist on high, revealing the blood-gorged heart cradled there. It was as red and lustrous as a polished apple. "Then your eyes shall be opened," his voice assailed the impassive walls, "and ye shall be as gods, knowing good and evil."

For a long while there was silence upon the deep.

Then, in answer, the great portal of House Tremere swung wide to receive her prodigal son and his precious double-edged gift.

As her heart was carried over the threshold of the pyramid and into captivity, Chessie screamed and passed into merciful oblivion.

Jacqueline froze. Her first instinct was to dive for the cupboard door. She could still make out the sizzle of arcane energy stretched taut across the tiny opening—a sign that the temporary passage back to the vestry was still operational. She could probably scramble through the low door and, assuming the vertigo was not so severe that she blacked out entirely, slam the corresponding vestry door shut behind her, severing the connection. But this flurry of activity would certainly alert whoever had entered the adjoining room that there had been an intruder present.

Her second thought was to stealthily move around to a position behind the door. From this vantage point, she might fall upon anyone foolish enough to enter the sanctum and take them unawares. She had already taken two light steps in that direction when it occurred to her that she did not want to be anywhere near that ward when the door opened.

She stopped again, feeling awkward and exposed in the middle of the room. The light in the outer office clicked on. The brightness sliced under the door, the glaring artificial light stretching across the floor in a shape like a guillotine blade.

Jacqueline cursed silently. Stupid. If that was not the security team—traipsing through the front door, poking around in Foley's office and flipping on the lights—then they would not be far behind. Whoever was in the next room was either stupid, careless, or…

The glyph on the door flared suddenly to life. Already, Jacqueline was diving, not for the cupboard (now precisely two full steps too far away), but for the protection of the solid worktable. There was a sharp cry from beyond the door, followed shortly by the sound of something heavy collapsing to the floor. On the inside of the door, the glyph drifted away from the wood and fell gently to the floor in a trail of spent ashes.

A stillness settled over Foley's chambers. Forgotten, the adjoining door swung slowly inward.

Jacqueline scrambled for the cupboard. If she were lucky, that concussion would have knocked the unwelcome newcomer out cold. The security team would have their intruder and Jacqueline would hear all about it tomorrow. If she were not lucky…

Perhaps unwisely, Jacqueline spared one quick glance toward the open doorway and Foley's office beyond. There, across the threshold, lay Eva, shaking her head groggily and struggling to pick herself up off the floor.

In that instant, their eyes met.

Damn.

Jacqueline abandoned her mad scramble and with visible restraint, composed herself. There was no point in running now. She turned upon the fallen novice.

"You little twit. What could you possibly have been thinking?" She took the girl roughly by the arm and made to haul her to her feet. "Can you stand?"

Eva nodded and pushed her away. "I'm sorry. I heard someone inside. The regent was quite specific. No one—not even the security team—was to enter these rooms while she was away. What were you…? Oh."

"I might ask you the same question. But my guess is that we've only got about two minutes before we'll have even more unwanted company." Jacqueline found her hand unconsciously straying to the carefully rolled parcel concealed beneath her robes. *Blood of black cat; heart of black cockerel. Company's coming.*

She cursed herself and then turned her outrage upon Eva. "I can't believe you. Walking right in through the front door. Flipping the lights on and off. Just what exactly did you expect to…? No, never mind. Don't answer that. Look, here's your story.

"You were passing. You heard a noise. You could have gone for help, but then it might have been too late. Against your better judgment, you decided to try the door…"

"But that's exactly what *did* happen."

"All the better. But if they decide to double-check your story, you insist on seeing the regent before you let them open a vein. You're her favorite; everybody knows that. They won't risk it—her displeasure, I mean. They'll probably just put you away under the keystone for a few days until she gets back. Now listen.

"You came in here, got as far as the sanctum door and bam! When you came to, you knew you had to stay put and report the whole incident to the security team. You never saw anyone or anything. You understand?"

"I'm not stupid and I'm not a child." Eva straightened her robes. Without looking up, she asked, "Why did you kill Foley?"

"Look you, I didn't kill anybody. You understand me? I'll go under the knife on that point and the blood will run true. I didn't like Foley—God, I *hated* Foley—but I didn't kill him."

"Then why are you here? How'd you get in here, anyway?"

"No time for that now. Tell me we've got a deal so I can get out of here."

"Why should I cover for you?"

Jacqueline rose over her. "Because I am your superior, *neophyte*. I can make things easier for you or…quite difficult."

"Not if I don't cover for you."

Jacqueline calculated quickly, weighing Eva's stubbornness against the time remaining. Not worth chancing it.

She rolled her eyes in dismissal of the threat. "All right, look. There are some things here that are just not right. But I had to see for myself. To be sure."

She expected an argument on this point, but getting none, she hurried on. "I can't go into a lot of detail right now. The wardings, they're not missing, they've been erased. Now the notes, *they're* missing. Foley made a great fuss over his photographic memory, but he always wrote everything down. He was obsessive. He couldn't do his laundry without making a list.

"And the gem is gone. You've figured out that much at least, haven't you? The one he kept in the fleur-de-lis box. The one he had those three novices flogged down to the bone over. That's really what this whole ritual was about, the gem. The Keyhole, he called it. Ugly little lump. Red with black smudges at the poles. I told him I didn't know what he saw in it and he laughed at me. He said whenever you peeked through a keyhole around here, all you saw in it was another eye, staring back."

"*And if you gaze for long into the abyss, the abyss gazes also into you.*"

"What?"

"It's nothing. Something the regent told me when

we…found him."

"Look, you're trying to find out what happened to Foley. I can tell you more about the ritual. About what should have been here, but isn't. I can help. But if the jackals find me here, I'm just another victim. Do you understand? Do we have a deal?"

Jackals, Eva thought. *Anubis. Pyramid security.*

"Deal. But I need to talk to you—to talk to somebody—and soon. I think someone's been…"

There was the sound of purposeful footsteps approaching.

"Tomorrow night. Midnight. The refectory." Jacqueline pressed her hand, held it to retain the novice's attention. Already Eva was worriedly craning toward the outer door. "If you don't show, I'll know they've got you under lock and key. In that case— listen to me—in that case, they're not going to let you out of their sight until the regent returns. You'll be safe enough. And we'll meet on the night of Sturbridge's return. Do you understand? You're going to get through this. You're going to be fine."

Eva nodded and Jacqueline gave her hand a reassuring squeeze. "Now get out there and buy me some time."

Eva carefully closed the sanctum door behind her retreating co-conspirator. Turning, she put on what she hoped was her bravest face to meet the jackals.

Chessie thrashed wildly, fighting the sensation that she was drowning, buried beneath a ponderous weight of water. She heard a familiar voice.

"It is enough, she is coming around at last."

Chessie felt something massive uncoil from atop her chest. His eyes flew open in alarm, but her sight was filmed over with blood. She had a fleeting impression of a gnarled branch twisting away into one corner of the room and disappearing into rafters with a rustling noise.

"You have returned to us, Miss Lyon. I was beginning to fear for your safety."

"Professor Sturbridge." She blinked repeatedly, trying to clear the haze from her eyes, but found them wet with new blood. "What did you...?"

"It was nothing, Miss Lyon, I assure you. Nothing I would not do for any novice entrusted to my care. Can you sit up? No, slowly. Better."

Chessie wiped at her eyes with the back of one hand. "I apologize. I fear I am unwell."

As vision returned, she surveyed the wreckage of the fireside seating arrangement. The remains of an end table, its lamp, the crystal decanter and both goblets had been hastily swept to the side—leaving a clear spot on the floor. Chessie lay in the eye of the storm. "I'm sorry. I don't know what..."

Sturbridge waved dismissively. "It's nothing. I should not try to stand as of yet."

Chessie was forced to agree with her assessment and crumpled back to the floor with what dignity she could muster. "It seems I find myself in your debt. You called me back."

Sturbridge regarded her curiously. "Called you back?"

"Yes, back from the…tell me, was I dead? I mean, *really* dead."

"No more so than anyone else."

"Please, Professor, this is quite distressing. You called me back from the bottom of the sea, from the very center. From the *Interiora Terrae*."

Instantly, Sturbridge's playful tone vanished, replaced with concern. "Well now, you *did* go a long way." She stooped and took Chessie's chin firmly in one hand. She prised open first the left eyelid and then the right, studying her eyes intently for the telltale gleam of delirium.

"Tell me about the bottom of the ocean. It must have been very…peaceful there."

Chessie recoiled as if struck, but Sturbridge maintained her grip. "Peaceful? The water was thick with bodies, corpses. They wouldn't let you be. They kept poking at you, prodding, leaning into you. And their faces. Oh, if you could have seen their faces."

"*Eyes as round and bright as moons…*"

"What's that?" Chessie shot back.

"Nothing. An old dream, a poem, a snatch of song. It is nothing. You were telling me about the children."

"The children?"

"The Children down the Well."

"No, no, you are not listening to me. There were no children. There was no well. I was telling you about the bottom of the ocean, about the Drowned Man."

"I am sorry. I misunderstood. Please, continue."

"…At least I think it was a man. It may very

well have been a serpent. A sea serpent. Yes, I seem to remember a sea serpent. And a shipwreck. Oh, you will think me a very great fool by this point. What nonsense. What utter nonsense!"

With an effort of will, Chessie teetered to her feet. Sturbridge moved to help her, but the young woman's look said very clearly that assistance would neither be necessary nor welcome.

"Not at all, Miss Lyon. Your tale is not so strange as you might imagine. You have my attention. Can you tell me about the Drowned Man?"

"Tell *you* about him? But you were the one telling *me* about him. 'Our beloved oracular serpent,' you called him. 'Our Prometheus, our Lucifer.'"

"The Light-bringer. Yes, I see. But what was he doing? Did he do or say anything…unusual?" Her look became shrewd, predatory. "What did he tell you?"

Chessie hesitated, taken aback by the sudden intensity of Sturbridge's interest. The young woman could feel it boring into her like the heat of a flame. She shifted uncomfortably, but could see no advantage in keeping this knowledge from Sturbridge.

"He told me…he told me to visit the center. *Visita Interiora.*"

A broad smile spread across Sturbridge's features. Chessie exhaled slowly in relief, seeing the familiar Sturbridge return to her.

"Vitriol. He gave you the cup of vitriol? Are you quite sure, Miss Lyon?"

"Cup? I didn't say anything about a cup. It seems to me that it was *you* who gave me vitriol to drink. I have not yet recovered from the effects of your concoction, and I am not entirely certain that I ever shall."

"No, you misunderstand, Miss Lyon. Vitriol.

V-I-T-R-I-O-L. It is an ancient alchemical formula: *Visita Interiora Terrae, Rectificando Invenies...*"

"*Occultum Lapidem.* Yes, his exact words. Strange. It seems an odd sort of thing for me to dream, don't you think, Professor? The chances of my accidentally stumbling onto some disused occult proverb, well, you must admit it seems unlikely."

"Do you think it coincidental, Miss Lyon?"

"I do not," she replied pointedly.

Sturbridge chose to ignore the tone of accusation. "Good. I will suggest to you, then, that it was no accident that you discovered this particular gem, this *occultum lapidem*, on your first journey inward. It is a road map, Miss Lyon. It will be a great comfort to you in the years to come, on your journeys into that inner country. It is also a promise—a promise that you will return there."

"I am not entirely sure I wish to return there. It was not a...pleasant place."

At this Sturbridge laughed aloud. "It is *your* place, Miss Lyon. It is the place from which you arise. It is the place you carry with you, even now. It is the place to which you must, eventually, return. But not tonight, I think."

Chessie's suspicions, however, were not allayed. "If you will forgive me saying so, Professor, it did not look like my place at all. It looked suspiciously like *your* place. It was filled with your forebears, your rituals, your symbols, your occult mutterings. Even *I* did not feel like me. I felt like some player in an ancient story—a story of your people."

"Perhaps you still do not understand. You think that I have taken advantage of you, that I have doctored your drink, knocked you out and whispered hypnotic suggestions into your ear."

There was an uncomfortable silence before Chessie replied, "I have suggested no such thing."

"But you have. Listen to me, Miss Lyon. The things you saw, they were not of my creation. I did not know you had journeyed to the *Interiora Terrae*, I did not know you had met with Gora...the Drowned Man, I did not know what he said or did. It is not my voice that has been whispering to you, it is the singing of the blood."

Something in her words both rang true and simultaneously filled Chessie with dread.

"It is in the blood," she recited hollowly, "the power is in the blood."

Sturbridge nodded. "The blood that fills you, the blood we shared tonight, it is the blood of the Tremere. The Blood of the Seven. The mortar of the Pyramid. It is ancient, it is potent, and it speaks to each of us—in visions and in nightmares. In ancient words and lost ritual gestures. And in the quiet places, where no others may go, the blood whispers to us."

Chessie felt a sinking sensation, a hole opening up at her very core. Anger bubbled up to fill the void.

"I did not ask for this! I came here in good faith, because you asked me to come. And this is how you have treated me? You would visit some measure of your curse upon me? You are a monster, a creature of deceit and of treachery. You would poison me with your tainted blood?"

Sturbridge held her gaze, felt the fever burning there, saw the hint of the earlier madness gaining full rein.

Chessie flung herself toward her. Sturbridge did not try to ward her off. An embrace fired by a warmth very different than that of two lovers.

The blood sang between them.

A cloud passed before the moon and the rows of tombstones vanished, replaced with the more mundane jumble of broken boulders that littered the ascent. Far away, in a luxurious hotel room near Central Park, Nickolai's body deftly shifted the bowl he was carrying to his right hand and sketched a complex sigil in the air with his left.

He caught himself in the act and cursed his own foolishness in a long-forgotten tongue. In the many lifetimes since his demise, he had never quite managed to shake the ridiculous superstitions of his mortal life. It was a tenacious peasant magic. A thaumaturgy of dung and onions. To Nickolai's embarrassment, no amount of sophistication could quite suppress it. No true power could shout it down.

Perhaps it was another trick of the light or the lingering grip of visions, but it seemed that the tracery of his fingers hung there before him in midair. Nickolai scrutinized the familiar glyph.

The sign against the Evil Eye.

With greater deliberation, he pricked the tip of his index finger with his thumbnail and retraced the symbol in blood. The delicate network of lines devoured the precious vitae and then blazed suddenly to life.

Elsewhere, high within the Adirondacks, another aspect of Nickolai took a step backward in alarm and nearly fell over the nearest tombstone. He caught himself in time to see the last of the flaming remains of the glyph gently raining down upon the rocks below.

The moon, drawing back its cloudy veil, fixed

him with an accusing stare. He could not abide the intensity of her visage and quickly turned away. He thought for a moment that he caught a glimpse of a retreating gossamer form among the tombstones. Nearby he heard the trickling laughter of a brook fleeing down the mountainside. Resolutely, he turned his back upon the snares and distractions of the night and began the last leg of his ascent.

The path between the tombstones (boulders, he reminded himself) led him to the lip of a precipice. He was very near the summit and looking down into a wide depression, a hollow carved out by an ancient spring. The floor of this bowl was crowded with crude obelisks of rock jutting up at improbable angles. It was as if the entire floor of the hollow had been pierced from below by uncounted spear thrusts from an angry mountain god. Disturbed, no doubt, in the midst of his stony sleep. Nickolai was envious of the slumbering god. Each night, he grappled with the temptation to sink into the earth's arms and surrender himself to her embrace and stony sleep. To be free of the dangers of the Final Nights, of the manipulations and covert dangers of the Jyhad. Of the hunters, and of the hunters of the hunters. To sleep, to forget, perchance to be forgotten.

But Nickolai was the last and he now must bear the responsibilities of his House. Alone. He scanned the broken ground for a likely avenue of descent.

Not far from where he stood, one of the mammoth obelisks had fallen like a lightning-struck oak. It leaned drunkenly against the wall of the precipice, its tip extended well above Nickolai's own height. It should be possible, Nickolai thought, to descend its sloping side to the floor of the depression.

As he neared the fallen giant, Nickolai began to

get a sense of its great age. Its sides were pitted with evidence of the slow passage of trickling water and years. He thought immediately of stalagmites and stalactites. He had never, however, seen such intricately carved columns of rock above ground before. He would have thought that the indiscriminate hand of the rain would obliterate all such delicate chiselwork.

Nickolai put one foot upon the great column of rock to ensure that it would not shift under his weight. Unlikely, he thought. If the giant were in the least bit unbalanced, it would have collapsed long ago under its own mass.

He looked to the spot where the pillar had impacted and settled into the wall of the precipice and was surprised to see newly broken earth. It was as if the impact of the colossus had taken place a matter of days ago rather than of centuries. Nickolai put his hand to the stone and ran his fingers across the deeply gouged surface. Was it his imagination or was the stone warm? For a brief moment, it seemed the stone still trembled slightly as with the remembrance of its precipitous flight through the earth's surface, its first glimpse of sky and the impact of its calamitous fall to earth once more.

Nickolai shook his head as if to banish such nonsense, but he could not quite shake the picture of the angry mountain god, awakened from its slumber.

There were other powers, Nickolai thought, as he picked his way down the treacherous slope, that slumbered deep beneath the earth. Dark powers. Angry powers.

It occurred to him that he might be traipsing barehanded into the lair of just such a mountain god. He searched back through his memory for tales or stories of the taming of a mountain. In the vain hope that he might find some efficacious weapon.

Saturday, 28 August 1999, 5:42 AM
Lord Baltimore Inn
Baltimore, Maryland

Without a word or backward glance, Sturbridge eased the door closed behind her.

Chessie was sleeping now, at last, her face buried in the bloodstained pillow. Sturbridge had waited for the gentle sobs to subside before slipping from the chamber. She crossed the sitting room to the closet near the hall door and withdrew the larger of two businesslike suitcases. She heaved the case onto the table one-handed. The latches sprang open in response to her low whisper, revealing precise rows of neatly pressed garments.

Sturbridge packed up the last of her things and tied the series of satin ribbons that held everything in its precise place. She leaned down hard upon the lid of the suitcase and the latches sealed with two distinct pings. She had turned to shoulder the suitcase from the table when her eyes lit upon the wreckage of the seating arrangement by the fireplace. Broken glass lay scattered in a glittering arc reaching out toward the room's center. The wave of glass had broken more abruptly upon the hearth and arrayed itself in larger jagged shards.

Sturbridge started instinctively for the closet for a broom to set things in order. She stopped with her hand upon the knob.

She would go now. A cab to the airport. A plane back to New York. And safely home before sunrise.

She thought of the nights of sneaking back into her parents' house, racing against the first hint of the sunrise. Charged on adrenaline, jazz, infatuation and bathtub gin.

Home before sunrise, she thought. The romance

of the idea had begun to wear a bit thin after nearly a century. Her surreptitious early morning races had taken on a hard, ugly aspect. The consequence of losing that race now was far more severe than her mother's displeasure. She had known of those, of course, who had been caught out by the jealous sun. Who had not? It was a critical part of a novice's education. It was one of the Portals of Initiation.

But the steady progression of years had turned the tables upon Sturbridge. As the regent of the Chantry of the Five Boroughs, she more and more often found herself in the position of the anxious mother, waiting for her wayward daughters to return home. She had even—she remembered the incident with excruciating clarity—once ordered the door of her house barred against the return of an unrepentant and irreformable novice. The sun had caught her upon the doorstep.

Home before sunrise.

And six impossible things before breakfast.

She thought of *Alice*, and of Maeve. She thought of the nights of reading aloud the stories of the Caterpillar, the Duchess, the Griffin, the White Knight, to her little girl. Her beautiful child. Her magical child. Lost to her and gone. Disappeared down a hole in the ground.

In a wonderland they lie
Dreaming as the days drift by
Dreaming as the summers die
Ever drifting down the stream
Lingering in the golden gleam
Life, what is it but a dream?

Sturbridge swung the suitcase off the table in a great arc. It banged angrily against the wall before succumbing to the pull of gravity. She heard an answering stirring from the inner room, but Chessie did not awaken.

It was perhaps a small cruelty to leave her like this. But she did not repent of it.

It was difficult to say how much of this evening's ordeal the girl might remember when she awakened. Would she recall what Sturbridge had done to her? Would she be able to call to mind the unique savor of the Blood of the Seven—its power, its compulsion, its madness? Would she be able to reconstruct the shards of memory from her journey inward—the touch of the Drowned Man, the majesty of the Pyramid, the terrible betrayal of the Sacrifice?

More importantly, Sturbridge found herself wondering if Chessie would recall her own weakness in the wake of potent vitae. The suspicions, the unreasoning rage.

Almost as an afterthought, she paused in the doorway. Crossing to the writing table, she extracted a sheet of creamy stationary and the fountain pen. In a bold, unquivering hand, she wrote:

Come to New York. Delay will bring only fever and torment. You are not alone.
—A.S.

She folded the note neatly in half and stood it on the mantle like a pyramid.

Running her hand affectionately over the wood of the ancient door, Sturbridge shouldered her cases and took her leave. The hallway and the rest of what had come to be known as the Witch's Wing was, as might be expected, deserted. Only after the door had sighed shut did Sturbridge allow herself to doubt.

Eva was late, hurrying and obviously shaken. Twice she stopped abruptly, her ears straining to pick out the telltale sound of stealthy footfalls shadowing her. She was not altogether certain what she would do if her suspicions proved justified.

It was too late to turn back now. Where would she go? To chantry security? Somehow Eva did not relish the prospect of another confrontation with Helena and her jackals—especially one in which she would have to explain how and why she had slipped her tether. Her memory of their recent encounter was still far too fresh in her mind.

No, better just to get this over with and get back before her absence was noted. She would meet with Jacqueline. She would explain her suspicions and enlist Jacqueline's help. With Sturbridge away, Eva was coming to realize just how vulnerable her position here really was.

Her agitation was not eased in the least by the fact that her path to the refectory—and her covert meeting with Jacqueline—would take her directly past the secundus's chambers. They were just ahead now, around the next bend. She could actually feel their presence like a weight pressing against her, holding her back. Eva realized her pace had unconsciously slowed to a reluctant crawl.

Purposefully, she forced herself to turn the corner. She felt the first gentle touch of dread caress the nape of her neck.

part three:

the children
down the well

She tried to ignore it. She kept her eyes fixed rigidly forward and counted off each quick measured pace. One, two, three...she was even with the door before she realized the source of her apprehension. The keyhole.

And if you gaze for long into the abyss, the abyss gazes also into you.

She closed her eyes tightly; she knew of no other way to keep herself from peering back at the keyhole. She willed herself forward. She pleaded with her feet to take just one more step. To lift, to fall, nothing more.

It was no good. She could feel the heat of the dead man's all-seeing eye—squinting at her through the keyhole. Boring into her. Where it touched, it burned with the brilliance of sunlight, of truth.

Eva knew her continued existence depended upon shadows, upon murky reflections, upon misdirection and half-truths. She could not endure the searing intensity of that unblinking stare.

She might have screamed. She remembered picking herself up off the floor—ignoring the fresh pain of bruised knees and battered forearms—and stumbling blindly down the corridor.

She arrived at the refectory trembling and out of breath. She was certain the sound of her wild flight had attracted unwanted attention. Jacqueline would curse her (or worse) for allowing herself to be followed.

Marshalling her apologies and excuses, she pushed open the refectory door.

Even before she laid eyes on Jacqueline, all of her carefully ordered rationalizations had deserted her. She shut her mouth stupidly, backing away from the headless body crumpled before the stainless-steel double sink.

A murky swirl of blood floated atop the soapy water. The cupboard above the sink was open and empty. Eva pressed one sleeve to her face in a vain effort to block out the pervasive smell of spilled life. The scent of blood muddled her thoughts, picked away at the frayed edge of reason.

Faced with the sudden and overwhelming presence of yet another corpse, Eva did the only thing she could do. She threw back her head and howled. She summoned the jackals.

Leopold carefully picked his way over the pocked, bleached landscape. He could not see his footing clearly through the glare. Progress was treacherous. An unbroken expanse of gleaming white stretched away before him. Bones. As far as the eye could see, nothing but bones. They jutted up sharply like obelisks. They leaned like palm trees in a strong wind. They cascaded to the ground in crashing waterfalls. They rippled outward in concentric circles of rambling ruins.

Leopold found himself returning longingly to the cool, silent recesses of the Cave of Lamentations— and of the masterwork he had wrought there. But all that was lost to him now. *Stolen*.

He had come to his senses half-blind and hysterical—groping at the wound where the Eye had been. Through the haze of pain and outrage, he was struck by the unsettling sensation of someone standing over him, shaking him awake.

The figure flickered uncertainly in the dim light of the cavern and was gone again almost before it registered on Leopold's senses. The artist caught only a momentary glimpse of a stern figure balancing a beaten copper bowl brimming with blood.

Leopold's first thought was of recovering the Eye that had been stolen from him. It was not difficult to follow its trail back down the mountainside and away to the south—toward the gleaming white towers of bone in the distance. The Dragon's Graveyard.

Why here? Leopold thought. *Why do I always find myself here?*

He again wiped the blood-sweat out of the raw, gaping eye socket. His silk shirt was already soaked through. It hung about him like a second and ill-fitting skin.

The shirt bothered Leopold. Not just in the way that it clung to him. Rather, it was the fact that it was already ruined. A distant part of his mind was nagging at him, telling him that having only just arrived in this dismal place, the shirt should still be fresh.

No, that is not quite right. Even as he formed the thought, a second and conflicting memory imposed itself. He distinctly recalled battling through the heat all morning long. Past the Whispering Fields, through the Witch's Shins, across the Sea of Dust. He remembered them all distinctly, but somehow removed. Like a story overheard at a crossroads.

The glaringly bright heat of the noonday sun seemed to hang above him, circling lazily. He was an easy target—the only moving object above the horizon. The oppressive heat marked his progress, bided its time, coaxed out drop after drop of life-sustaining moisture.

The light of the sun? Something was quite wrong. Leopold's every sense screamed danger, deception. He shook his head as if to clear his muddled thoughts.

Somewhere, tall, silent ladies in satin slippers were gliding through cool corridors of marble. Leopold closed his eyes. He could hear the gentle rustle of silk, the sound of distant laughter, the hint of a reel drifting up from the ballroom below. It all seemed so real. So very close.

As if only the thinnest of barriers separated the two impressions.

Leopold opened his eye again into the glare of the harsh noonday sun. The air went out of him. There was something behind the wall of life-sapping heat. A purpose. A hunger. Leopold could feel its breath against his skin.

Somewhere at the heart of the sun-blasted landscape—a flickering, twirling maelstrom of hunger. An unappeasable, longing emptiness. The stirrings of the Dragon. It broke over him like a wave, like the sound of distant keening.

Leopold shook his head to banish the thought, scattering precious drops of life on every side. He could ill afford to think about hunger. There was precious little hope of any sustenance in this inhospitable place. He tried to focus his thoughts on more immediate concerns. It must be nearly noon. He had to find shelter soon.

If he could just outlast the afternoon sun, he might have enough strength for one more attempt to free himself. To slice through the skin-taut restraints of the desert heat. To slip between the bars of his own skeleton, his prison these thirty-three years. To take one step back from the clumsy canvas of flesh and bone and, surveying it with an artist's eye, make it anew.

Overhead a solitary desert bird caught an updraft, banked, and vanished against the face of the unforgiving sun.

Talbott glided across the threshold, advancing precisely three footlengths into the room. He stopped, pivoted smoothly to the east. His body inclined forward at the waist, bowing in the direction of Vienna. His every gesture was an exact movement in an ancient and intricately choreographed ritual. He pivoted again upon the balls of his feet and flowed forward with aching patience and grace toward the room's focal point.

Sturbridge was seated upon the floor at the far side of the gathering. She alone, of all the assembly, faced the open doorway. She had certainly noted the opening movements of Talbott's approach. She made no motion, however, to rise, or even to acknowledge the newcomer.

The other members of the chantry were carefully arrayed about their regent. Each sat upon the floor in exactly the same pose of relaxed alertness—sitting back upon the right heel, with the left knee upright and folded closely against the chest.

The assembled radiated outward from Sturbridge in sweeping semi-circles, each member's place strictly dictated by rank and tradition. The innermost arch, seated at the very feet of their regent, now consisted solely of Helena and Johanus—the two adepts assigned to the chantry.

Sturbridge was painfully aware of the novel asymmetry that had been introduced into the carefully ordered assembly. Once there had been three arrayed directly before her. This was the first formal gathering of the chantry since Foley's entombment.

In three, there was strength, completeness. God manifested himself in a Trinity—Father, Son, Holy Spirit. Similarly man, fashioned in His image, was triune—mind, body, soul. The Graces, Fates and Furies were all three in number.

By comparison, two was an ugly number. A divisive number. Good and evil. Truth and falsehood. Us and them. Sturbridge studied the faces of her two adepts, searching for the telltale stirrings of envy, avarice, ambition. Neither would meet her gaze.

Sturbridge could not help noting how the adepts had closed ranks, filling the empty place left by their recently deceased comrade. She was instinctively distrustful of this apparent solidarity. How *quickly* they had closed ranks. Nature had rushed to fill the vacuum left by the absence of their fallen comrade. Sturbridge suspected that it was their base nature. To an outsider, there would be no sign that there had ever been another among them. Sturbridge checked herself and forced down her rising, and perhaps unjust, resentment.

Sturbridge knew each of her adepts was a force to be reckoned with. Each had progressed through all seven circles of mastery prescribed by the Rule. They had traveled widely before accepting this prestigious and dangerous posting. Each had further honed her talents in the crucible of constant conflict with the Sabbat that was the special legacy (and curse) of this chantry. Each of them was being tried, and tried severely.

Sturbridge knew that conflict between the two might well rend the already war-torn chantry apart.

Without exception, the adepts assigned to C5B were the best of the best. Foley, she could not help thinking (with some bitterness), could have led his own chantry, and done a far better job than some existing regents that she could name. She could have very much used his support, somewhere nearby—Jersey, Connecticut…. But what was the point of such conjecture now? Instead of growing a sister-chantry to bolster the Tremere line against the rising Sabbat tide, Foley was dead.

Foley was *killed*, she corrected herself.

Sturbridge looked hard into the faces of her two adepts. Each of them might, in time, aspire to her own regency. Each of them was now precisely one step closer to fulfilling that aspiration.

This was foolishness. Sturbridge knew full well that the adepts were innocent of Foley's blood. It was the duty of adepts to prepare against the day when they might be called upon to assume the mantle of regency. Just as it was, in turn, Sturbridge's job to make sure these two survived long enough to get that chance. She had failed Foley. She was not accustomed to the company of failure.

Her gaze grew hard. It drank in the whole of the assembly. Beyond the inner circle of adepts were arrayed those who, through centuries of toil and intrigue, had achieved the coveted rank of master. Within each of the seven circles of mastery, the members were carefully arranged according to their status, seniority and precedence.

Beyond the closed ranks of the masters sat the seven circles of the novitiate.

Beyond the novices lay only the door to the

outside world and the battering of the Sabbat upon the portal.

Judging by the muted whispers among the assembly, it was clear that Sturbridge was not alone in being acutely aware of the secundus's absence. The worried murmurings were only further fueled by Talbott gliding into view of the rearmost rows of novices. He proceeded straight toward the regent, oblivious to the waves of seated figures through which he soundlessly cut. All eyes were upon him by the time he pierced the innermost circle of adepts. Talbott stopped, pivoted again toward Vienna, bowed. He then bowed to Sturbridge and settled gently to the floor. Despite his advanced years, Talbott effortlessly assumed the pose of the rest of the gathering. He waited with head still bowed.

"Yes, Brother Porter," Sturbridge acknowledged.

"Your pardon, Regentia. There is a guest without. He says he would speak with you without delay."

"Who is this guest, Brother Porter? Is he of the blood? If so, you may bring him before us presently. If he is not, you may escort him to our sitting room where he may await us."

Talbot seemed to hesitate. "Yes, Regentia. He is of the blood. There is no denying his credentials. But perhaps it would please you to speak to him privately. He is from...he has come a great distance," he finished awkwardly.

"If our guest wishes to rest and refresh himself, you will see to his needs. If he would come before us directly, you may bring him here."

"But, Regentia, he is from..." Talbot began, obviously agitated. Then he recollected himself. "As you wish, Regentia."

Talbot rose in a single motion without apparent

effort. He bowed to Sturbridge, turned east, and bowed nearly double. Still facing toward Vienna, he glided backward from the hall.

He was barely out of the room when the sound of a disturbance from the corridor broke in upon the uneasy silence. Two distinct voices could be heard—one raised in challenge, the other pitched soft and conciliatory. A number of novices were already craning around to get a better view of the doorway. When the door at last cracked open, all that could be seen was the broad expanse of Talbott's back. He was still deep in discussion with the figure just beyond him—apparently trying to interpose not only his words, but his bulk between the other and the door.

Having won some momentary advantage, Talbott seized upon the opportunity to slip deftly through the opening. He turned to face the gathering, blocking the still-opened doorway with the breadth of his back.

He took only a moment to collect himself. Clearing his throat audibly, he announced in a broken voice, "Your pardon, Regentia. We have guests. Please allow me to present, from Vienna, the Lord…"

Talbott's voice choked off abruptly and he wheeled as if struck from behind. Only the head of the newcomer could be seen peeking around the crack in the doorway. He held one crooked finger to his lips. The withered hand trembled slightly as with great age or palsy. Talbott tried to speak but all that escaped his throat was a harsh animal squawk and a fine spray of blood.

The newcomer held Talbott's startled gaze for only the briefest of moments. Satisfied, he lowered the admonitory finger and leaned heavily into the door. It swung open fully, spilling him a few shuffling steps into the room. Almost as an afterthought, he turned back toward Talbott, muttering to himself.

"No that is quite all right. You are dismissed, Brother Porter."

Talbott staggered backwards as the newcomer shuffled past him into the midst of the assembly.

He critically surveyed the entire gathering—their carefully orchestrated ranks, their precise and identical pose, their military precision honed by many lifetimes of service.

He muttered aloud in a voice dripping with age and vitriol. "Discipline, lax…security, lax…" He continued his damning litany the entire length of the hall. He did not pause until he had penetrated the inner circle of adepts. He then turned upon the gathering. His entire form shook with the intensity of his emotion and effort to speak.

"Children! I have crossed oceans to come here and all I find within this house are children. Unkempt, undisciplined, unmannered children. Where is the regent of this house?"

An uncomfortable silence settled over the hall. The stranger had positioned himself so that he stood between Sturbridge and her subjects. Not only had he purposefully turned his back upon her, but she was the *only* person in the room so slighted. Furthermore, he had interposed himself squarely between her and her people—as if attempting to eclipse her from view.

A calm and clear voice broke the silence.

"Be welcome among us. I am Aisling Sturbridge; you may address me as Regentia. You have come a great distance and are no doubt fatigued. Sit. Rest." She gestured to a place beside her own. Her voice dropped into a reverential tone as if reciting words of some ancient scripture. "The shadow of the Pyramid is long; there is room enough for one more to shelter beneath it."

Her words were calm, precise, unruffled. Behind this barrier of outward composure, however, Sturbridge's thoughts were racing. *A representative from Vienna.*

Never in all her time of stewardship over the Chantry of the Five Boroughs had the "home office" in Vienna seen fit to pay a visit. An unannounced visit. No, this certainly did not bode well.

She had heard the stories of course. Everyone had. Of how certain undesirables within the hierarchy were suddenly "recalled to Vienna"—disappearing entirely from Tremere society. Dropping off the face of the Pyramid.

But that kind of thing always took place somewhere else. Somewhere very far from here. *Please, not here.*

It was the assassination. That had to be it. The assassinations.

First Atlanta, then Baltimore, and now here. Of course it wouldn't do the higher-ups much good to drop in on the Atlanta chantry to throw a little weight around. Surely the ashes had cooled enough by now to allow safe passage, to gaze upon the blackened remains, to search for some clue as to what had gone wrong (gone so horribly wrong). But to what end? There was no one left in Atlanta to hold accountable. None to render back to Vienna what was Vienna's.

And what of Washington? Sturbridge wasn't even sure who the new regent in D.C. was now that Chin was dead, and Dorfman...unavailable. Something unpleasant nagged at the back of her mind, but she pushed it down. Was the besieged D.C. chantry even now suffering under the unwanted and unannounced attentions of their own legate from Vienna?

Her guest turned upon her very slowly. Freed from the spell of the stranger's attention, the adepts quickly regrouped and rose up as one. Sturbridge took little comfort from this display of unity.

She wondered what they might do, her ambitious adepts, if they did perceive a direct threat to her well being. Would they leap to defend their regent, or would their loyalties fall along more established party lines? Sturbridge sat calmly as if unaware of the silent conflict of interests that must be playing itself out inside the private thoughts of each of her adepts.

"Sit? We do not," the visitor pronounced each word separately, "*sit* on the same level as novices. It is unbecoming and erodes proper discipline." He scowled over the seated Sturbridge. "We shall stand."

Sturbridge ignored this rebuke and spoke past her accuser. "Talbott, please bring our guest a chair. It is uncharitable to keep him standing so long."

Although Talbott was at the far end of the chamber, the room's acoustics were such that the regent never raised her voice. Talbott seemed grateful for the opportunity to slip from the room and recover himself.

Sturbridge had been steadfastly refusing even to consider the alternative—that the representative from Vienna was here for some other reason, for some very personal reason. That was cause to fear.

She had taken great pains, of course, to be circumspect in her inquiries into the Tremere role in resisting the Sabbat offensive. Of course she was puzzled, confused, frustrated by the Tremere's almost systematic refusal to take any hand in the resistance.

But what if word had gotten back to Vienna about her *private* doubts about this matter? Of her covert conversations with leaders of the Camarilla council in Baltimore? Of her interview with Jan Pieterzoon, leader of the council? Of the "bargain" struck during that interview?

In hindsight, that rendezvous was, perhaps, a miscalculation. Not a mistake, *per se*. But perhaps not as subtle an approach as she might have taken. The home office was most comfortable when their carefully selected regents stayed where they were very carefully put. Yes, they would certainly inquire further into her trip to Baltimore.

Bracing herself, she smiled up at her guest and posed the question she most wanted to have answered and that she least wanted to ask.

"We are flattered by this unmerited attention. To what do we owe the honor of this visit, Lord…excuse me, Talbott did not have opportunity to finish your introduction."

These words provoked exactly the opposite of the disarming effect that Sturbridge had intended.

Raising himself up to his full height, the emissary choked out, "We are the Word of Etrius. We are grieved to learn of recent misfortunes at the Chantry of the Five Boroughs. We have heard the cries of our brethren and we have come.

"We are deeply concerned lest external influences jeopardize the harmonious operation of the chantry. In particular, our brethren have a solemn right to expect that within these walls, they shall be safe from all harm. Until such a time as this security has been demonstrably restored, we shall remain among you. Effective immediately, the Regent of the Chantry of the Five Boroughs will report to us directly, rather than through the normal geographic chain of command. We are the Word of Etrius."

Sturbridge sat stunned. She was not, as she had most feared, recalled to Vienna. She was not under sentence of death. They had not wrested control of her chantry from her. So why did she feel as if a great chasm had just opened up beneath her feet?

In silence, she tumbled headlong down the well.

Saturday, 31 July 1999, 5:15 AM
The Dragon's Graveyard
New York City, New York

Leopold placed each foot carefully, deliberately. Like a novice dancer, he picked his way among the jagged spikes of bone. His sandals would prove little protection against the wicked shards underfoot. He had no doubt that at the first misstep the flesh of his feet would be adorning someone else's bones.

He crept forward across the Dragon's Graveyard. Leopold tried to force himself to patience, but he was exultant. He had cornered his prey and the Eye was his once again.

The snake was a fool to ever think he could ever steal the Eye away for himself. Leopold focused his newly reclaimed Eye on the small stretch of ground where his next footfall must land. Grander details of the landscape were lost to him, beyond the scope of his world. His attention was consumed by an area precisely one pace long by one pace wide that lay directly before him.

Within that area, a diverse landscape spread out before him, played out in shades of black and white. The stark white of new bone, recently picked clean, thrust up sharply in cliffs and bluffs. The off-whites of bones left too long out of ground, exposed, rolled and tumbled upon themselves like hills. The stark black of each shadowed space between the bones lurked like ravines, gullies, badlands, ready to swallow the unwary.

Gazing into these pools of darkness puddled between the bones, Leopold could see that the bones ran deep. The field was made of layer upon layer of bone. The layers shifted, clashed, parted at each footfall.

Eric Griffin

A fistful of knucklebones rolled slightly underfoot. Some of the dislodged pieces slipped away into the gaps between larger bones. Rattling, rolling, sifting into the unknown depths. Leopold paused midstride to listen to the bones trickling down and away. He guessed that the layers of bone must go down at least the depth of a man. Leopold imagined slipping between the bones himself and sinking from view. Sidestepping the cruel sun. Gliding to rest a cool six feet under.

But there were other noises among the bones. Leopold couldn't help noticing (focused as he was upon the minute details of the ground in front of him) that sometimes the bones seemed to shift of their own accord.

As if some unseen footstep had passed ahead of him.

Leopold, however, suspected another source for these disturbances. His keen hearing had no trouble picking out the faint chattering beneath the surface strata. Crawling, scuttling, stirring on the undersides of the very bones he trod upon. Thousands of tiny footfalls that mirrored and magnified his every step above. Leopold was reluctant to put his foot down, lest it slip into the dark spaces between the bones. There was no telling what a single misstep would conjure up from the dark recesses.

As intent as he was upon his feet, Leopold only noted the bone outcropping because he felt its shade. A most welcome break from the deadly rays of the life-stealing sun. He leaned against it with one hand, summoning up his reserves of strength to continue his journey.

Instantly, he drew back, finding the surface he touched seething with life.

Nearly invisible white mites scattered in all directions. He wiped the back of his hand repeatedly on tattered jeans, but could not seem to shake the feeling of tiny legs scurrying across his skin, picking their way over the parched and broken landscape of pores and follicles.

With a cry of pure animal triumph, Leopold knew he had, at last, realized the great reversal and found a way to transcend the inferno of the boneyard.

"Hello, Leopold. I have been looking for you. My name is Nickolai."

Leopold turned to face the familiar voice and saw, in the flesh, one whom he had previously glimpsed in fevered sleep. "You are the one who awoke me in the cave. The keeper of the past. I remember you, although you once tried to eat those memories. It was you who..."

"Slowly, Leopold. There is so much you must know. But you must learn how to stalk knowledge—with calmness, detachment, patience. If you are ravenous, the prey will sense your hunger and escape you."

Leopold smiled. "How will my prey escape me?" In an instant, he had worked the Great Reversal. He was the Dragon's Graveyard. Nickolai and the city's millions of inhabitants scurried across his skin—picking their way over the parched and broken landscape of pores and follicles.

Deep within the bedrock of the city, something vast and unreasoning stirred in answer.

Nickolai felt the ground tremble. He took Leopold firmly by the shoulders, grounded him, anchored him. Leopold snapped back within his own bones. He suddenly looked very frail and shaken. "It seems the question is rather," Nickolai replied, "how will you escape it?"

Tuesday, 7 September 1999, 12:30
Regent's Sanctum, Chantry of the Five Boroughs
New York City, New York

The bolts of the outer door had barely hissed shut
when Sturbridge wheeled upon her guest.

"Do you want to explain just what the hell that
was all about?"

"I would remind you that you are addressing your
direct superior, Miss Sturbridge. I will brook no in-
subordination. Is this what passes for proper decorum
in this colonial backwater? Familiarity? Vulgarities?
I will not have it."

"I don't care if you're the archduke of Austria.
While you're in this house, you are my guest and I
will expect you to behave accordingly. Am I making
myself quite clear?"

"Perhaps you do not appreciate the gravity of the
situation. I am the Word of Etrius. I have been
charged to set this house in order. I will employ whatever means necessary to achieve this end. I will not
be thwarted, and I will not scruple to remove any
who resist the will of the council in this matter."

An overt threat. Sturbridge did not react well to
threats. "What you believe your mission here to be,
or not to be, is of little concern to me. I have seen
your credentials. What you are is an ambassador. And
I would remind you, Mr. Ambassador, that histori-
cally, diplomats who do not comport themselves with
dignity are summarily expelled and returned home
in disgrace."

"I assure you, Miss Sturbridge, that you have no
such authority in this matter." He smiled past cracked
lips and leaned forward confidingly. "What will you

do, have your porter show me the door?"

If he hoped to goad her into a more open display of anger, he was disappointed. "If you like," she replied with a honeyed edge to her words. "Will a noon wakeup call suit you?"

"I have taken certain precautions. To spare you the humiliation of having any harm befall me while I am in your care. I would not like for there to be any ambiguity in your mind on this particular point."

He picked up a thick volume from atop the nearest teetering stack of books. By the number of yellow sticky notes peeking from its pages, Sturbridge could tell it was one of the works confiscated from Foley's chambers. As Sturbridge watched, the notes began to brown along their exposed edges. A thin tendril of black smoke curled upwards. Before Sturbridge could react, or even protest, the book burst into flames.

She heard the telltale sound of the room's autonomic defenses clicking in.

"Override!" she barked.

"Override confirmed," a disembodied voice responded. "Sturbridge, Aisling, Regent. Response team dispatched. Defensive systems lock: Fire. Defensive systems lock: Arcanum. Defensive systems lock: Intruder.

"Fire systems warning: override status. You have 180 seconds to manually extinguish fire. Depressurization commencing.

"Arcanum systems warning: override status. Unauthorized thaumaturgic effect. Overt. Pyromantic. Retaliation: approved and armed. Triggers: delta proximity, delta temperature.

"Intruder systems warning: override status. Please

immediately identify unknown persons to maintain override status."

"Etrius, Logos, Ambassador." Sturbridge glared at her guest. "Address as Mr. Ambassador. Authorizations: guest quarters, owner-level clearance. Common areas, resident-level clearance. All other areas, restricted—access only when accompanied by Sturbridge, Aisling, Regent or Fitzgerald, Eva, Novice. Chantry ingress/egress, prohibited."

"Confirmed. Visitor record added. Please supply voice ident to complete record and cancel Intruder systems warning."

Sturbridge's voice dropped to a whisper. It was unnervingly calm and measured. "Mr. Ambassador, you have been acquired as a target by three separate autonomic defense systems. Please listen carefully.

"It is imperative that you refrain from any sudden movements that might be interpreted as hostile. I would also recommend that you immediately extinguish the burning book. The blaze will go out of its own account, of course, in just about two and one half minutes—when the remaining oxygen is forcibly ejected from the room. I assure you that this depressurization produces a singularly unpleasant sensation, even in those such as ourselves who would not dream of wasting air on anything so mundane as breathing.

"Also, if you could spare a few inspirational words for the voice recognition system—three or four sentences should suffice to register your vocal pattern—the alarm system will stop referring to you as an intruder. There are certain advantages to this arrangement. I highly recommend it."

"You must teach your guardian spirits better manners," he replied. "Such presumption! And I will advise you in turn, Miss Sturbridge, to call off your dogs. As I was explaining before we were so impertinently interrupted, this little demonstration was arranged solely for your edification. If any harm should befall me while I am under your protection..."

He allowed the arm that clutched the burning book to drop a few degrees toward the floor. The flames nipped eagerly at the billowing sleeve of his robes, caught and chased each other around his forearm. Sturbridge had a momentary glimpse of exposed skin blistering, cracking, blackening. She managed to take a half step toward him before the pain slammed into her. She doubled up, fire racing through her veins like molten metal.

"Enough!" Trained to their master's voice, the flames shrank back, withdrew and flickered out.

"Voice ident confirmed," the mechano-musical voice was unruffled. "Etrius, Logos, Ambassador. Welcome. Defensive systems alert: Intruder—canceled. Defensive systems alert: Fire—canceled. Defensive systems alert: Arcanum—canceled. Response team *en route* and attempting contact."

"Cancel response team." Sturbridge's voice was harsh, hollow. She repeated herself, conscious of the effort to draw enough air to form the words properly.

The ambassador was still talking, as if unaware of the mechanical interruption. "Fire and sunlight are such clumsy, imprecise tools. It is always difficult to say if they will strike true, or fell some innocent bystander. Like you, perhaps. We are bound together, you and I. You know that now. I have been promised safe conduct to and from this house. You are the surety of that pledge."

Sturbridge steadied herself with one hand and

straightened. She took a single cautious step forward, testing her balance.

"I don't know how the hell you did that, but you can be absolutely sure that it's not going to happen again. Security systems programming," she called. "Proximity alert, individual. Subject: Etrius, Logos, Ambassador. Subject suffers extreme vulnerability to light, heat. If subject approaches within twenty feet of open flame or sunlight, immediately incapacitate and extinguish. End."

"I am touched by your concern for my safety. Still, this guardian spirit of yours is nothing if not fickle and perverse. I will have its true name within the fortnight; you may rely upon it. Then we shall teach it some manners."

When Sturbridge did not rise to his barb, he continued. "I had been considering commandeering these chambers for the duration of my stay, but the company does not at all agree with me. I think the secundus's rooms will suit our purpose. The longer they lie untenanted, after all, the more the rumors and superstitions will fester among the novices."

"Of course, Mr. Ambassador. I will have the wards removed and the room made ready for you this evening. In the meanwhile, I imagine you will want to review all of the evidence relating to the secundus's death as soon as possible. Shall I have it carted down to the *edificium* for you? I would have it taken to Foley's quarters, but I'm not certain we would be able to get it all back in again. "

"You are quite mistaken, I assure you."

"I beg your pardon?"

"I said that you are mistaken. I have no desire

whatsoever to reopen this case. I have read your preliminary report on this unfortunate chapter in the history of this chantry and it is my considered opinion that the sooner we close that particular book, the better."

"But there have been new developments since that report was written. Another death for starters, and..."

"Another assassination?! This is intolerable. It is gross negligence. What is being done to protect the chantry from outside threats? And I don't mean this farcical Intruder Defensive System nonsense I've been subjected to here tonight. I believe I have seen enough of that. Why aren't your guardian spirits securing the perimeter instead of accosting the guests of the chantry?"

"Mr. Ambassador," Sturbridge's patience was beginning to wear. "There is strong evidence to suggest that Foley's assassin did not breach chantry security unaided."

"What precisely is it that you are trying to say, Miss Sturbridge? If you are merely trying to deflect attention from your own failings..."

"Our investigation turned up certain papers on Aaron's body—the novice that was killed just inside the *Exeunt Tertius* on the night of Foley's death. Papers that were removed from the scene of the crime. Surely you cannot fail to grasp the significance of..."

"Aaron was a hero." He spoke slowly and precisely. "He died protecting this chantry—a duty which I remind you, Miss Sturbridge, properly falls to you. I will not stand here and listen to you speak ill of the dead."

"But surely you realize," she began, but broke off midsentence. Realization had been slow in coming, but had gathered force with the waiting. It broke over her like a wave. Aaron, a hero, despite all evidence to the contrary? Why was the representative from Vienna so firm on this point, unless...

"Oh, I see."

"What is it that you see, Miss Sturbridge?"

"It was not his treachery after all, was it? It was his loyalty. His loyalty to the clan, to Vienna. Yes, I had things quite backwards. Thank you for pointing out my error. This puts things in a very different light."

"Let the dead rest, Miss Sturbridge. You would do well to look to the safety of your novices."

"Yes, I see that now. Thank you."

Thursday, 23 September 1999, 10:49 PM
The Mausoleum,
Chantry of the Five Boroughs
New York City, New York

"She knows too much already, my Lady. And what she does not know, she suspects." The ambassador's hand was knotted in the front of his robes, keeping the hem from dragging through the powdered bone that covered the floor.

"Nonsense. You have nothing to fear from the regent." Eva considered a moment. "No, that's not precisely true. I should say that you have nothing *more* to fear from her. If you give her the opportunity, she will destroy you, of course."

"She is insufferable. She resists my very presence here and undermines me at every turn."

"Well, of course she does. She has enjoyed a very free hand to this point and now it is time to shorten the tether. This relative autonomy has been a necessary evil. The councilor is well aware of the price of maintaining a front-line chantry. It is a cost we have been willing to pay in order to hold the Sabbat at bay. But now…"

"Yes, now there are other considerations." They rounded a bend in the narrow passage. A gust of moist air from some hidden niche carried the scent of moldering bones. His face wrinkled in distaste. "Already the carrion birds begin to gather."

"A pretty image, that. I can picture them now. A flight of tattered justicars and archons descending upon the city in their flapping black leather trench coats. But we must have a care not to frighten off our Camarilla brethren for the present. The political climate remains volatile."

He snorted. "I find it all more than slightly ironic. It seems a very short time ago indeed that our Camarilla allies were pouting, stomping their feet, and making all manner of dissatisfied noises—disgruntled over the lack of Tremere involvement in this conflict. Now, when they have at last uncovered evidence of our vigilance…"

"Tread gently. If you are referring to the rumors coming out of the nation's capital, we can give them no official credence. Still, your point is well taken. The Pyramid has already played a far greater role in reversing the Sabbat gains than any of our friends can yet imagine. Even our most vocal detractors must surely realize at this point that the chantry houses in New York and Washington are the last remaining bastions of defense for the our beleaguered allies. Yes, one must be very careful what one wishes for."

"I wish for an end to this damnable waiting. I don't like this little pantomime, never liked it. I'm the one hung out over the edge of the precipice here. If this thing starts to unravel now…"

"Nothing's going to unravel. You're not here to take a fall. You're here to…" She hesitated only an instant. In that moment's hesitation, however, he clearly heard the reading of his own death sentence. "To keep Sturbridge off balance."

He walked in silence for a time. "Even you don't believe that. Look, it's too dangerous keeping her in power here. She's already got hold of the frayed end of Aaron's secret. It won't be long before she worries it loose. We need to take her out of the picture…"

"Out of the question."

He raised his voice, talking over the top of the interruption, "…to take her out of the picture, if only for a little while. We could send her to Baltimore again."

"I can't encourage more interaction with Pieterzoon's *ad hoc* Camarilla council down there in Baltimore. It's too unpredictable, dangerous. We've already sown the necessary seeds among them. We've established Sturbridge as their 'in'—their link to the city, their chink in the pyramid. When they come to New York, they'll pay their lip service to Prince Michaela, but they'll come to Sturbridge for help. This chantry will provide them the intelligence, the expertise and the firepower they need to carry the city's liberation."

"You make it sound as if it's all a foregone conclusion. I envy your confidence."

"What you call confidence, I call control. Victory here will boil down to a simple matter of who can control the field of possible outcomes. By culling out the undesirable results now and nurturing the more rewarding ones, it will all seem like a foregone conclusion—after the dust settles."

He shook his head. "There are still too many uncertainties, too many permutations. I don't know how you can pretend to pierce the tangle enough even to discern a desirable outcome. You and I, we are far too embroiled in the painting to make out any of its details."

"The situation is complex, yes. In a sense, we will be fighting the battle on two fronts. It is not enough to win the overt battle against the Sabbat. We must also gain the upper hand in the covert struggle for prominence with our Camarilla brethren. We are fortunate (some might say vigilant) in that the Tremere are already far out ahead of the competition. We are on the ground. Our units are in position. We have been specially trained and equipped to fight this particular foe in this particular place in this particular way. All we have to do for the present is to be patient and to continue to remove the wildcards from the equation."

"Faster than our allies can introduce them, you mean. You know how I feel about this waiting game. There is so much we could be doing to prepare—and even more we might do with Sturbridge out from underfoot."

"You are still thinking in terms of logistics. Forces to marshal, supplies to lay in, rituals to enact. You are stockpiling certainties. I am disposing of uncertainties. I know this to be the only method to produce reliable successes in distilling our desired outcomes from the muddied waters of mere possibility. That is why your carrion birds do not concern me. Justicars and archons are monolithic, ponderous, predictable. One cannot commit a battleship with subtlety, nor withdraw it again gracefully once committed. They can be accounted for in the equation, factored out.

"No, it is the Foleys that worry me. Does that startle you? It is the Aarons and the Jacquelines that lie in wait for me when I close my eyes. The children. Their intrigues are more humble and therefore many times more damning. There is no telling how just one of their petty jealousies, their casual cruelties, might nudge the whole calculation in some previously unexplored and disastrous direction."

"So we eliminate them?"

"Certainly not. We eliminate the uncertainties. The uncertainties. The children, we draw them out, we force them to declare themselves and sometimes, to slip. When they have revealed their fomenting ambitions, their fears, their desires, then we have them."

"You turn their passions against them. You must admit, my lady, that it amounts to much the same thing. Foley is dead. Aaron, dead. Jacqueline…"

Her gaze grew hard. "Some passions we allow to run their course. The predictable ones. The ones that advance the inevitability of the final calculation. Are you suggesting that we are somehow responsible for Foley's death? I would be a bit more hesitant to put forth such a ridiculous and perhaps even subversive opinion if I were in your position."

"Ridiculous? Are you saying that we are blameless of Foley's death? If true, this would be welcome news indeed. It is one of the things that weighs most heavily upon me. I hope you might further put me at ease on a few other small points. Perhaps you can tell me how Aaron, a cloistered novice, managed even to make contact with that most ancient and dread brotherhood of assassins. Or how he came by the savvy to convince them not to kill a hated warlock on sight? Or how he came by the not inconsiderable financial resources that would be required to contract a murder in what may very well be the single most dangerous building in the Northeast to carry off such a transaction? Do you know what I think?"

Her voice was cold, distant. "I could not imagine, but I feel certain you are about to tell me."

"I think we are not blameless. At this point, even I feel implicated in this murder, soiled. I have spent the last two weeks sleeping in a dead man's bed. And now, I am convinced that I have killed him."

"You are unwell. It is the air down here. There is

something unhealthy about it—a bad humor, Sturbridge called it. Come, we must be getting back. You will go first, and I will follow at a ten-minute interval."

"Yes, something in the air. The entire chantry has fallen under the miasma. Like the thick, stagnant air down a disused mine shaft. Or the moist, pregnant atmosphere down a deep well. I don't think there is anyone under this roof who is not affected, who is not culpable. Not one soul who is blameless of these three deaths."

"Listen to me. The Tremere are not in the business of killing our own novices—of eating our young. Do you understand me? Do you understand?"

But already he was lost to her. His eyes glazed over, seeing, not the orderly accumulation of the centuries of bones piled high around him—a monument to monolithic tradition, solidarity, continuity—but another, humbler memorial. Before his eyes, he saw only the endless procession of the young, bright faces, eyes as round as saucers, trapped beneath the weight of black waters.

Friday, 10 September 1999, 2:24 AM
A subterranean grotto
New York City, New York

The flame of a single candle affronted the surrounding darkness. Calebros, staring at the dancing nimbus, felt his large pupils alternately contract and dilate with each hiss and flicker. He searched for answers in the fire, but the illumination served only to deepen the surrounding shadows.

10 September 1999
Re: Eye of Hazimel

6/11 Atlanta—statue delivered to High
Museum of Art.

6/21 Atlanta—Rolph hands over to Vegel;
Vegel destroyed, Eye lost in Sabbat
attack.

6/22 - 7/25—unaccounted for.

7/26 upstate NY—Gangrel massacre (at
hand of Leopold!?).

7/28 upstate NY—Hesha removes Eye from
inert Leopold.

7/31 NYC—Leopold attacks and seriously
injures Hesha, reclaims Eye.

8/1 - present—unaccounted for. Hesha
unable to trace (as during earlier
unaccounted for period).

Why? Who/What is shielding
the Eye?

"That will not be necessary. You may leave him where he lies. Please step away." Sturbridge's voice was flat and dispassionate in the darkness. The only light came from an opening high above. Another passageway.

They were deep within the catacombs. Down near the vaults that housed the remains of the chantry's founders. Passages that had, long ago, lost any justification for trafficking with the waking.

"Oh, thank goodness! The ambassador, he is hurt. Quite badly I think. I was afraid to move him. He fell from the gallery." Eva pointed toward the distant light above. "It took me some time to find my way down."

Sturbridge circled warily. "It was foolish to come down here alone. Whatever inspired you to…?"

"The ambassador insisted. He wanted to examine the remains. Of Aaron's body and of Jacqueline's. I'm afraid we took a wrong turning. Several, actually. I tried to summon help, but I guess the security systems just don't operate down this far."

"Clever. Go on."

"Something came over him. He seemed haunted, hag-ridden. He was raving about some miasma hanging over us. Do you know what he told me? He said he had spent the last two weeks sleeping in a dead man's bed and that he was now convinced that he had killed him. That's what he said. I begged him to stop, to let go. I told him he was frightening me. But he…" She was close to tears.

Eva wiped angrily at her face. Her sleeves slid down to reveal battered and bruised forearms.

"You pushed him away," Sturbridge supplied.

"Yes. No! Not like that. I did not push him over the…" She swallowed hard. "I pushed free of him and ran. I could hear him coming after me in the dark. The hollow sound of the scattered bones underfoot suddenly taking flight and careening wildly off the walls as he came. Somehow I lost him in the dark. I found an alcove. Stumbled into it, actually. It was one of the larger and (thankfully) untenanted niches. I crawled into it and curled in upon myself. Shutting my eyes tightly, hoping it would all just go away.

"I could hear him as he blundered past. I felt the stale air stir at his passing. I smelled the salt tang of his exertion. And then he was gone. It was not long after—certainly before I dared to move, or even hope that I might be safe—that I heard the long dwindling cry and the echo of the reverberating impact."

"A very convincing performance. I must congratulate you. Yes, it would be quite easy for me to fall back into believing your enchanting stories."

Confusion and then hurt flickered across the novice's features. "But I don't understand. Why would you say such hurtful things? Look at me!" She brandished battered arms, framing her bloodstreaked face.

Sturbridge returned her stare levelly and slowly shook her head.

The novice was close to hysterics. "You don't believe me. What do you believe? That I lured him here, to the edge of the precipice, and hurled him over? Look at me. I cannot even budge his damned unconscious and unresisting form. Do you seriously think that I could have…"

"It is enough, Eva. It's over, now. It's all over."

"Oh Regentia! Then you do believe me. He'll confirm what I told you, I know he will. When he is himself again. You will make him tell you, won't you?"

"The ambassador will not be coming back to us from where you have sent him."

Sturbridge spoke with certainty. She could feel the shock of icy water coursing through her veins. She knew instinctively the watery depths to which his spirit had been committed. Even if there remained some faint spark of unlife within the broken shell of his body, the one they had known as the Logos Etrius would never again return home to warm himself before it.

"There you are wrong, Regentia. He will be coming back. They will all be coming back. Surely you, of all people, must realize that."

"The ambassador is not coming back, Eva."
Sturbridge nudged the unmoving corpse with the tip of
her shoe. With a sigh, the entire torso crumbled inward
in a cascade of gray ash and yellowed bone. "Nor is
Jacqueline, nor Aaron, nor Foley." Sturbridge glared at
her protégée as if daring her to debate this point.

"You really do not yet understand." Eva's tone
was one of wonder, rather than of apology.

"I understand well enough. I have been slow in
coming to that understanding and it has cost me
dearly. You have snatched three of my little ones from
my hand. You may well have robbed me of my chantry.
You have broken my trust. And you must now attempt to take what little life remains to me."

Eva shook her head. "There is a morbid humor
in the air down here. A fetid reek of melancholy, distrust, self-pity. I can feel its breath through the broken
teeth of these neglected crypts. You are quite right to
warn others away. But you are mistaken if you really
think that I would want you dead. You are my regent, my protector, my benefactress."

"I do not know what you are," Sturbridge replied
coldly. "Once, I thought you were…someone very
special. But I am a foolish old woman. You are as
commonplace as death."

Eva recoiled as if struck and seemed about to re-
tort angrily. Then she visibly calmed. "You do not
mean that. I know you don't. You are not yourself.

It's this place, it is so…" She shivered. "Come on, let's get out of here."

"We're not going anywhere until you have explained yourself. Not until I understand why you are doing this."

"I'm not doing anything. And you must realize that you cannot possibly be in any personal danger at this point, much less from me! If the murderer had wanted you dead, there would have been no need for all this chicanery. Foley would still be at his post. Aaron would have had his promotion and been quietly shuffled out to another chantry. Jacqueline, well, Jacqueline hardly merited the attention of anyone outside this house, now did she? Make no mistake, Regentia, someone has spared no effort to bring you safely to this juncture."

"You have brought death into my house; you will not lay the responsibility for these murders upon my doorstep. It's not my fault that they are dead. I know that now, although this was another realization that was too slow in coming. I have felt the weight of their blood upon me. The sleepless days of wondering if there were anything I could have done differently—anything that might have saved them. Rest assured that you will be held accountable for each of those days in the final reckoning."

"Now you are frightening me. Please, Regentia, let us leave this place at once."

Sturbridge ignored her. "Their blood slips between my fingers. I cannot hold it and it, in turn, refuses to cling to me. There were nights, of course—nights that I wallowed in their spilled life, trying to drink it down, to claim it as my own. This is my house, damnit, and anything that happens here is ultimately

Eric Griffin

a reflection of me, of who I am. Everything that goes on under this roof happens with my approval—either explicit or implicit. I believed that I was responsible for allowing Foley to be killed and that by failing to find his murderer, I had doomed Aaron and then Jacqueline as well."

"But that is only more nonsense, delirium." She took Sturbridge by the hand. "Come on, we will go to Helena, she will know how to help. You're going to be fine."

Sturbridge would not be moved. "No, the logic of self-condemnation was undeniable. I am responsible for all that transpires beneath this roof. Foley, Aaron and Jacqueline were murdered beneath this roof. Therefore, I am responsible for their murders. Q.E.D. I could not break free of the damning syllogism. That is, not until your accomplice arrived. That was your first real mistake."

Jacqueline let Sturbridge's hand drop. "My accomplice?"

Sturbridge scuffed impatiently at the pile of ash and bone with her toe. "After his own fashion, the ambassador reminded me that, despite my rank and title, I was not mistress of this house. The deed to this chantry was not signed in my blood. There is nothing I have here that Vienna cannot take away in a single night."

"I'm not sure I'm following you. So you're saying that since you realized that you were not really responsible for all that transpires here, it was possible that you were not responsible for these three deaths. Is that it?"

"And that started me back to looking around for who might be responsible. The ambassador again came to my rescue. In talking to him, I realized that he—and by extension, Vienna (for he was exactly what he claimed to be: a mouthpiece, nothing more)—they all considered Aaron a hero. Now why would that be?"

Eva opened her mouth to speak, but Sturbridge continued before she could interrupt. "We knew Aaron had escorted an assassin through the chantry defenses. Despite all the wild speculations of infernalism and rampaging demons, the one who struck down the secundus entered the chantry by more mundane means. He was led down from the *Exeunt Tertius* and made his escape along the same route. Aaron could not have realized, of course, that the assassin would claim the novice's own blood as well.

"But here is the curious part. Instead of being branded a traitor, Aaron was being hailed as a hero. It didn't add up. Now, about the only thing that merits that kind of honor around here is giving one's life in the line of duty. So I began to wonder.

"I could never quite swallow the idea that Aaron had been motivated by treachery. The proposition simply did not bear up under scrutiny. Even the greenest neophyte knows how swiftly and mercilessly the entire pyramid falls upon the first hint of disloyalty. Aaron could not have hoped to escape discovery. Rather, he was relying on something else to spare him from the consequences of his actions.

"It was not until I spoke with the ambassador that I realized the 'hero' had died for his clan. He was not motivated by treachery, but rather by loyalty—and perhaps the promise of a rapid promotion and a one-way ticket out of this war-torn house. He was carrying out a rather dangerous (and unknown to him, suicidal) mission for his superiors. He was taking his orders directly from the motherhouse in Vienna."

Eva finally broke in upon her. "Now you have lost me entirely. Your speculations seem to raise more questions than they answer. Why would Vienna want Foley dead? And even if they did, why not simply 'recall' him to the motherhouse where a more private disappearance could be arranged? And why introduce an outside and hence unreliable assassin, instead of ordering Aaron to kill the secundus himself? And how could Aaron be expected to..."

"Your questions are spurious. You already know the answers. But perhaps you would like to discern whether or not I know them. Very well. I suspect you did not so much want Foley dead as you wanted an excuse to take a more direct hand in the affairs of this chantry. With a pair of unsolved murders hanging over the premises, you could rely upon minimal resistance to your coup. By inserting a special legate from the motherhouse in Vienna—and breaking the regional chain of command—you would have secured a very free hand in directing chantry affairs. You would be accountable only to the council itself.

"I'm not entirely sure why Five Boroughs is so important to you, but I would suspect that it must have something to do with the Sabbat war. You are clearly a seasoned intriguer. You are an insider, intimately familiar with how to best play the system to your personal advantage. And you do not scruple at ruthlessly striking down any who oppose you, or get too close to your machinations, or even prove unreliable. At this point, my best guess is that you are an aspiring robber baron, intent on plundering the resources of this chantry. You certainly fit the profile, if not the particulars. Will you redirect our assets to fuel the fight to reclaim Washington? Or will you simply siphon them off until the last pocket of resistance left in New York collapses under the rising Sabbat tide?"

Eva stared at her in open disbelief. She seemed to be caught midway between concern for her mistress and fleeing to get help.

"What are you?" Sturbridge repeated pointedly, her speculations having come round full circle.

Eva was silent a long time. When at last she found the words, her voice sounded soft and far off.

"Come and see."

Without turning to see that she was followed, Eva led the way into the deeper darkness between the ancient bones.

Friday, 24 September 1999, 12:30 AM
Beneath the Mausoleum,
Chantry of the Five Boroughs
New York City, New York

Sturbridge struggled to keep up without falling over the scattered remains and other nameless debris that littered the narrow tunnel. There was a darkness that clung about these deeper passages. A petty, vindictive darkness that had lain undisturbed for many years. It jealously guarded its secrets. It snatched at her ankles. It battered at her hands and arms with unseen turnings.

Sturbridge fumbled along in Eva's wake. She could no longer see her one-time protégée, but she could make out snatches of her voice, muffled, battering against the pervasive dark.

"A robber baron. Very romantic. But the truth is nothing quite so mercenary, I assure you. Your grasp of the political situation, however, shows great promise. In other circumstances, it would merit future observation."

Sturbridge was not at all certain she like the implications of that last turn of phrase. She felt she was being drawn inevitably down an ever-narrowing spiral. There was a presence at the bottom of that gyre. A force gathering, rolling storm-like in its depths. Sturbridge leaned into it and struggled onward and down.

"In a sense, I suppose you are correct. It would have been quite impossible to bring in 'my accomplice' without a scandal for him to ride in upon. Foley's murder was that scandal. He died for you, but I have told you that already."

Sturbridge had heard that line before. Some-where up ahead a distant flame flickered to life. "I can't accept that. All right, a quiet disappearance back to Vienna would not suit your purposes. No scandal, no need for such drastic intervention. Therefore, you contracted with the Assamite to kill Foley. But why Foley? And the whole business of going to the ancestral enemy strikes me as a bit too splashy. Gaudy. I take it this added touch was intended to fuel the already colorful controversy?"

"Again, the merely pragmatic escapes you. There was no room for error; we sought out and retained only the most qualified professional available. Do you think that this is the first time that members of our clan have conducted business with the infidels?"

Sturbridge reached the outskirts of the faint light. She had hands once more. Then she could pick out knuckles on those hands. And then the lines of vestigial, disused veins. There was blood in her still, but it no longer flowed along the traditional pathways that God and nature had designed. It was a false image, that network of lines. A still life.

She could not keep the note of bitterness from her voice. "Then Aaron was only the unwitting contact, the prearranged fall guy, victim number two."

"You were fond of him?"

The question caught her off guard. "Damnit, I was *fond* of all of them." Sturbridge stepped out of the low tunnel and rose to her full height. Dark as a battle raven and straight as a pin. "Maybe you don't know what it's like to be responsible for..."

Then she caught the first real glimpse of her surroundings and her words trailed off into their own dim afterimages, echoing up the empty tunnels—

sputtering through the chantry's own vestigial, disused veins.

"I think I have some passing familiarity with the burdens of command. But come now, you were explaining to me about Foley's murder. About how Aaron circumvented the chantry's security system."

Sturbridge blinked uncomprehendingly at the vast, rough-hewn cavern, doubting the evidence of her eyes. She would never have guessed such an expansive space could exist below the cramped confines of the chantry. The light that Eva held aloft was a small, lost, fragile thing against the immensity of that emptiness. The pinprick of a single star against the entirety of the night sky.

"He circumvented *most* of the security system," she replied in a hushed tone. "He could navigate through the chantry defenses. He could disarm any troublesome mechanical systems, but he could not take the human element offline—the security teams, Helena…"

"And yourself. Yes, very true. But the watchers failed to note anything out of the ordinary that night. Until it was too late. And you, yourself, were otherwise occupied…."

Sturbridge was acutely aware that she had come to the still point, the very center of the downward spiral. She could feel the weight of mountains looming over her.

"Yes, trading words with that fool storyteller. I have not forgotten that you were the one responsible for drawing me into that little exchange. You were blatantly fishing for information about me, about my past—and you were goading Talbott into a story that he knew better than to relate in so public a forum. And while I was occupied with trying to suppress the worst of Talbott's tall tales and wild embellishments, Foley was dying."

"Yes." The voice was almost a purr of satisfaction. "Not exactly fiddling while Rome burned, but I think you are on the mark."

Sturbridge forced down the unsettling thought of tons of granite and limestone poised above her and defiantly struck out into the cavern, aimed directly at the source of the accusation. The darkness seemed to resist her every step.

"You had caught me unawares once. I was not about to be so outmaneuvered again. You must have realized this. You waited until I was safely out from underfoot, at the council meeting in Baltimore, before you struck a second time."

"Your appointment to the council was not simply a fortuitous coincidence. But no, we had no intention of 'striking again'—I assume you are referring to removing Jacqueline—at least, not until she became a wildcard."

Eva's words were coming to Sturbridge only sluggishly now, as if the darkness they struggled through were thicker than mere air. Minutes had passed already as the syllables fought their way across the intervening distance. But Sturbridge could not let that monstrous assertion go unchallenged. She knew she must make some response, else all was lost. In the final reckoning, it was not, however, the need to speak out against the injustice of Jacqueline's death that drove her. Nor any compulsion to condemn the casual brutality of it. Nor was it the reflex to defend herself, to rationalize her own failure. No, the need that drove Sturbridge to answer was something more humble and less noble. Her response was her only means of clinging to that tenuous lifeline of words that connected the two antagonists. That bond was all that kept each of them from being isolated, swept away, lost amidst the rising dark.

"Damn you. Damn you to hell." Sturbridge's voice shook. "A wildcard? A random element? She was a person. A novice of your own order. A sister. A childe. We do not eat our own young. It is one of the few points on which the laws of God, man and the Pyramid all agree. Each of them reserves a special dark hole for monsters like you.

"What did Jacqueline do to you? What could she have done? She came upon you going through Foley's things. She saw something," Sturbridge accused.

Eva's voice was unruffled. "Quite the contrary. It was I who came suddenly upon her. I think she was doing a little investigating of her own—in addition to removing evidence that might later incriminate her, of course. But that was to be expected."

Her tone became contemplative. "It is perhaps ironic. But I think Jacqueline may have been the only one of the secundus's would-be murderers who actually harbored any ill will toward him. By all accounts, he was far too unpopular an individual to be done in for such impersonal reasons, don't you agree?"

Hand over hand, Sturbridge slowly closed the distance between them.

Eva ignored her struggle. "Jacqueline's own death was another story altogether. In her clumsy efforts, she had stumbled upon certain inconsistencies in the story we had chosen to cover Foley's murder. She knew too much about the ritual, about its preparations, about Foley's predilections...."

266   TREMERE

Sturbridge felt the darkness break over her like a wave. She sagged against the lifeline, nearly losing her grip. Somehow, she managed to find her voice. "It was Jacqueline who realized that the protective wards had been erased, that Foley's notes were being suppressed, that you knew altogether too much about the secundus's secrets—his 'eye', his treasure box. She realized that she was not the only one falsifying evidence."

Eva shrugged and continued with her preparations. "I had been waiting for her to make her attempt. She had been obviously anxious and behaving in a suspicious manner since we first questioned her. It was really only a matter of being patient until she had gathered enough courage to put her head into the noose."

Sturbridge closed her eyes against the callous litany of crimes. She plodded steadily forward, counting off the precise number of paces between her and retribution.

"What I did not expect," Eva's voice thrummed along the umbilical, "was for Jacqueline to pull off a full-blown translocation to gain entry to Foley's sanctum. Such unexpected promise; such wasted potential. So few of the novices nowadays have the necessary prudence to ensure that their gifts have the opportunity to mature and develop. It is one of the signs of the decline of our order. I fear the Final Nights are at hand for us, *Aisling*."

Sturbridge recoiled at the sound of her own name—at the familiarity taken by the novice. Even under less threatening circumstances, it would have struck a jarring note. "Jacqueline, at least, was not intent on hastening that decline through sheer force of attrition. You will receive your reward for your part in this, you know. Just as Aaron received his, *kinslayer*."

The hissing invective brought Eva up short, chalk poised midstroke. "We are a race of kinslayers, Aisling. Our founder was the first of a long and distinguished line of kinslayers. Oh, not the old wyrm caught in the throes of nightmare beneath motherhouse in Vienna, but our First Father. He was the first murderer and he ushered Death himself across the threshold and into this world. That is a weighty responsibility that we all must bear each and every night."

Sturbridge had more than a passing familiarity with Death. The mere mention of that name conjured up a wave of unwelcome thoughts—thoughts of her own death and of her daughter, Maeve. She felt rather than heard Eva's words. A vibration transmitted along the ghost-vein, the trailing strand of life that bound them. Pleased with herself, Eva put the finishing touches on the *diagramma hermetica* with a flourish.

"Come now, Aisling. What is the fall of one novice compared to such a solemn charge? Do you know that, for all my patient waiting, Jacqueline still nearly managed to escape me. Her adaptation of the translocation ritual (which she stole from Master Ynnis, incidentally) was an unexpected turn. But in the end, I think it actually worked to our advantage. By coming upon her in a clearly compromising position, I was able to pressure her into making a covert appointment with me—alone and in an out-of-the-way place. In effect, I allowed Jacqueline to choose the time and place of her own death. There are many who might envy her that gift."

Sturbridge strained to pick out the faint light, gauging her distance. It bobbed slightly like a lantern swinging from the bowsprit of a ship far out to sea. It seemed further away now than when she had

first begun. In another, this might have been an opening for despair. But, with great deliberation,
Sturbridge planted her feet, leaned into the rushing
darkness, and loosed her grip upon the lifeline.

The light swung wildly, now overhead, now behind her. Sturbridge tumbled through the darkness.
Eva's voice was still there, an anchor line amidst the
maelstrom should Sturbridge only choose to reach
out for it. The words streamed past her in a blur, barely
registering upon her consciousness.

"It was her wild tales of Master Ynnis and his
translocations that led me to the method of dispatch-
ing the troublesome novice. I do not think it dawned
upon her, even in those last moments. Even when
she reached up to close the cabinet above the sink,
which had swung open, seemingly of its own accord.
Even when she saw the flicker of metal and felt its
hot kiss upon her throat. Yes, you should have been
there. Her expression remained unworried, even as
her head rolled free of its pedestal and splashed into
the sink, vanishing beneath the murky waters."

Sturbridge tumbled end over end, caught in the
riptide, buffeted, borne down. Her lungs filled with
dark water.

She managed to gasp out (or imagine she had
gasped out) "You seem to have acquired a taste for
casual atrocities. Tell me, the ambassador, did he lose
heart, threaten to betray you?"

Eva waved the question aside distractedly. "He
had become unstable. He was teetering on the brink
of the abyss and had been staring too long into darkness. His utility no longer justified the uncertainties
he introduced into the equation."

Sturbridge felt the calculated indifference of the silent waters close over her head.

As the light receded, she became gradually aware of the swarm of wriggling shadows surrounding her. The sea was alive with writhing, struggling forms. Hundreds of drowning bodies all frantically clawed towards the surface. The blue and bloated limbs of those who had already succumbed to the struggle snatched at her, clung to her, bore her down.

Sturbridge tried, in vain, not to pick out the familiar faces among the drowned—their features reproachful, distorted, water-gorged. She knew precisely where she would be confronted by the one she could not face. She could feel her presence behind her like the ache of a raw tooth.

Still, Sturbridge could not help twisting to peer through the press of bodies, trying to catch a single glimpse of the receding figure. She caught the barest hint of gawky girlish lines, limbs long and straight as a pin, tresses dark as a battle raven.

Sturbridge writhed in her attempt to free herself from the icy press, to pursue the fleeing figure. A swollen face, its eyes bright and round as saucers, interposed itself and pressed uncomfortably close to her own. It bobbed gently, aimlessly, from side to side, its hair fanning out in the current. It regarded her with a clinical, almost serene detachment. Thick, sausage-like fingers experimentally probed and prodded her. Sturbridge batted at the corpse, trying to dislodge it. Draped languidly in fetters of clinging seaweed, it embraced Sturbridge, entangling her flailing limbs as the pair tumbled over and over.

There was something familiar about the Drowned Man as he pressed uncomfortably close—a lover bent on confiding a dark secret. Its chill lips brushed her ear.

"*Visita Interiora Terrae, Rectificando Invenies Occultum Lapidem.*"

Her thoughts flickered inward for the briefest of moments and then flared out again with renewed fire. Sturbridge turned the warmthless kiss upon the startled Light-bringer and, with a crow of triumph, kicked out toward the surface.

Clinging hands fell away from her on all sides as she realized that they were much like the sea. And the sea was much like the pervasive darkness. And the darkness was much like the weight of mountains. They were not external threats, but merely shadows of the true threats—the internal ones. Eva had laid her snares well. Yes, she was indeed familiar with the burdens of command. She had reached into Sturbridge's uncertainties and drawn out the weight of the regency—of Sturbridge's failures to guide her novices safely through danger—and brought it crashing down upon her with the weight of mountains.

She had opened the floodgates of Sturbridge's ignorance—of her inability to unravel the brutal murders that threatened to tear her chantry apart—and very nearly drowned her in a sea of pervading darkness.

She had turned a hand offered in trust—and perhaps even a genuine affection, as monstrous as that possibility might be among their kind—into the bloated and groping hands of the drowned.

And she had very nearly succeeded.

Visita Interiora Terrae Rectificando Invenies Occultum Lapidem.

Sturbridge broke from the dark water like a stone skipped inexplicably *out* of the well.

She found herself, not in a vast cavern mantled

in darkness, but in a small, disused crypt, deep within the bowels of the chantry. Eva was waiting for her there.

She smiled. "I had hoped you would come through. But you were taking such an awful time about it I feared I would have to fall back upon the contingency plan. No matter, I have completed all of the preparations. All that remains is for you to speak the words."

Sturbridge lowered her head and started forward, toward her young protégée. Vitriol streamed off her like water. Eva held up a hand in warning.

"Careful, please. I cannot advise you to break the line of the *diagramma*. The ward was not really designed with you in mind, but rather those who must follow. I did not anticipate that you would use such a circuitous route to come to me. It would have been far more efficient merely to pick your way through the tombs like anyone else. Sometimes you can be quite exasperating.

"But since you have come by way of the Well, you are bound by the same prohibitions as those who will come after you. Now, if you would simply recite the words that have been entrusted you…"

Sturbridge ignored this demand, but stopped short of the ritual warding. A seething fury peeked through the cracks in her composure. She glared at Eva, only a few inches and a crude chalk line separating the two antagonists.

"You have the temerity to make demands of me? Make no mistake, little one. Of all the things you have entrusted into my care—your calculated deceits, your feigned compassions, your casual betrayals—there is none that you would care to have returned upon you now."

Eva spoke slowly and deliberately, as if addressing a particularly slow child. "All the words that have passed between you and me to this point are nothing. The empty exhalations of the grave. The muttering of the wind through two exhumed skulls.

"No, the words that are required were entrusted you long before we ever met. The Words of Fire and of Blood. It is time to loose what has been bound. It is time for the nightmare to end."

A feeling of vertigo crashed over Sturbridge. Her eyes refused to focus. Ghost images flickered in the periphery. Ancient verses and snatches of song hopelessly intermingled into a uniform muttering, pitched just below the range of her hearing. It was if two competing worlds vied for her attention.

"The Words of Fire and Blood," Eva prompted again. Sturbridge recoiled from her. Staggering backward, she caught the sudden impression of something vast rising up behind her. She spun upon the Well.

Something dark brooded over the silent waters— an ancient and unappeasable hunger that refused to be contained within the cramped confines of the mausoleum. It rose head and shoulders above the crypts, ignoring the protests of intervening walls and ceilings.

Sturbridge caught a momentary glimpse of an immense rough-hewn idol, the cool black stone of its feet worn to a perfect smoothness by the passage of centuries of blood.

"*Too much blood already,*" she thought aloud, not knowing from whence the words arose, or that they had already been uttered once, long ago. "*Blood of the firstborn. I know you, Cromm Cruaich. You were their Moloch, their Kinslayer, a nightmare of an older order. Chidden of God, you were banished to the dark places of the earth, sheltering from the light of life-giving day. You have had centuries to brood in those shadows, marking time by the spilling of blood into your dark well."*

Somewhere, far beneath them, the Dragon stirred.

Sturbridge tried to fight off the sudden ambush of the mythic, to cling to the literal. She could almost imagine that the Well was only the dry and empty shell of a broken crypt. She could pretend that the blasphemous features of the Stooped One were nothing more than the play of shadows and torchlight upon the rough-hewn walls of the crypt.

She closed her eyes and clung fast to that image. "This is what it is all comes down to, then, isn't it? It's all about the Children. All the lies, the betrayals, the murders. It was never about the revenges of abused novices, or the ambitions of would-be journeymen. It's not about intrigues or infernalism; assassinations or political maneuverings. It's not even about manipulations from Vienna or the damned Sabbat war. It all comes back to the Children."

"You only have to say the words," Eva coaxed. "You can call them forth, they will answer to your voice. My calculations have been exacting, they cannot be mistaken on this point. The Children will hear your call and they will not refuse you. And then all this," she made a broad gesture intended perhaps to indicate their current predicament, or perhaps the chantry itself, or perhaps the carefully ordered ranks of crypts—the Tremere dead, their history, the sum of all their struggles. "Then all this doesn't matter anymore. We will finally be free of the nightmare. Say the words, Aisling."

Sturbridge's voice began faint and unsteady, but grew in confidence with each syllable. "Logos Etrius,"

Sturbridge recited. "Jacqueline. Aaron. Foley..."

"No! You fool, you will ruin..."

"The Children are your accusers, Eva, not your redemption. Can you not hear their voices? They clamor for your blood." Sturbridge's own voice rumbled through the crypts. The ancient walls rang with her authority. "As regent of this house, it is my judgment that your blood has been tainted with the unabsolvable stain of kinslaying—and is forfeit. May God have mercy upon the quick and the dead."

Eva drew back as if struck. Sturbridge instinctively reached out to her, shrugging free of the mantle of judgment as quickly as she had donned it. In her eyes, concern for her young protégée found room enough room to coexist with the determination to see justice served.

"Come, Eva, it is time to go home. The nightmare is over for you now." Sturbridge's hand extended awkwardly, hesitating just outside the faint chalk line.

With a mounting cry of fury, Eva snatched the censer that swung lazily above the central altar. Like a dark angel, she scooped up the fire of the altar and swung the censer three times in a wide arc. Loosing her grip, she hurled the blazing comet into the earth, into the very heart of the dark well. The waters roiled in answer with a cry as of many voices. The thunder danced above that cry and the earthquake rumbled beneath it.

Sturbridge could only look on in horror as her carefully-constructed grip on the mundane was shattered. In the turbulent light bubbling up from the well, she could already pick out the familiar features of the Stooped One taking form. The idol's ebony body writhed in time to the music of the flames. Sturbridge saw that the sculpture was not formed of a single block of polished stone as she had first imagined, but was composed of dozens of lesser beings—their bodies twisted, frozen in time, preserved in attitudes of horror, defeat and despair. Their features were crude and animalistic. Their gaping wounds still oozed blood. The moans of their broken bodies, grinding one against the other, rattled the old bones scattered across the crypt floor.

Sturbridge shrank back from the hundred-handed one, trying to avoid the piercing single-eyed stare. She felt the icy weight of dread clutching at her. She tried to flee, but found that she was caught from behind. Clumsy bloated fingers knotted in the fabric of her robe. Her feet splashed and nearly slipped as she struggled free from the drowned one's grip. The Well was disgorging its own.

"Say the words, Aisling."

Sturbridge tried to turn toward the voice but found that the scene had again shifted. She was lost in a limestone landscape—a vast cavern carved out of the mountain's heart by centuries of trickling water. The cave was a boneyard of scattered stalagmites and stalactites. It gaped like a raw mouthful of broken teeth.

The moaning was stronger here, echoed, redoubled. Sturbridge tried to shrink back from the clamor, to draw inward. The piercing wail ruptured her defenses. It broke in upon her sanctuary and dragged her back out.

She felt herself being drawn bodily toward the center of the cavern and the blasphemous sculpture that squatted there. Leopold's sculpture, she realized with growing apprehension. His masterwork. His still life.

This is what Foley saw, she thought, *just before he...*

Her eyes could find no purchase upon the tangled

remains of the massacred Gangrel. Her gaze traveled uncomprehendingly along the shifting line of twisted and broken bodies. Her mind could not seem to encompass it all. One victim flowed into the next, all distinctions blurring in that perfect marriage of the flesh. One in body. One in blood.

Sturbridge realized the sculpture was not so much a monument to the dead as an indictment of those, like herself, that still lingering here among the living.

"You can free them, Aisling." The voice chorused from a dozen shrieking mouths, as if the entire statue was nothing more than some grisly pipe organ for Eva to play upon. "You can undo this atrocity. You can end their nightmare."

"Stop it! Why are you doing this?"

"Think of the Children, Aisling." Then the voice took on a more ominous tone. "Think of your own child. Think of Maeve."

The scene shifted again and she found herself teetering at the very brink of the dark well. She flailed and only narrowly caught herself on the slick stones. The waters that had already overflowed this bitter cup lapped over her feet, soaking the hem of her robes.

It was not Sturbridge's cry toppling over the brink of the well and down into the darkness, but that of a child. A small, frightened child.

Sturbridge lurched toward the sound, knowing already it was too late. Years too late. She leaned far out over the gulf, clutching desperately at fistfuls of nothingness.

Her face pressed against the damp stones, her eyes screwed tightly shut. She could not bring herself to peer over the edge, to look upon the faces she knew would be awaiting her there. She sagged. Her voice was a broken whisper, lacking all certainty. "No. She is…they are gone, lost. Lost to us, long ago."

"Call her, Aisling. She will come to you. She wants to come home. They have lost their way, that is all. But they want to come home. They are ready to come home now.

"Maeve?" Sturbridge mouthed the word, but all that escaped her lips was a broken animal sound.

"That's right. Now louder, so that she will hear you. How can she follow your voice if she cannot hear you? How long has it been since you last saw her, Aisling? How long since that day when she was lost to you?"

"Night." Sturbridge answered woodenly. She seemed lost in memory and unaware of her surroundings. "It was night. She lost her way, in the dark. I called to her. Told her to come back. Pleaded with her."

"But she wouldn't listen," Eva supplied. "If only there were something. Something you could have said."

"My beautiful child," Sturbridge sunk to the ground and curled inward, elbows hugging knees. She ignored the rising waters. "My magical child. Too late. It was already too late. I tried to follow her."

"Of course you did. You could not have known that she had gone. But there is still time. Call to her, Aisling. Call to her and she will come back to you."

Sturbridge rocked slowly back and forth, moaning softly. Despite herself, her ears strained to pick out the sound of a distant voice, a lost cry, a familiar need. "Maeve." It was more a sob than a call. "If I had known. If only I had known. No, she will not come back. Not now. She knows what I have done. What I have become."

"But how could you have known?" Eva coaxed. "She will understand. She will come back to you. You are her mother. She loves you."

"I never told her." Sturbridge pushed herself uncertainly to her feet, struggling against the dead weight of her soaked robes. She turned toward Eva, words and water streaming from her. "But I thought it would be all right. I thought it would all turn out right. Just like in the Bible, with Abraham and Isaac. Abraham never told Isaac either, you know. Never sat the boy down and explained to him what had to be done. How can you explain something like that? That's all I was reading those last nights. Must have read the story over a dozen times."

"Then you knew she was going to die?"

"No," Sturbridge's voice was sharp, defensive. "I knew *I* was going to die. It is the price of being initiated into the secrets of this house. A distant echo of the sacrifice of our Founder and the Seven. It is our devil's bargain, the contract signed in our own blood. To be transformed, to die, to rise again. But I never realized that when I died... I thought that she..." Sturbridge came up short, the words catching in her throat. Eva's accusation had found its mark. The cruel point bit flesh, twisted, broke off in the wound.

I knew she was going to die.

Dark wings buffeted about Sturbridge's face, the first familiar caress of Death, her longtime suitor. Wicked talons tore at her carefully constructed rationalizations. She tried to fend them off—the flurry of blows that neither cut nor bruised but rather seemed to smother. Her ears rang with the cry of carrion birds.

No! I did not kill her. I am no kinslayer. We do not eat our own young.

She must have spoken the words aloud. Eva moved towards her, making calming noises. "Quiet now. Easy. It's all right. But there is only one way to know if she will understand, if she will forgive you. You must say the words. You must open the Well. You must call her back. You cannot possibly turn back now, knowing that she is this close. How will you live with yourself if you do not at least reach out to her, if you do not at least make the attempt?"

Sturbridge curled in upon herself, doubled over the raw wound piercing her side. Slow and low, like a broken rumbling from the deep places of the earth, the name tore free of her. "Maeve... My child. My beautiful little girl."

Reluctantly, Sturbridge plunged down into that forbidden place at the very core of her being—the dark well in which she had so carefully drowned all those things she could never hope to face in her waking hours. Desperately she called out, floundering in the unfamiliar waters, casting about for some hint of the comforting image of her child's face. The fickle and vindictive memory eluded her.

She has to be here. She cannot have escaped me. I have gone to such pains to keep her here, to keep her safe.

A face rose toward her, streaming up through the dark waters. A wave of relief and regret washed over Sturbridge as she picked out the first hint of the familiar—the wreath of billowing hair, dark as a battle raven. The gawky girlish form that hove into view a moment later was no blue and bloated corpse; it was vibrant and straight as a pin. The girl met Sturbridge's imploring stare without flinching. Sturbridge could see that one of the girl's eyes was milky white with the witchsight.

Sturbridge's initial rush of elation died away. The girl's features, they were not quite right. As she drew closer, the lines of the girl's face resolved themselves into greater clarity. Sturbridge devoured those lines like a palmist, searching for meaning, understanding.

The tangle of lines drew suddenly into sharp focus. With a cry of denial, Sturbridge shrank back from both the realization and the figure before her—the image that was not her daughter's—was never her daughter's. But rather her own.

Angrily she kicked away from herself, twisting, calling Maeve's name over and over again. Already she feared that it was too late. Decades of rationalization and self-deceit unraveled. Sturbridge found herself grasping desperately at the retreating end of her Ariadne's thread.

Maeve is not here. Was never here.

She plunged deeper into the dark well of madness, seeking the comforting sands of oblivion in its depths. She had lost her child, her only daughter. And now even the memory was being taken from her. *Lost. Gone. As if it had never been.*

Sturbridge knelt at the very bottom of the well, frantically sifting through fistfuls of the sands of oblivion, seeking to unearth some shard of memory that had escaped the ravages of time. Some proof. Some vindication.

She tried to dredge up the day of Maeve's birth— a day that had changed Sturbridge's life irrevocably. The day that she had first awakened to her own magical nature. Nothing.

She tried to conjure up the images of those last

tense hours before Maeve's death, before she herself died and was reborn into the blasphemous society of the damned. Only more unraveling threads. Nothing Sturbridge could get a grip upon.

Already, some sense of the monstrous truth loomed over her, but she would not turn to face it. A birth that was no birth but her own. A death that was no death but her own. A child that was no true child, but the awakened flame of her own magical self, her alter ego, her avatar. That mystic part of herself that was so brutally snuffed out in her transformation. Ground out beneath the heel of the Stooped One, the Kinslayer.

Sturbridge felt the last shred of the pretense fall away. There was no point in resisting further. Her voice sounded small and lost amid the vastness of the tombs.

"*Visita Interiora Terrae Rectificando Invenies Occultum Lapidem.*"

Eva was only dimly aware of Sturbridge's voice, hollowly reciting the words entrusted to her so long ago by the Light-Bringer—the Words of Fire and of Blood. She had already spun, quick and predatory, intent on catching the first hint of scrabbling bluish fingertips emerging from the rim of the Well.

The waters roiled and sloshed violently over the brink. There was a sudden rush of air and a radiant figure, bright and pale as moonlight, erupted from surface of the brooding waters. Eva staggered back. With a piercing cry, the gleaming figure broke free and rose triumphantly above the well, unfurling wings of purest flame.

For a moment, Eva had the distinct and unsettling perception that the figure above her was rendered entirely in the negative. It did not seem to protrude into space in the same way that a normal person or object would. It had no depth to it, no thickness. Rather, it seemed to be a human-shaped rent in the background of the room. An aperture through which a piercing light shone.

Eva felt the searing heat of that light fall upon her, felt the scrutiny of that all-consuming eye. She screamed and clawed at her face.

In those final moments, staring directly into the deepest recesses of that shining well, that brilliant hole between the worlds, Eva had the most peculiar impression. She thought, if only for an instant, that the entire world she knew—a world unambiguously bounded by somber crypts and chantry walls, by pyramids and hierarchies, by ritual formulae and an unbroken line of victims (their watery eyes bright and round as saucers)—that her carefully ordered world was only a sad, tattered sort of pasteboard backdrop. That only the thinnest and most hastily constructed veneer protected the inhabitants of this world from the ravenous scrutiny of the divine.

The last thing she heard before the light consumed her utterly was Sturbridge purring quietly, monstrously to herself, "My child. My beautiful little girl."

About the author

Eric Griffin was ushered into the bardic mysteries at their very source, Cork, Ireland. He is currently engaged in that most ancient of Irish literary traditions—that of the writer in exile. He resides in Atlanta, Georgia, with his lovely wife Victoria and his three sons, heroes-in-training all.

His other works include **Clan Novel: Tzimisce, Three Pillars** and **Castles and Covenants**.

For more information on the best-selling Clan Novel series, please feel free to visit the author's site at http://people.atl.mediaone.net/egriffin, or White Wolf publishing at http://www.white-wolf.com.

The Vampire
Clan Novel Series.................

Clan Novel: Toreador
These artists are the most sophisticated of the Kindred.

Clan Novel: Tzimisce
Fleshcrafters, experts of the arcane, and the most cruel of Sabbat vampires.

Clan Novel: Gangrel
Feral shapeshifters distanced from the society of the Kindred.

Clan Novel: Setite
The much-loathed serpentine masters of moral and spiritual corruption.

Clan Novel: Ventrue
The most political of vampires, they lead the Camarilla.

Clan Novel: Lasombra
The leaders of the Sabbat and the most Machiavellian of all Kindred.

Clan Novel: Assamite
The most feared clan, for they are assassins of both vampires and mortals.

Clan Novel: Ravnos
These devilish gypsies are not welcomed by the Camarilla, nor tolerated by the Sabbat.

Clan Novel: Malkavian
Thought insane by other Kindred, they know that within madness lies wisdom.

Clan Novel: Giovanni
Still a respected part of the mortal world, this mercantile clan is also home to necromancers.

Clan Novel: Brujah
Street-punks and rebels, they are aggressive and vengeful in defense of their beliefs.

Clan Novel: Tremere
The most magical of the clans and the most tightly organized.

Clan Novel: Nosferatu
Horrific to behold, these sneaks know more secrets than the other clans—secrets that will only be revealed in this, the last of the **Vampire Clan Novels**.

......................continues.

War rages in—and beneath—the streets of New York City. Now that the Sabbat realize they have been duped by Jan Pieterzoon and Theo Bell at Baltimore, can the American Camarilla survive the loss of vast tracts of the eastern United States? Or will their plans be ruined by a single Toreador pawn, Leopold, and his unseen masters? Hazimel has plans for his Eye, but so do others.

In the World of Darkness, reality is seldom what it seems, and no one knows that better than Calebros, elder of the heinous Sewer Rats, the unobserved observers, the keepers of secrets. He has been watching and influencing events from the start. The stars of other books still have roles to play as well: Victoria, Hesha, Ramona, Jan, Theo, and Aisling all have ambitions and goals to realize.

The best-selling Clan Novel series culminates with **Clan Novel: Nosferatu**. Find out why uncovering some secrets can be more dangerous than staying in the dark.

CLAN NOVEL: NOSFERATU
ISBN 1-56504-835-0
WW#11112
$5.99 U.S.

next: nosferatu